FEELINGS MUTED

Susann Svoboda

Copyright © February 2023 Susann Svoboda

All rights reserved

The characters and events portrayed in this book are fictitious. Any similarity to real persons, living or dead, is coincidental and not intended by the author.

No part of this book may be reproduced, or stored in a retrieval system, or transmitted in any form or by any means, electronic, mechanical, photocopying, recording, or otherwise, without express written permission of the publisher.

Cover design by: Susann Svoboda

FEELINGS MUTED

~

Day X

How in the world had she gotten into this entangled, uncomfortable, hopeless situation? She, Marisa Keach, an ordinary woman, totally unremarkable and insignificant in this big world, was tied to a radiator by her hands through the thinnest but most effective cable ties. She, the silly one, was half-kneeling, half-sitting by the radiator on the second floor of her own building in the dark.
She, who after all was supposed to be married in two weeks. A few days ago, her life had been completely normal and had not made any big waves. How could it be that she of all people was in this mess?
All because of this stupid vacation.
Because of these 21 days.
And one night.
Shit.

~

Day 1

Year after year.
For over twenty years she has spent her time here in the mountains. Not necessarily here in Kilnovech, maybe in another winter camp. But definitely in the mountains, in the snow. In the beloved cold. What had started then as family vacations had now become her own tradition. What she had not appreciated then as a child had now become her salvation. This year was no exception, even if a few things had changed in the last few weeks, days even. For the better, of course, she reminded herself.
Marisa Keach looked at the man at her side and almost had to pinch herself to make sure she wasn't daydreaming after all. George Rashdy was an attractive man, in his mid-forties. His hair short-shaven, his grey-white five-day beard was neatly trimmed. He was sitting next to her with his reading glasses on his nose, frantically trying to solve the round of Sudoku with the highest level of difficulty, without looking in the back of the booklet for some help. She grinned at the sight of it and then turned back to the white landscape.
Their journey had gone well, no traffic, no breakdowns, and once they left Germany and the cities behind, the magnificent splendour could finally be seen from afar. It wasn't like it used to be, that you were guaranteed to have meters of snow in front of you in the winter. It was a load off her mind to discover the snow-covered mountains.
When the coach stopped in front of the beautiful wooden huts

with the skilful manoeuvres and purposeful steering, Marisa heard a pleasant tingling in her stomach.
And the same feeling of contemplation and peace spread through her as in all the previous years. A little sadness came with it at the moment, but she knew that he would have wanted her to continue skiing. Even without him.
Father. I love you.
And she would do the same for the next 3 weeks.
With stiff bones, the passengers got off one by one, making sure to gather all their gear and leave nothing behind before the bus had to leave again to bring in the next skiers and winter vacationers. They had a relatively short journey after all, but many visitors were not so lucky and looked very exhausted from the trip. Marisa smiled encouragingly at one or two as she helped them with their suitcases and skis. A good start to the vacations was important, the less stress and chaos there was today, the better the first day on the slopes, completely rested and prepared. She herself could hardly wait. The staff at this popular resort were super dedicated. As soon as you entered the enormous magnificent alpine hut, everyone got the feeling of being in the right place. In the background, one could see the fireplace that would definitely give them warmth in the late, cold evenings. One overlooked the large room with plenty of seating, comfortable and inviting after a long day on the slopes. There were tables in the corners to play games, there were sofas and armchairs to read comfortably by the fire after choosing a new story from the tall bookshelves. There was a television, of course; but in all the years she had spent here, she had never sought the digital distraction. Instead, there were other opportunities to relax further away. Plus, you couldn't forget the fancy dining room, the small but nice swimming pool, and the sauna next door from the bar and pool tables.
Marisa loved this place. Here she lacked for nothing.
"I hope they have free Wi-Fi here," George muttered to himself. He looked around impatiently while the other guests were

being taken care of by the staff. His eyes roamed over the furniture and decorations, but his expression never changed. Marisa stroked his shoulder encouragingly and just laughed at his comment. He was only joking.
"Ah, that reminds me!"
She felt no rush, she didn't mind that they had to wait a bit. On the contrary, she used the moment to read through her work email one last time and then shut it off. In an emergency, her colleagues would know how best to reach her; until then, her cell phone was no longer needed. Except for the numerous photos she would take of her ski vacation, which she would show to her mother traditionally, as if in an old-fashioned slide show.
Of that first vacation as a couple.
Crazy times!
Good times.
Finally, it was their turn, and the receptionist turned his full attention to them both.
Johnny Pitt hadn't changed a bit. His eyes literally gleamed as soon as he too recognized Marisa and he welcomed her with a friendly hug.
"Marisa, has it been eleven months again?" he said delightedly, and the laugh lines on his eyes deepened greatly. A man who knew how to have fun, someone who enjoyed life.
Marisa laughed back.
Johnny now stood somewhat reservedly in front of the man at her side, a little unsure how to greet her companion. A hug didn't seem appropriate, a handshake would have to do.
"Mister Rashdy, welcome to our magical resort. Johnny Pitt, hello, I'm the manager in charge of your vacation here with you. Marisa, I'm sure has already told you what adventures await you here and how much you will enjoy your vacation time here."
George smiled kindly and accepted the hand. He didn't get to say anything, the other man was only too eager to continue the conversation with Marisa.

"So, as I explained to you on the phone, your accommodations will be a little different this year. With the last-minute change in your vacation booking, we are able to offer you a double alpine lodge. Which means that you will be accommodated with another couple in one of our best alpine huts. A dream of a cottage - believe me!"

George was about to raise his eyebrow doubtfully when Marisa lovingly and at the same time warningly put her hand on his arm. And he repressed the need to challenge this man. After all, this was just a mountain hut in the midst of other mountain huts in the deepest snow. What could be so exciting about that?

"I am very grateful to you for being so accommodating so that we can visit your resort together."

Johnny smiled deeply pleased with himself and gladly accepted the thanks.

This man had a positive attitude, you couldn't believe it.

"Come with me, we'll take our snow buggy to your lodging."

A little while later they had loaded up all their gear and suitcases and unloaded them after a five-minute ride.

The cabin was secluded from the other cabins, and from the common areas where they had been just a moment ago. The icy cold air burned on their warm faces, but Marisa didn't feel it. She looked spellbound at the cabin, which even from the outside, just looked like it had been cut out of a romantic book or movie and set among its mountains. In front of the door was a small porch, the roof above it cut to a point like an A. Smoke was rising from the chimney, they were already firing. The sun had already disappeared behind the huts, only the light red between the trees and mountains could be seen.

Marisa grabbed George's hand to share the moment.

Johnny sucked in her satisfaction deeply. He had been right after all. It was pure paradise for them. Unlike all the years she had been here. She hadn't known this remote side of the resort at all. Usually always staying in a very simple hut, and today here.

Unique.

Johnny led the way, carrying gear and bags, and skis and what he could stand. And despite him blocking most of her view, she saw enough of the inside of this cabin.

It confirmed her first impression. It was fascinatingly beautiful, spacious, and inviting. There was a large living room, with a laid-out kitchenette. She noticed a bathroom to her right as she entered and assumed the other bedrooms were on the second floor.

Johnny talked in a tour, mirroring her thoughts in his words. She agreed with him on all of them.

"So, you can see why we could almost call it our honeymoon hotel suite."

He grinned mischievously at her, and she couldn't help but laugh.

Johnny set the suitcases and things all down for her before turning back to the two of them.

"I'm afraid you'll just have to share it with another couple. But other than that, it's like a dream."

Marisa recognized the regret in his voice and had to admit that she hadn't actually felt that regret until now. The place was magical enough. George and she would make the most of it. Besides, they would spend their days on the slopes, skiing, hiking, sledding - you name it. They probably wouldn't run into the other couple that often.

Marisa set her things down on the side of the living room, as did George. She heard Johnny talking to someone else and assumed it was the other couple. That was good timing, that they could get it over with right away. A quick hello and brief appropriate information exchange, and then they could get to unpacking. Once they knew who they would be sharing the vacation with here, they were ready to go. Marisa again felt a tingle in her stomach at the thought of being able to ski at her heart's content for the next few weeks. That's why she was here, no matter how crazy or poopy boring the other two were. This little hurdle was absolutely no problem.

Holy fuck.
Marisa had taken three steps, three small steps into this beautiful, perfect alpine hut and instantly wanted to turn around and run a thousand miles away.
She swallowed dryly and tried convulsively not to stare like a lunatic at the man in front of her. It didn't quite work; her body had lost contact with her brain and didn't want to react to anything it was screaming at it.
Shit.
"So here we have Maureen and Vincent." Johnny talked on cheerfully, stopping without further ado in front of the two, followed by George, who, without stumbling, was able to approach them.
And she. Yes, she did the same to him. Kind of.
"This is George and Marisa." he continued. He said a little more about it, but Marisa couldn't hear another word.
Seconds passed, what felt like an eternity.
Marisa regained consciousness and looked up.
Into ice-cold, blue eyes. Into a face with cold, deep features. Blond, short hair that fell tangled in his forehead. She saw a man who could break all women's hearts, just with one look.
What did he see?
A woman, with brown hair, brown eyes. That was it. What more was there to see in her? Stinking normal. Definitely not a blond, perfect beauty like ... Maureen.
George noticed nothing. Instead, he eagerly set about befriending the other couple. He smiled kindly at the others and even extended his hand to them. As if she were a spectator, she saw him touch their hand and stroke their skin with his thumb. The other woman laughingly shook her long blond hair and ran her other hand through her shiny curls. Both were laughing, had said something to each other.
Marisa put her hands in her pants pockets. She couldn't do the same to George. Her nervousness was rising. A wet handshake was less than appropriate.
Vincent's eyes didn't leave Marisa's and a twinkle lit up at

her defiant and unambiguous gestures. Even though she had her eyes on Johnny, she felt exactly his presence, his mockery. If there was even a meter of distance, she felt exceedingly hemmed in and wanted to escape.
Fortunately, there was Johnny, and he provided a distraction.
"Make yourself comfortable. And once again, personally from me, congratulations on your engagement."
Ah, not the best distraction. More like unwanted attention focused on her again.
Vincent looked up at the remark. Any sparkle gone from his eyes. Interest piqued.
"Congratulations." were the first words he spoke to her. His voice low.
She herself didn't seem to know how to put words and sentences together anymore.
George on the other hand, put his hand proudly on her shoulders and squeezed lightly.
"Thank you, still very fresh."
"According to that, no ring yet." Vincent finished the other's statement, causing a moment of uncomfortable silence. After all, he had immediately noticed her hands as she had put them in her pockets. Stupid mistake.
"Don't be so picky. Why don't you tell us more? How did he ask you to marry him? A little romance is good for you, isn't it?" beamed Maureen.
She looked openly at George; her chin slightly lifted. A gesture that did not go unnoticed. By everyone present.
Johnny looked theatrically at his watch and interrupted the spell.
"I wish you another good stay. Meals and entertainment are available around the clock, as your brochure also states. We look forward to serving you for the next three weeks."
As the man finally let the door fall shut behind him, a sense of panic overcame Marisa. She turned to George, who was only too eager to strike up a conversation with Maureen.
"Next time." she finally replied, glad that her voice was still

quite the same. No tremor. No wavering. "George? We should get our things into the rooms."
"I'll show you where the rooms are."
"You can tell us where it is, too." Too abrupt. Too cold. Damn.
"Oh, we're already at the 'you'. Much better!" stopped Maureen. And Marisa could have cursed herself. "That's a good idea. It'll make it much easier for the next three weeks. After all, we'll be spending a lot of time together."
Her green eyes sparkled at her insinuations, and she laughed. Then at the same moment she walked up to Vincent and put her arm around his shoulders. A little saucy kiss on his cheek did not go unnoticed. By everyone present.
"Our bedroom is in the back on the left. You guys are in the front on the right."
Marisa couldn't watch any longer. She felt sick and funny. She turned away abruptly and grabbed what she could. She had distraction enough for the next couple of hours with unpacking and preparations for tomorrow's departure. Her thoughts were all over the place. Her head was spinning. All she wanted to do was focus on her vacation here. On her time with her fiancé. Nothing else.
Focus on that!
Three weeks of skiing.
His voice.
Sleeping in that beautiful mountain cabin for 21 nights.
He had hardly changed.
Shit.

~

It smelled of ice and snow. And mulled wine.
The bitter cold nipped and pinched at the cheeks, sometimes the only piece of skin that was not covered. Otherwise wrapped up thick and warm, everyone made their way to the hustle and bustle. There was little else going on in the small town, but at Christmas there was a lot going on. The town centre was magnificent to behold, with an illuminated Advent calendar in the mayor's windows, opposite a beautifully decorated giant fir tree. So was the superhumanly large carousel, which was a popular attraction for young and old alike. Typical Christmas delicacies and specialities were sold, as well as traditional wooden figures and Christmas decorations.
But all this aroused very little interest in Marisa. Instead, she walked arm in arm with her friend Danielle, swaying along the ice-slicked paths to reach the somewhat secluded stalls. To the small, quieter stalls where one could safely enjoy a hot drink before or after checking out all the other special features.
The young girls laughed light-heartedly as they arrived at the church square. This was where they spent every day, before or after school, which was right next door. Several schoolmates were just as out and about, standing away from the stalls in small groups.
"There he is." giggled Danielle suddenly, making them both stop. She turned to Marisa, taking off her cap before frantically trying to arrange her hair. Excitement was high, her plan had worked. Her crush was actually here at the market too. So, they hadn't been wandering aimlessly for the last two hours after

all. Marisa was happy for her friend. Finally, she could keep an eye on this hot boy too. She had heard so much about him, but not seen him.

"What should I do?" Danielle fidgeted nervously.

"We'll order something to drink!" suggested Marisa, pulling her friend with her. She had nothing to lose, was least worried about her own hair, which she had hastily tucked under her woollen cap. If it had been her darling, she would have run away.... Instead, she pretended to have the utmost self-confidence in front of her friend. Ha, as if.

It was already dark, but the snow and the twinkling Christmas lights made everything seem bright. Bright enough to see everything.

Him too.

Marisa knew immediately which boy her friend had been raving about. He was standing at the booth, at the table. And looked up just as the two of them approached.

For a lightning second, Marisa looked into ice-cold blue eyes. And the moment was gone.

But irreversible.

Danielle seized the moment to step in front of her, full of confidence and elegance. She ordered a mulled wine, paying with the knowledge that he was watching her. She had an attraction that Marisa herself would never have. She stayed in the background, just watching the action. And then...

...her friend became uncertain again. The hot cup in her hand, her plan negotiated, now what? Leave again and she would have blown her chance to talk to this guy again. That would be many long hours wasted thinking about what she could have done.

"Is there any room here?" asked Marisa out of pity.

Danielle looked at her in shock.

The boy with the cold eyes, even more so.

"Enough."

And so it came to pass that the two girls were now standing with their crush. Without having put the right sentences and actions in place.

"Do you go to this school too?" Danielle chattered happily in response. Marisa held her breath.

"You're asking me that?" he replied, almost offended. "You always follow me into the schoolyard at break time. You know perfectly well that I go here too."

He looked at Danielle, who would have preferred to sink into the ground.

Marisa raged inwardly.

What an ass! What's his problem?

"You're so right. We know all about you, Vincent McDormant. We adore you." Marisa immediately jumped in to pull her friend out of this miserable situation. She just wasn't sure if she was thanking her for that right now or not. Her expression was a mixture of shock, anger and total panic.

Vincent was instantly speechless. His gaze fixed only on Marisa.

"And you're who? Your sidekick?"

Marisa's eyebrows drew together. She couldn't quite interpret or condone his behaviour. She turned fully to her friend, who was just sipping her mulled wine to show him exactly what she thought of him and to get their attention exactly.

"Let's go drink our wine somewhere else."

Danielle looked at her in confusion. A hundred questions and arguments sparkled in her eyes.

But this was Vincent here beside her! The love of her life. The reason she was breathing.

Why shouldn't she take this chance to stand somewhere else?

His comments hadn't been that bad after all.

Marisa only slightly cocked her head to the side and threatened in the same way with her gaze back.

He's not worth it. He's totally arrogant.

'I'm Danielle. Do you want to go to the movies sometime?"

Marisa took a step back in disappointment after Danielle had unceremoniously and really cleverly made her decision. Nothing could be done about that. Just hope she wouldn't cry

about him for weeks.
Vincent looked into her eyes one last time before turning his full attention to Danielle.
Those icy blue eyes.
The ones she had never forgotten.

~

I can't wait to spend the next few weeks here. I need a new challenge. I need something naughty, something illicit.
Who should I give my attention to? Which woman can I see to the skin with my eyes?
Icy cold days, hot nights. Someone will want my strong, horny body.
I need more, much more than mountains and snow. Who can I pursue in the night? Overcome their defences and conquer them ice cold.
Fresh meat.
I am ready for the new challenge.

~

The next morning finally came. She had hardly slept. With tired thoughts, she persuaded herself that she was just excited to finally be able to ski again. That's why she had stayed awake for hours, that's why she hadn't found any rest.
Early in the morning, Marisa had all her things ready, waiting patiently for George.
Unfortunately, Vincent and Maureen came first.
"Did you sleep well?"
Their cheerful voice was nerve-wracking. Marisa had to force herself not to just ignore them and turn away.
"Fine." she brought out with difficulty, finding it even more troublesome to ask politely. "You?"
She didn't want to hear the slightest thing about how the others had slept. It didn't interest her at all. She didn't want to be reminded with a syllable of how they must have spent the night.
"You're all early risers, aren't you?" George interrupted the conversation when he finally appeared with his backpack and things. Thank goodness for that. "Why don't we have breakfast here together and we can get to know each other a little better?"
His gaze landed on the blonde woman in front of him, with the tight jeans and short jumper, until he remembered who was standing next to him. He put a warm hand around her waist and gave Marisa a fleeting kiss on the cheek.
Marisa instantly tensed at his proposal.
"We should go to the main buildings. The first few mornings are critical for the next few weeks. We need to make sure we

find the right ski group, etc. We have other opportunities to get together." she countered instead. That was the truth. It was essential to be there for the next few hours and not miss anything.
Especially not to get to know each other better. No, thank you.
"Enough." agreed Vincent.
Marisa stared at him in surprise. Maureen noticed the silence but covered it up with her endless cheerfulness. Love.
"Well, go on then. I'll drive the snow buggy."
After a few long minutes they were finally at the alpine hut, where it was safe to take breakfast. The dining room was big enough that you didn't have to deal with others if you didn't want to. George and Marisa spent a few pleasant minutes together, just a normal holiday.
Shortly afterwards, the staff made sure all the guests knew what the day would bring. They were all driven to the practice hills in minibuses. The different visitors were divided into smaller groups. During the morning, everyone was given a crash course in skiing. Most of them had enough experience and were able to move up to the next group in no time. Some had not been on skis for a long time and needed the whole morning or day to get used to it again. Little by little, you could see what level everyone was at. Eventually, the ski instructors would divide everyone according to their qualifications. They insisted that you never ski alone. Taking risks was unacceptable.
Marisa loved the smell of the pressed snow, the new snow, the ice. It filled her heart with joy and an impatience she could barely suppress. The guilty conscience came up again, she knew she was here with George. But it had never been planned that way. George had persuaded her that he would accompany her, he was a good skier himself.
But from the side, she saw him struggling with the skis. He needed help with unbuckling and buckling his skis. He landed on his backside more than expected. At his side, always Maureen. Beautiful, perfect Maureen. Her ski suit was bright

red and fit like a glove. Even with helmet and sunglasses she looked like a model.
But skiing wasn't her thing either....
Soon the couple was several degrees of difficulty apart.
So was Vincent. He could ski.
Shit.
Too late, he too had spotted her in the group and came up to her without any problems. Just what she needed, that he now wanted to start a conversation with her here alone.
"Marisa, good to see you."
Lucky again.
Now she recognised the ski instructor in front of her. Mitchell Burgess waved at her, letting the other skiers rehearse braking on the downhill as he approached her.
"Mitch. Hello." She smiled at him and was one step closer again to a normal winter holiday as she knew it.
"I heard you were back. Not alone this time. Is that your fiancé?"
The ski instructor was pleased to meet the man in front of him, standing stiff and still beside Marisa.
"No." she jumped in before Mitchell could shake his hand. Vincent didn't move an inch, watching her panic. An interesting spectacle.
"No." Less eager and defensive this time, she continued. "George is in another group. For now."
Mitchell laughed back and looked off into the distance. There was no sight of the others. It would probably take longer for them to catch up. All the more time with Marisa. Vincent recognised the joy in the latter's eyes.
"Go down the mountain. Glide, brake, glide, brake." he suggested to Vincent, looking after the others with satisfaction. He did him the favour, leaving the two of them alone. This time.
Marisa exhaled deeply in relief when she was finally out of his presence.
"How long are these practice sessions this year? I would have

thought we could at least get on the blue piste today?"
Her impatience and discomfort that Vincent was still at her heels became clear. Why did he have to be so much better than George right now?
"The training programme has changed a bit. Most of the tourists take a little longer with the new snow, it's all fresh. You know, we have to make sure everyone is safe."
"I'm really looking forward to finally skiing, can't I skip a group or two?"
Mitchell cocked his eyebrows tensely.
"Unless you cheated and went to another resort last week, in which case you haven't skied in the last eleven months either and you need this crash course."
Marisa nodded slightly, feeling a little embarrassed. She shouldn't have begged him for it. What was wrong with her? She was a grown woman who would naturally be fine with Vincent being in the group with her. There were two or three other skiers she had seen who did the training course just as effortlessly. She just had to hang on to them and stay on Mitchell. She wouldn't even notice him.
In theory yes, she wouldn't. In practice ... shit.
Vincent was waiting for them at the end of the day in front of the minibus. His face red from the cold, his eyes all the bluer. She did not look any better. Several strands of her hair had come loose from the braid and were hanging in her face, despite her cap and sunglasses.
She could no longer ignore him. As much as she wanted to.
"There was a time when you used to run after me during breaks. Now you run away."
Marisa felt everything inside her tense up. The memories of those times hurt.
"Not us. Danielle." she clarified, completely ignoring his second insinuation. And was inwardly pleased with her confident answer and strong voice.
"How is she?" He narrowed his eyes slightly to better interpret her reaction. "Has she still not forgiven you?"

She pushed out some air in disgust.

"Are you serious?" She felt deep anger rising inside her. Her jaw clenched tightly to avoid uttering another word.

"I'm just trying to bridge the silence. What do you want to talk about?"

She shook her head dismissively.

"The silence bothers you? Not me. You and I don't need to talk at all." she countered him and went off to talk to the other skiers.

Vincent watched her from afar as she laughed and talked. The people here all seemed to know her, to know her well, and also to appreciate her presence. But especially this Mitchell. If he didn't have his eye on her, he wouldn't know anything.

~

"He broke up with me." Danielle cried bitter tears into her pillow.

Marisa sat next to her friend and tried to calm her down. She didn't have much she could say, at that moment the emotions were still so raw she didn't want to hear anything either.

"At least you don't have to buy him a Christmas present," she just said, pragmatically.

Danielle only cried louder.

"I already did."

Marisa fell silent, concerned. She was not surprised. Hadn't her friend already talked about true love after their first date. Of course, she had already bought a present, and certainly written a love letter to go with it. She swore to herself at that moment that she would never do such a thing herself. True love! Ha, as if that already existed for a seventeen-year-old!

"Why did he break up with you? Do you know?" Again, Marisa tried to make sense of the conversation. If she knew the background a little, maybe she could speculate and help.

"I don't know. He just doesn't love me." Danielle blew her nose loudly and intently. Her make-up was all runny, her dark curls not lying perfectly for the first time. Her eyes were all puffy and red. "We were together for a whole ten days, weren't we? How can he just break up like that?"

Marisa stroked her friend's back. Yes, that was how you counted the days and time with your crush when you were a teenager. From the first conversation at the Christmas market until today, it had been a whole ten days. But in fact, they had only met twice.

But Marisa wouldn't say that out loud now. Ten days were ten days. If she ever got involved in a relationship, she would know exactly when it had started and when it had not.

After a couple of hours, Danielle had calmed down enough to fall asleep, holding a teddy bear she had wanted to give him, of course. That was sweet.

Marisa quickly made her way home, it was already dark, but luckily, she only lived two new-build blocks away from her friend. As she stepped out of the front door, awkwardly handling her scarf and gloves at the same time, she suddenly found herself face to face with Vincent.

Marisa stood rigidly at the top of the stairs in front of the new-build block, Vincent quietly at the bottom. His gaze never strayed from her. Probably because her scarf hadn't been all the way around her neck, and her gloves slipped out of her hand, landing halfway between them.

After the first few seconds, she got a grip on herself again, admonished herself inwardly why the hell she was staring at him like that, and went down the few steps to her gloves.

So did he.

Oh.

"Danielle definitely doesn't want to see you right now," Marisa said distractedly.

His nearness made her all nervous. Hastily, she grabbed the traitorous glove and without another word, ran back down the rest of the steps and towards home, away from him.

Vincent hesitated for a moment. Cursed himself a thousand times and followed her.

"I knew you'd be with her." he said as he ran beside her.

The cold air fell on her neck, and she fumbled with her scarf. She had never had such problems with her winter clothes.

"Oh, so... who's chasing who now?"

"You have no idea." he said honestly.

Marisa drew her eyebrows together in confusion.

"Should I call the police?"

He laughed out loud.
And thus, it was done. She was lost.

~

Guilt.
Feelings of guilt.
Emotions so powerful that you can't just go on living. This feeling keeps coming back, this feeling reminds you of the past, of something you can't change and so it destroys the present. It affects the future.
You have to learn to deal with it. And in the same step, you feel guilty for wanting to get this emotion under control. A vicious circle.
Marisa felt the past rising up inside her, making every day, every hour a little more difficult. She tried with all her might not to think about her first love. She didn't want to be reminded of her missteps. But his presence alone sent her thoughts into a whirlwind.
Danielle ... he had asked about her. He had mentioned her name as if he didn't know exactly how guilty she had felt at the time. She had fallen in love with her friend's ex-boyfriend.
Unforgivably.
Irrevocably.
At the time.
She had carried that guilt alone for a long time. In her young mind, she had deserved the nightmares and sadness. Accordingly, the suffering lasted a long time.
And here she stood now. In front of the minibus with her ex-boyfriend within easy reach. With the first great love.
And immediately only the worst feelings came up.
Guilt.
Guilt hit her. She should have been a better friend. Then they

all would have been spared a whole bunch of other feelings. Even the good ones...

Marisa shook her latest train of thought away. No way would she credit him with anything positive. No, she would not think of that now. If only George, her *fiancé*, would finally come off the little practice slopes. If only she finally knew that he, her *fiancé*, had finished well, so that they could ski the steeper slopes together. That was why she was here, after all. To feel the cold air on her face as she sped down the slope. To feel the adrenaline when she just barely scraped the curve with a short turn. Feeling alive after all these years when she could just deal with herself and nature and tackle an extreme downhill. Because she was good enough. She wanted to ski so badly, with or without George.

Guilt.

A powerful feeling. At that very moment she knew that she had selfish ideas and that she was acting selfishly in her thoughts.

Unforgivable.

Who knows... maybe he just needed to get back into it and had just been hiding his talent.

Maureen and George came walking back together. In deep conversation, laughing. It wasn't until they were standing right in front of them that they paid any attention.

"So, how did it go? Did they give you a clear for the blue pistes?"

Marisa had stood in the cold long enough without having done anything useful. Her patience was wearing thin.

George weighed his head back and forth. With his gaze half on Maureen and half on Marisa.

"The ski instructors agreed that we should spend another day on the small slopes. He's hopeful that by the end of the day we'll have skied our way back in."

Marisa swallowed dryly. In her jumble of thoughts, she had no adequate answer. She smiled a small smile but wasn't sure it looked friendly enough. To make things even better, Vincent came running over to them. His mood had obviously not suffered, a hot drink in his hand. She looked longingly at the cup from which a sweet steam was rising. A hot cocoa would really have been a great idea. Instead, she had refused to have a conversation with him, exposing herself to her freezing guilt. She was cursing herself right now.

Vincent listened with little interest as far as skiing was concerned. He found it more exciting to tease her with his drink. His gaze did not leave her eyes for a second as he took a long sip. Marisa no longer knew what she was actually seeing at that moment. There was a little twinkle in the blue; he was making fun of her.

This asshole. Nothing had changed.

It was time to sit down in the warm minibus, next to her fiancé and put all the superfluous things out of her mind. After the long hours, they finally made their way back to the alpine hut for dinner, where she could indulge in her fiancé's serene, familiar routine. His manner she knew, she appreciated. His quietness in the evening, where they read a book together, or answered emails was soothing. She did not need more.

Maureen, on the other hand, was apparently looking for entertainment and before she could say anything, they were all sitting together at the table. The blonde in a smart outfit with her hair laid in a fine coiffure, her make-up immaculate. Far too fine for a resort like this, in Marisa's humble opinion. But of course male visitors as well as females took a liking to her appearance and demeanour. No surprise.

No envy either. If she wanted to, she could get all dolled up and walk around in high heels. But not here, in the snow, in the cold, in front of her handsome ex-boyfriend. Her simple looks and practical clothes would have to suffice. She had no intention of impressing anyone.

"I had such fun on the slopes. I think our ski instructor was rather fed up with us in the end."

Slope? More like a bump.

"He didn't even try to show us the right position at the end," George agreed with a laugh. The two of them got on brilliantly.

Marisa concentrated on her food in front of her. This conversation was making her angry. Wasn't he going to ski properly? How were they supposed to spend the holiday together if he got stuck on the kiddie slope.
You stay by his side and help him get better.
I won't.
Guilt.
"Which slope should we tackle tomorrow?"
Marisa looked into the blue eyes. He looked stunning. His blond hair even wilder after a day in a helmet and cap. Couldn't her hair look as playfully loose?
Shit.
"We?" She heard the coldness in her voice herself and broke off immediately. George and Maureen didn't really need to overhear the distaste she felt for him. She cleared her throat slightly.
"Mitchell usually has two or three runs in mind for the first day. I'll join his group and see what happens. If it gets too strenuous, I'll change the slope. If it gets too easy, I plan another run or two."
Vincent nodded slightly, his gaze resting on her. His hand on his glass of water as if he were thinking. Marisa wished he would finally stop looking at her like that. He knew exactly how she avoided direct eye contact. It was all the more difficult for her to show her reluctance... and to feel it.
Or had he forgotten?
She felt sick when she realised that perhaps he had long since forgotten all that concerned her. He had probably repressed all that long ago and never thought about it again. That was almost embarrassing that she had assumed their relationship had meant something to him. As if he had wasted a second on her.
"Good idea. I'll bring my cards." he agreed.
"That fits like a glove, Mary. You two can have fun on the black or pink piste and Maureen and I will still practice together and then meet you later."

Black? Pink? Had he no idea at all?
Vincent raised an eyebrow challengingly at George's joyful words but did not address the reason for his amusement.
"You're not going to rip each other's heads off for the couple of hours, are you?"
Marisa looked at the other woman in shock, not quite knowing what she was alluding to.
The other laughed and placed her hand possessively on Vincent's arm. She leaned seductively against his side so that her breasts pressed against his upper arm.
"I can see you haven't warmed to each other yet. Come on. Try to get to know each other. I know you had planned your holiday differently from sharing it with us. But George and I are making the best of it too, aren't we? Vinny is really cute!"
She rounded her lips as if she were talking to a baby and then pressed them firmly and unabashedly to his mouth.
It made everyone a little uncomfortable, or at least it did for George and Marisa.
"Why don't you tell us about yourselves a little? How long have you been together? When's the wedding? Was it love at first sight?"
Marisa felt great panic rising inside her. The evening had to end, as soon as possible. The other woman kept patting Vincent's face. His cheek, his ear, his neck. She hadn't moved back an inch either, sitting halfway on top of him. Her gaze fixed directly on George with every touch. Unbelievable.
She breathed a sigh of relief when Vincent took her hand, breathed a kiss on it and made a little more room for himself. Maureen didn't seem to resent him, on the contrary she used her free hand to pour some more wine.
"Definitely love at first sight. I knew from the start that we should get married." George replied, stroking Marisa's hand tenderly.
Marisa would have loved to jump out of her skin.
Just what is going on here? Are we all trying to prove to each other who is sleeping with whom?

Unnoticed, she slid a few centimetres away from him instead of towards him. She searched frantically for a reason to leave this place and escape to her mountain hut.
"This is like something out of a romance novel!" the young woman reacted immediately.
Just believe that there is such a thing. When you're old enough, you'll realise they're just fairy tales.
George smiled contentedly. Yes, it had worked out that simply.
"We will get married as soon as possible. Just a little ceremony, that's all."
"Such a hurry?" challenged Vincent. For a split second a shadow fell over his face, but he immediately got himself under control again.
"Why wait? What argument is there for that? Our relationship is solid, strong. We're old enough to know what's right for us."
His answer had sunk in. Was George indirectly addressing the age difference between Maureen and Vincent? After all, she hadn't known him like that.
Crafty.
And what a compliment. They had a *solid, strong relationship*.
Was that supposed to be a positive thing? Or synonyms for old and boring?
The handsome man with his cold demeanour just smirked at the remark and accepted defeat. Until the next time.

~

Their relationship had by no means been a bed of roses.
Oh no. It had been an absolute whirlwind.
It had been the experience of a lifetime.
Vincent would turn up the other night and upset everything. It wasn't a *regular* relationship. Sometimes they had a date, sometimes not. Sometimes he was late, sometimes he didn't show up at all.
Initially, they never showed up at events where you might see other classmates. It was going to the cinema, or riding bikes in the park. It was at her house or his. But not in front of everyone.
Marisa was under his spell and let herself be pulled along. When something exciting happened, she would float in seventh heaven. Only to fall lower when he would then not contact her for days. She vowed to ignore him, to give him the cold shoulder.
But she had only been 17 years old. Too inexperienced, too in love to stay strong. And his eyes. His blue eyes seduced her every time. This tingling in her belly, this eroticism was unbearable.
And addictive.
In the six or seven months she learned how hopeless and in love played together.

~

So much temptation. I can hardly hold myself back. It was far too easy to be near you, to watch you. To stand by your side without you suspecting anything. You smile at me. You accidentally touch my shoulders, but a hot fire burns inside me.
When will you become mine?
Your eyes say yes, your closeness says yes. I should take what you offer me. I see myself with you, deep and hot together. You send me little signs that you feel the same way I do. It doesn't matter if there's someone else. He's not important. He can't give it to you or you wouldn't move your hips so provocatively.
I'm ready.

~

Day 3

It got off to a good start. George and Marisa set off together and independently for breakfast, as well as the slope. There was great anticipation in her. They started the day on the blue run, near the practice slopes. Which meant that Marisa was never too far away from George and he could join her as soon as he had passed his integration stage. She immediately felt more comfortable, knowing that they would both make the most of it. And she couldn't wait to go down the slope, see Vi - no, George and do it all over again.

There was one small hitch in that Vincent was in the same group as herself.

She couldn't deal with that at that moment, though, because it was all about getting up the mountain. Even though she had been skiing for so many years, drag lifts worried her. She had once gone off track as a child and had to ski down the middle of a slope. Since then she had the utmost respect for these ski lifts and needed every brain cell to get her coordination in order.

She gritted her teeth in annoyance that Vincent was lining up next to her. These lifts didn't give you much personal space. On the contrary, as they waited, their arms touched. She didn't feel anything, the insulating ski jackets protected her from actual contact. Fortunately. But what was happening in her mind was inappropriate.

Marisa knew how close he was to her in those few minutes. Her concentration on the tracks, not getting right on the ski lift and going straight down, was intense.

She was jubilant to have finally reached the top of the mountain.

Mitchell steered all his skiers towards the start of the slope. He briefly explained how the signs were divided in this area and reminded everyone that they should not ski alone under any circumstances. Without further ado, the others found someone to ski with.

Mitchell looked hopefully at Marisa. She smiled approvingly.

Vincent had not missed this moment.

"He's as happy as a little kid." he said condescendingly. Marisa drew her eyebrows together in annoyance.

"And that bothers you?"

"Not at all, MK." he replied just as coldly.

Marisa reacted poorly to his choice of words and scooted as close as she could. With a warning look and clear voice, she addressed him.

"You know I don't like that pet name."

"So you think it's better if your fiancé calls you Mary?"

Marisa took a deep breath. Where was this conversation going to lead? Talking about the past, about their relationship, she wasn't up to it.

"No. I just haven't told him yet."

"I also know you tolerated him with me. MK." he reminded her as well. Her heart contracted painfully at his suggestion.

"You haven't been in that position for a long time that you should even think him."

With the words, she slid effortlessly towards Mitchell and got ready to take off. She was going to enjoy the next few hours. Not want to think. But even out of the corner of her eye, she could make out his tall form. She made out his dark blue suit and felt his gaze boring into her back.

With one remark, with one name, he had thrown her completely off track.

Bastard.

~

It really seemed like the perfect idea.

Her relationship with Vincent had been very fresh. So new that she didn't even know if they were actually boyfriend and girlfriend. He showed some interest in her, he sought her out, he seemed to want to spend time with her. The question, of course, would never be asked outright as an inexperienced teenager. Instead, one assumed it was. The problem came with it being close to Christmas, and what to buy. Or was that too much? She could ill ask her friend Danielle for advice.

Hey, what had you already bought your ex-boyfriend for Christmas? Oh, and now that you don't need it anymore, why don't I give it to my boyfriend? Yeah, that's right, your ex-boyfriend. I'm seeing him behind your back.

That was out of the question.

A letter to him would settle everything. She didn't quite want to call it a love letter, but at some point it did seem to her in the end that she had accidentally written something similar. She just wanted to make it clear that she really liked her time with him and that he could visit her more often. Unfortunately, she also wrote a few lines about his eyes and his hair. How much she liked them.

You idiot. How utterly embarrassing.

Even today she couldn't understand why the hell she had put all that in writing.

No wonder the whole thing had backfired. Somehow the letter had not only ended up in his hands, but also in those of his friends. She still felt sick at the thought of that day at school. Danielle and she were walking along in the schoolyard as usual when she recognised his group from the side. She wanted to shyly peek in his direction just to see him without his friends or Danielle noticing.

Instead, they all burst out laughing.

"Isn't that your ex? Maybe she wrote you that letter. Hey, show the love stuff again!" the guys shouted excitedly, laughing rudely. They literally snatched the piece of paper out of his hand.

Marisa could clearly see their purple stationery and pink handwriting. Why had he brought the letter out here to the schoolyard? Had he made fun of her the same way he had just made fun of his best mates?

Danielle looked shocked at the group and then offended at Vincent. She still had feelings for this boy, it was clear to see in the sad eyes.

"Is that why you broke up with him?" Her voice was trembling, but she stood confidently in front of him. Marisa rather less so. She remained somewhat in the background, shivering herself, not from cold, but from guilt.

Vincent looked away from her friend and then at Marisa.

All the colour drained from her face. For the first time, she didn't just feel the deep tingle in her stomach when he was near her. This time it wasn't his eyes she wanted to lose herself in. She had to think frantically how she would get through the next few minutes.

And after the Christmas holidays she had to transfer to another school.

"No."

"*You look so cute with your blue eyes.*" read out the tall, thin Karl. He giggled as if to himself and with his hand he crumpled almost the whole sheet. It had taken her hours to draw the little flowers and hearts. Couldn't he be careful with it.

Concentrate on what's important here, she admonished herself.

"*I'm looking forward to seeing you more often during the Christmas holidays. Maybe as a boyfriend?*" he read on in a higher pitched voice. "Ooooh, that sounds exciting. What's she up to?"

The others all laughed. Vincent finally took the letter from him and carelessly put it in his jacket pocket. That one too!

"The letter is from my girlfriend." he finally admitted.

Marisa pleaded with him silently with her eyes.

"You have a new girl? Who's that? Are you sure it wasn't that one?"

Danielle looked heartbroken. She turned to her friend for comfort.

Shit.

"Do we know her? Who is she?" poked Otto. He didn't even notice the other girls anymore. He was only interested in who Vincent was having fun with.

"M ... K."

"M? Like Emma? Oi, Karl do you know an Emma? MK?"

"At the comprehensive school, maybe? There's the new girl we saw from the bus the other day. Man, she looked cool."

No one noticed in all the commotion. The boys were chattering loudly about Emma, what she would look like. Busty, tall, slim. Hot. A good red herring.

They would never, ever come up with Marisa Keach.

"Vin, come on. Ignore those two. Give us details."

All this time he hadn't taken his eyes off her. She was immensely grateful to him for that.

She had fallen a whole lot more in love with him.

~

What a welcome déjà vu!
At the end of the day, Vincent was waiting at the minibus and no sign of the other two.
Marisa was in no hurry to join him, instead she stayed close to Mitchell and tried to engage him in conversation. It seemed the easiest thing ever, he seemed to enjoy her company. She thought he was nice too and managed to relax a little, despite feeling *his* eyes on her.
Damn it!
It wasn't long before Vincent was fed up with being ignored by her. She noticed him moving out of her hearing and sight. She took a deep breath and smiled at Mitchell. Her attention had suffered somewhat, but now she was all ears again.
"When was the last time you tried cross-country skiing? We're expecting some fresh snow in the next few days. I know of some people-free trails we've got freshly groomed."
"That sounds ideal. Maybe the end of the second week?"
Too soon to rejoice. Vincent was back again. This time he didn't keep his distance and came straight up to the two of them. Without asking, he held out a cup to her and kept another in his hand. She just stared at it. Hesitantly.
"Hot chocolate." was all he said. And his eyes sparkled. "Or would you prefer mulled wine?"
Marisa was speechless.
You!
Her eyes warned him he was on thin ice. Why did he have to poke around in the past again?
Mitchell looked in surprise at the two of them and at the

outstretched hand with the smoking drink. It probably looked silly that she still hadn't accepted it. Pure peer pressure made her accept the drink.

It smelled delicious. And she loved the warmth on her hands, which, despite professional equipment, were the first to get cold. Once again Vincent had seen more than she had wanted to admit. Yesterday she had already longed for a hot drink. Very thoughtful.

Or sneaky?

"Can I borrow cross-country skis?" continued Vincent their conversation as if he were part of it. She gritted her teeth angrily, openly showing her distaste for his own invitation to the activity. "Maureen and I would be interested."

And that had hit home. There she had embarrassed herself to the bone again. How had she assumed he wanted to go cross-country skiing with her? How embarrassing. He didn't want to spend time with her any more than she wanted to spend time with him.

"Of course. We have all sorts of things. Sledges too." He laughed at his remark and took a quick look around. Most of their group had arrived back, without any bad injuries or dislocations. A successful day.

The short drive back to the shelter was leisurely and private. Finally, time alone with George again. Finally being alone with him and hearing about his day.

It didn't bother her that he had spent it with Maureen. It was natural that he mentioned her in every story he told. The most important thing was that from tomorrow he was also allowed on the blue slopes. They could finally ski together.

Although she had actually already toyed with a few ideas for downhill runs on the red slope. She didn't mind...

What she did mind was his suggestion to have dinner with the other two again....

"Mary, we must not forget that we share the mountain hut with them. If we worry too much about ourselves, it will only make our stay with them more unpleasant."

"I don't think so. We still have several evenings ahead of us where we can eat with them. The first two days on the slopes are exhausting, we might as well stay here."
George wasn't letting go so easily. He had made a decision, for both of them, and so would they.
"If you're not well, then of course we'll stay here, darling."
He stroked her shoulders good-naturedly. But the silence that followed said more than words. He gave her a hint of a kiss on the cheek.
The silence grew.
"I can still stand, see? Think of my legs here. Didn't I practise falling and standing up for two days?"
Marisa smiled at him. How bad could it get?
It was bearable.
Barely.
The table George had chosen seemed much smaller than all the others. The seating plan had been badly chosen. How and why did Marisa find herself right next to Vincent?
His aftershave was in the air. She had loved it back when he had struggled to smell good as an adolescent male. Now she could have condemned him for it. To make matters worse, he had taken a quick shower just before leaving and his hair was still half wet and a total mess in his forehead.
Damn. It!
Her thoughts ran amok. She had loved that look. That hair, those eyes had softened her back then.
Why the hell were they doing the same to her now? What was wrong with her? It had to be because too much in her past had gone unspoken. Her mind just couldn't rest. That was why she felt like she was in a quandary.
She forced herself to sit a little further away from him and concentrated on the conversation at the table. George was just enquiring about his housemates' line of work. Maureen was currently between two jobs, undecided whether she would make more money as a tourist guide or a model. Vincent's answer was rather vague, that he was looking into the law.

A safe topic.
"I've always been interested in the digital world. If you have any problems with your mobile devices, give me a call."
That almost sounds like flirting to me!
Marisa ignored their laughter and relaxed mood. Maureen had totally outdone herself again in her choice of clothes. If you had the figure for it, you could wear anything. Even a far too short jumper over skinny jeans. Of course. Why hadn't she thought of that?
Because she much preferred to hide her feminine curves with thick woollen jumpers than to highlight them. And she had no fashion sense at all.
"Technology that inspires." Vincent just murmured from the side and Marisa almost spurted out some of her water again. She cleared her throat quietly to regain her composure.
And that almost sounded like a joke. Had he noticed the flirting too?
His eyes shone at her reaction. His gaze penetrated deep into her.
Shit.
Your eyes are cute as shit.
Shh!
"Did he help you out of a critical internet situation too?"
She wanted to ignore his question from the bottom of her heart, wanted to talk to him as little as possible. Couldn't avoid it. She picked up her glass of water and leaned back slightly in her seat. A mistake. She had come a very little bit closer to him with her shoulder. Maybe she should open the wine after all, and worry less about everything.
"I can turn the computer off and on myself, thank you."
This time he was about to smirk.
Double shit.
"Two IT experts, then. I know who I'll be calling then."
She sent him a quizzical look. Warning, disapproval or panic. One of those, or all three.
"Don't you have an IT department where you work?"

"A badly overworked, insufficiently manned team. Help usually comes too late."

Marisa was silent. She had to admit that curiosity drove her. She was only too keen to know where he worked. At the time, he had graduated from high school with a 1.3. Where had his results taken him?

But she didn't ask him. Didn't want him to think they could just be nice to each other again. She was here as a favour to George. Not because she had forgiven him.

"What do you do for a living?"

"I work in a children's nursery." she replied. And found deep pride in herself as she thought of her place of work and her dear colleagues who will keep everything up to date for her for the next few weeks.

"Of course." was all he said.

Marisa felt a chill run down her spine. She just managed to excuse herself before standing up abruptly. The table shook, glasses clinked, fortunately everything stopped. Maureen and George looked up in surprise. Luckily, they had been so engrossed in their conversation that they hadn't seen anything. Until now. George was taken aback.

Without another word she ran almost blind with rage to the toilets and found refuge in them. She didn't know how long she must have spent in the toilet cubicle. Not enough time to sort out all her emotions and thoughts. Disappointment. Sadness. Panic. Pain. Love.

But worst of all was the thought of having to go back to the table, back to the mountain hut.

Her heart contracted; she felt the panic rising inside her.

Deep breaths. Think of what's good for you.

George.

Breathe.

He brings calm and order to your life.

Breathe. Forget. Survive.

After half an eternity, she plucked up the courage to seek out the others again. With any luck, the other couple had already left and all that was left was George, who was waiting lovingly for her.

This was not quite the case. The situation had improved somewhat when they joined them at the bar. Away from the cramped table, towards the noisy bar and alcohol.

Good idea.

Marisa walked towards them full of strength and less anger. She would suggest to George that it was time to go. He would understand and the evening was over.

But it was Vincent who saw her coming first. And it was he who was now coming towards her.

What the hell?

Afterwards she didn't know why she turned around like a child and ran away again. She turned around on the spot and went back to the toilets. This time, however, she was not alone.

"MK."

And in one fell swoop, the pent-up anger she had so painstakingly brought under control in the toilet was overflowing again.

That son of a bitch.

"Don't do that." she warned him, clearly unimpressed.

He didn't listen to her. Within seconds he was standing right in front of her. Fire in his eyes, the same anger, a thousand questions.

So close in front of her.

"What just happened?"

"Don't pretend you don't know what games you're playing here."

He raised his eyebrows arrogantly.

"Games? What the hell are you talking about?"

"You keep alluding to our past. You can't let it go. Danielle, mulled wine, MK!"

Her brown eyes were dark. She shook with anger, wanting to shake him.

He just looked at her bizarrely.

"Really? That bothers you?" he gave his answer like an echo

from this morning. He had known it after all, that she remembered that time as well as he did. Alas.

"I can't stand your presence."

"You don't say."

He took an exasperated deep breath. Her nearness distracted him a tiny bit. He cursed every second longer he stood here with her in front of him.

"You're not seventeen anymore. We were a couple, we broke up. Get over it!"

She stepped up to him, close. Too close, but her emotions were wild.

"We didn't *just* break up, Vin."

Vincent heard his name, heard her accusations, knew what he'd said wrong. Had always known.

His eyes fell on her mouth, her lips slightly parted. He saw her breathing in and out. Literally felt her warm breath on his face. Seventeen years was a hell of a long time, but at that moment he remembered exactly how sweet her lips had tasted. How erotic her kisses had been. How much his body had reached for her.

His breath caught too, her breathing quickened.

He stepped back from her.

"And yet it was over. It is over. Deal with it like an adult."

She froze instantly. This time it hadn't been anger that had vibrated her body. But all at once she was back in reality. And full of hatred and dislike.

"Go to hell."

Marisa was shaking inside and out as she stalked off with her shoulders held high.

Asshole. How could he?

~

She had expected him to kiss her. There, on the spot, no matter who would see or think what. But he didn't.
No matter how close they got, no matter how many times Marisa stood perfectly in front of him, he held back. Surely, they were not boyfriend and girlfriend? After all, wasn't he interested in her in that way? After all, he had said it loud and clear in the schoolyard. Surely he had to know that she had heard it too. Had that also been an act in front of his mates?
In any case, she had fallen for it just as much. Too much so.
She longed to be kissed. She wanted him to take her in his arms and touch her in places that had been totally taboo until now. In all those teenage years, she had only lusted for when that moment would come for her. She was ready. But only if he wanted it too. Therein lay the problem.
He was so unpredictable with his dates, so untouchable when he didn't want to see her. She couldn't find the courage to go for it herself. Perhaps there was a grain of truth in the fact that he didn't find her attractive enough after all. From what she had heard and seen, she was totally not his type.
Even her friend was the complete opposite of her.
That had to be the reason.
She didn't appeal to him.

~

It's so fucking cold here, my dick is freezing. Standing on the slopes all day, just so I can see you for a few seconds. I need hot thoughts. Just the thought of you, mastering the turns with a skilful, slinky swing of your hips. Ah, you know I'm watching you. You see the desire in my eyes. I can't hide it any longer. You are always in my mind, but you should be moving back and forth at the tip of my cock. Your smile, your lips, and I'm getting hard. Ah, better. The fucking snow didn't ruin everything. You make everything good again.

~

Day 4

Marisa had not slept well. All her emotions, self-doubt had followed her into her sleep.
George noticed her silence, reacted to it. As a fiancé should.
But she felt all the worse for it.
What would she have done if Vincent had come closer to her after all? How would she have stopped him?
... Would she have stopped him?
Her guilty conscience dragged her down deeper and deeper. Nothing had happened. Nothing would happen. And yet she was plagued by the knowledge that her heart had beaten faster in his presence.
It was enough.
Today George and Marisa were on the slopes together.
If only he could hurry, they had already wasted an hour where he couldn't find his gloves.
Marisa smiled patiently at him. Don't mention it.
Then they had to wait for the next minibus.
Then it took them a while to find his way around the drag lift. Also like them then, he got out of the tracks twice. The third time, they almost made it to the starting point of the easiest blue slope.
No problem at all. They were together, spending a particularly good time together. The descent was pleasant, calm and as planned.
Just the way George liked it.
And what Marisa needed in her life.

And yet she could not suppress her longing for the mountains, for carving, for the right turns. Towards afternoon, she finally heard the redeeming words.
"I need to rest a bit. Shall we go for a coffee?"
George took off his gloves at the same moment, took off his sunglasses and helmet. He had really had enough, no matter what Marisa's answer might be.
Just at that moment the other group of skiers came rushing up. Even just the fresh breeze of snowy air they conjured up as they ploughed down the snow gave her an inward thrill.
"Marisa, we're going for another run on the red slope? Are you coming?" Mitchell's eyes were invitingly friendly. His face red from the cold, especially now in the afternoon when the sun was beginning to set and the temperature was dropping.
"Go on. I think Maureen and Vincent just went into the café. I'll sit with them."
Marisa felt the greatest relief and guilt in one fell swoop. She smiled at him. He gave her a quick, insignificant kiss and walked stiffly towards the café.
Marisa turned to her favourite ski instructor in a flash and beamed all over her face.
"Let's go!"
In the background, George was now hurrying to join the others without his skis and poles, just as Vincent watched his group drive away. He too had a bit of an appetite for a steeper descent and instantly apologised to them.
He had no worries they would have a blinding conversation without him. There was no kiss. He felt inexplicable haste enough to follow the others. Mitchell noticed him first and pointed delightedly in the direction of the slope.
Marisa was quite confused as to what Mitchell was doing with his sticks, and made the mistake of turning backwards during the brisk lift. Before she could do anything, a ski pulled her off track and she had to drop sideways out of the tow.
Shit.
Firstly, it was incredibly embarrassing in front of the other

skiers in their group, and secondly, they hadn't quite reached the top of the slope yet. Damn. What on earth had distracted Mitchell? And then her?

"You all right?"

Marisa looked up from the snow in shock and met ice-cold eyes.

What the hell?

She hadn't seen him in the group earlier. He must have left George and Maureen sitting in the café. Had Mitch waved at him?

He had landed her in the snow. That only made things so much worse. She had far from forgiven him for his comment. His accusation that she was the stupid one here played on her conscience. He had meant that she had made far too much of their relationship. Had he forgotten the ending? Repressed it? How could he?

She refused to take his hand and not very gallantly got herself back up as quickly as she could.

"Are you trying to suck up? You were welcome to drive all the way up the hill. I don't need any help."

He just looked coldly at her snowsuit, which was the first time it had really been broken in, this year. Certainly not for the last time. Especially if she could finally get onto that red slope now.

"You know we're not supposed to ski alone. Mitchell will thank me."

He didn't respond to her. His voice neutral, no emotion on his face. And great distance.

She wanted to be angry with him for much longer. She wanted to throw everything she could at him, and tell him clearly what she thought of him and his leaving then. But she also wanted to go skiing.

He was right.

With difficulty, they made their way up to the starting point. Vincent used his map to guide them along the most direct path. Once again, she appreciated the drag lifts, even if they gave her nightmares every time, they didn't make climbing halfway easier. She was so exhausted that she had no strength left in those long minutes to loathe his presence. But she would make up for that as soon as she could breathe again.

The sun was barely visible, the cold nipping at her cheeks and fingertips.

When they finally arrived at the departure point, no one from her group was in sight. Mitchell had already accompanied them down. He knew Marisa was competent enough to find the way. And Vincent had also proved to be very experienced and sensible.

With the new, unfamiliar slope ahead of them, they had to put aside their differences for the moment and concentrate on the map.

Marisa looked intently at the markings on the slope, ignoring the fact that Vincent was standing inches away from her. He had slid his sunglasses onto his helmet to see the lines properly. He looked focused at the map and was professional in his actions.

Man. She could have listened to him all day.

"We don't have much time with the sunset. We'd best practice our carving. Mitchell thought it would be appropriate for all of us today. I think we can do it."

To which he said, he folded the map back up and tucked it into his breast pocket in his suit. Marisa glanced down the slope.

If she was honest, she couldn't wait. The whole day had felt like she was giving lessons on the children's slope. Now it was going to be much, much more interesting.

She would never admit that out loud, of course.

"George can't ski." he now abruptly changed the subject. He had to seize the moment when she was just standing in front of him so openly and without being defensive.

Marisa immediately moved away from him a little and got ready to go. The abrupt change of subject caught her off guard.

"He's doing his best."

"Why did you go on a skiing holiday together when you obviously can't spend the time together."

She didn't like his questions. He seemed to be looking for a deeper reason.

"You couldn't care less."

"You've been skiing here for years. Mitchell knows you and loves you more than anything. But he hasn't heard of George."

Vincent wanted to know more at that moment.

She didn't give him the satisfaction of elaborating.

"How exactly did you two meet? How long have you been together? How long engaged?"

"I feel like I'm being interrogated."

This time he moved a little closer to her. Her reluctance to answer him was driving him crazy.

"No ring, newly engaged. Newly in love?"

Marisa needed to get away from him. His persistence made her uncomfortable. That and his body right in front of her. Best she give in so they could finally get going.

"The beginning is a little unclear, when our relationship started."

"Oh really? You know it down to the minute."

She fell silent.

"At least from the moment you had sex?"

No answer.

A thousand thoughts jumped out at him. His eyes sparkled. His emotions tripped.

"Did you have sex on your first date?"

Marisa narrowed her eyes. Not to admit it, and not to answer it. "Think what you want." And with that she pushed off with her sticks and made her way down the slope. She just barely had the direction in her head, hearing his skis cutting the snow behind her. And within seconds she had lost herself in those sounds, in the icy wind. She loved the movements, the speed, the tight turns. It was a challenge, something new. She could be herself here.

Halfway down the slope, she stopped and signalled Vincent to go ahead.

They were like a team.

It was a pity that even the most beautiful descent had to end. Too bad he had to ruin it with conversation.

Fortunately, the others had stayed down on the mountain until all their group members were safely back. The excitement was great. There was a certain rush of adrenaline, pride at having survived the first red run and anticipation of more to come.

Marisa and Mitchell glanced fleetingly at a few more runs on his map, talking eagerly about tomorrow's plans. Vincent just watched them from afar. Shortly after, other active skiers joined them, laughing and discussing tomorrow with Marisa.

Her smile was genuine. Her charisma much more intoxicating than the skiing itself. No one noticed the numbing cold and how darkness had slowly but surely fallen upon them.

After half an eternity, the others recollected themselves and made their way to the minibus. Vincent was aware of how she deliberately stayed as far away from him as possible.

It drove him crazy that she did not smile at him or seek his suggestions. He would have liked to shake her until she finally looked him in the eye too; without hatred or reproach.

Arriving at the alpine hut, they unloaded all their equipment and backpacks. Slightly late, they finally arrived at their warm, welcoming accommodation.

George and Maureen were sitting comfortably on the sofa laughing just as Marisa and Vincent entered quietly with an iron stare. Somewhat reluctantly, George rose from his seat and helped his fiancée with her things.

"We've had to wait for you for a while." he said quietly when they were alone in their bedroom.

Marisa carefully hung up her things and attentively straightened her accessories. She heard some annoyance in his voice, but couldn't quite interpret it as to why he would be angry with her.

"Sorry, yes. The descent did take a little longer in the end. We had to trudge up the mountain on our own first and then find our way down safely. It all took longer than expected."

"You and Vincent?" His question was quiet but clearly what he was pointing to.

"Originally our group together. We found them again at the end."

George was silent for a moment.

"Maureen and I have already eaten." He finally added.

It hadn't seemed to her that he hadn't enjoyed his time with the blonde beauty. Apparently, he did.

"That's no problem." she replied kindly, walking towards the man in front of her. His grey eyes dark, not particularly warm at that moment. "We can make ourselves comfortable here and rest."

George looked at her for a long time, attentive and concentrated. The silence was heavy in the air. She was unsure what or if she should say something. His gaze did not waver, did not become affectionate or forgiving.

"I am very tired. Tomorrow is another day." A small smile hung on his lips, but it was not genuine. His eyes remained cold.

Marisa nodded her head slightly, a little confused as to why her proposal was not accepted. Hadn't she just proposed something quiet and together?

"Fine. You're my fiancée, Mary. I don't want you to forget that." George kissed her lightly on the forehead. Then he set about getting ready for bed.

When he was in the bathroom, she dropped onto the bed, perplexed. He had been nice to her in the end, had talked her down. But his words echoed in her head.

Had she forgotten?

~

"Did you forget we were supposed to meet?"
Marisa only half turned towards him. Her pace didn't slow down a bit, on the contrary she walked all the more purposefully up the hill.
"Did we?" she countered annoyed, not letting her bad mood distract her. Unconsciously or deliberately, she chose the path that led her through the Hammer Valley. Not the best way. She had heard many bad stories about how a young girl shouldn't go up there alone. But it was much shorter than the busy road along. And it was secluded from other people, but especially classmates.
"MK! Why don't you stop and talk to me?" He grabbed her thin arm and forced her to stop in front of him. His fingers on her even though her jacket, jumper and T-shirt were in the way. It was the first time he had come close to her. And then under such unattractive circumstances.
Therein lay the problem. She wanted more.
"Why did you want to meet me?" she brought out, jerking her arm free. Even that brief touch caused numerous butterflies in her stomach.
Vin looked at her in confusion. Had he missed anything here? After all, that had been the agreement for a couple of weeks. They would walk home together when he had time.
"Then don't," was his defiant reply and he ran off.
Marisa had not expected this and had to decide in a flash whether to let him go or not. Or not. Her mind said concretely yes, it would not end well. Her heart literally pulled her into his arms.

She reacted as her teenage heart dictated. She ran after him until this time she stood in front of him.

"Why did you want to meet me?" she repeated her question clearly, her brown eyes shining. "To just talk about school and our career plans again?"

She swallowed dryly, her heart pounding in her throat. Her hands damp, and she was nervous as hell.

"Or as a boyfriend? Because we haven't even ... done anything that you do ... as boyfriend and girlfriend... I mean.... I ... you haven't kissed me yet."

Now it was out. How honest. How embarrassing. She couldn't take the words back. She just had to wait. Be patient. Freak out with impatience soon.

Vincent saw her in front of him. So sweet, so blind. Relieved. She had no idea what was going on inside him. Every day, every hour. And right now.

"Talk to Danielle." was his reply and she would have liked to scream out loud.

What the hell? What had she had to do with any of this? Was he back with her? Since when? How? That couldn't be. Or didn't he like kisses? No advances in general?

She just stared at him. Shaking her head, heart breaking.

"You're not making any sense. Danielle? Your ex-girlfriend?"

"*Your friend.* Every time you see me, you feel guilty. You fight a guilty conscience so you can't enjoy the present. You resist enjoying it. Tell her the truth. Tomorrow at school, the last day before the Christmas holidays. And then ..."

Vincent stopped. Unable himself to choose the right words without embarrassing himself. His blue eyes so clear, his gaze fixed only on her.

Carefully, as if afraid of hurting her, he raised his hand to her face and just very gently touched her cheek with one finger. Like a bolt of lightning, it went to her stomach. This tenderness, his closeness. His scent. She could not breathe, could not think. But she felt it deep inside her.

The moment was over again far too quickly, and he had made

his way out of her proximity. This time she did not run after him, but she knew she would see him again.

Not everything always has to go according to plan. On the contrary, the unexpected is the most exciting. I'll only think of you tonight when I'm playing with myself. It was a nice surprise. You feel the same way, don't you? Is this the beginning of our passionate relationship? Just one look from you and I feel the blood flowing to just one big part of my body. You're in my head, in my dreams. Will our first fuck be as good as my imagination? There's only one way to find out. Come to me. Spread your legs.

~

Day 5

Marisa bore him no grudge. Of course George wanted to spend the day with her. Of course, they would. Even if she had made all these plans to try two or three red runs today.
She didn't look sadly at the other group. She just smiled encouragingly at Mitchell. She wasn't here to ski all the risky slopes. She didn't need to feel the wind in her face as she sailed down the steep slopes, following gravity.
George was in no hurry to get up the mountain, instead he wanted to go for a hot drink first to warm up. Marisa looked longingly at the drag lift for a flash second. She hid her disappointment behind banal stories about her work and tried to show him that she wasn't suffering from this time together. The blue slope wasn't so bad. Just a little shorter, and flatter, and full of tourists.
"Are you having a nice day?" asked George around noon, putting his arm affectionately around her shoulders. They had again paused at the café for something to eat. So had a hundred other skiers. Untalented ones, beginners and children.
"Of course."
Shit. She had just flat out lied to his face.
And she wanted to run away, and ski for real!
"George, Mary - good to see you!" Maureen made her way through the rows towards them. Her snowsuit hung gallantly around her waist. Her top was tight and provocative around her round curves. She looked as if she had just modelled for a ski magazine, as if she had skied down a real mountain.

The pleasure was not hers at all.

"What are you doing now? I've lost my group and I'm looking for a partner." She winked at George.

Or maybe she did.

"I don't have a partner either. Poor Mary had to put up with me all morning." He laughed sanctimoniously. Indeed, she *had to*.

"Shall we ski together? We can help each other back up?"

George's laugh lines came up at his eyes as he conversed with the young woman. Of course, he liked her and she liked him. What was there not to like about his looks? He was only twenty years older than her. Nothing more.

"Mary, would you mind if I went on with Maureen's group?"

Marisa held her breath. She didn't want to agree too eagerly.

"No problem. I'd like to try some red runs myself." She admitted honestly and pulled out her map from her backpack. She showed them what she had in mind, but the other two were not interested or impressed by it at all. They only saw colourful lines in front of them, nothing more. After a short while they went on their way, so Marisa could finally leave too.

According to the plans from last night, they would just start the second piste. She hoped Mitchell would check his mobile before they left. If she was lucky, they would wait for Marisa, and she could join them.

Bingo.

Mitchell quickly texted her back and she was on her way to piste 109. Great excitement, relief but also a guilty conscience suddenly plagued her. She knew there was only one thing that would help ... she had to be honest with him and tell him she wanted to ski other slopes. He would understand.... And then her skiing holiday could really start. Oh, the mountains she wanted to ski down, the tight switchbacks she wanted to tackle and even if it got humpy one time, it wasn't going to stop her. She felt the greatest exhilaration at these thoughts on the way to the meeting point. She had a firm grip on the drag lift, made it to the top. Glided smoothly on it.

And her joy faded.

"Where are the others?"
"Already on their way. Mitch split us up."
Marisa refused to believe it. Of all the other skiers, he had to pick Vincent McDormant. Why not himself? Why him? Her stubborn, uncaring ex-boyfriend?
"Out of the question."
She glanced angrily at the slope in front of her, put on her sunglasses and made a quick decision. She would drive off without him. A stupid gesture, against the rules. Childish.
But she just wanted to enjoy this holiday. Not with him by her side.
Vincent cursed loudly as she pushed off with her sticks in a flash. She hadn't even looked at the map, and she wasn't even supposed to be leaving in this direction. With nimble hands, he folded the map back up, put on his gloves and put his glasses back on. Just as carelessly and annoyed, he ran after her. She had talent, he had to admit. She would be really good at slalom running. But so was he.
With some effort, he finally caught up with her. Skilfully and planned, he cut her off with his body and they both landed sideways in the snow. Everything happened so fast that Marisa landed hard and for a few seconds didn't know what was going on.
Then she saw and felt Vincent above her, and a thousand emotions rose in her all at once.
What the fuck? What was he thinking? Get off me! Stay away from me!
But not a syllable came out of her. And she did not move an inch. His face was so close in front of her that she could feel his breath. His body on top of her did not feel heavy. Her breath caught in her throat. But his eyes were covered, as were hers. The protective layer was like a protective wall. No one saw what the other was thinking or feeling.
Vincent broke the spell and straightened up again, unaffected. He refrained from offering her his hand this time. Those few seconds were enough to bring her back to reality and make

him feel her anger.

"Oh great. Now we're even further behind them."

"What the hell has gotten into you? As good as you are, you can't just drive off like that just to avoid me."

Marisa patted the snow off herself. She didn't hear a word. She lifted her sunglasses and shook out the snow.

"Nothing would have happened here. Your manoeuvre, on the other hand, could have turned out much worse."

"It was planned. I had to stop you somehow. Such a headless thing to do."

"Get over yourself. I was just trying to catch up with Mitch and the others so I could ski with them."

Vincent shook his head in annoyance and did the same to her. He looked different without the protection of the sunglasses. Colder, more distant. Unattainable.

"You're risking your runs here just so you don't have to be alone with me."

"Who are you? The ski police?" She had achieved just the opposite. She had to talk to him again and endure his attractive closeness. Vin looked at her sternly.

"If Mitchell had seen you straight up like that, with the sharp short turn straight down the slope, not knowing the route, he would have automatically suspended you for two days. No matter how fond he is of you. It's worth it to you?"

Marisa gritted her teeth in annoyance. She was about to burst. She had already wasted the whole morning by not skiing. Now again!

"I'm not here to chat and swap stories!" she spoke defiantly. "I'm here to ski. To have new adventures. To explore new slopes and just be free. And then you show up here and ruin everything."

"And *you* don't ruin *my* holiday?" he reminded her coldly.

She stared at him. Could this be happening? Did he feel exactly the same dislike towards her and just wanted to jump down her throat as soon as he saw her?

Ah, she hadn't thought of that.

Vincent did not expect an answer. Instead, he retrieved his map from his breast pocket and began to orient himself by the trees and hills. Somewhere he had seen a sign earlier. After a few minutes he knew where they were. He pointed in a general direction and nodded at it. Without so much as another word, they made their way back to a safe off-ramp.

Never in her life would she have admitted it, but she had never enjoyed skiing as much as she did today. They worked well together, taking turns leading, orienteering. She could switch off, could enjoy her beloved snow. Eventually they had caught up with the group and it was possible for them to go for one more run. For those hours, she appreciated his presence.

With tired legs and frozen faces, they returned to the minibus. Marisa laughed delightedly and said goodbye to Mitchell without a care in the world. He hugged her in response and gave her a kiss on the cheek.

"See you tomorrow. If you behave, there might be a black run!"

Marisa couldn't wait. With a happy smile, she turned to the minibus and saw George. His face closed.

"Did you have a good day, darling?"

Like a slap in the face, his question came and her smile faltered. He had already asked her that question. She had lied. Now it was obvious how much she had liked the day without him more.

Shit.

"Yeah. How was your afternoon with Maureen?" she answered honestly, trying to get something off her chest.

"Nice too." George took Marisa in his arms and hugged her tightly. "I just want you to be happy, after all."

A loving gesture. Kind words.

Why did it feel to her like it was a lie? Why did she feel like she had betrayed him?

~

"You went behind my back. You do that to your best friend?"
The conversation with her still-girlfriend had not started well. Marisa had wanted to start by saying that she considered Danielle her best and only friend. Then, not wanting to chicken out of the rest of the truth, she talked about the night Vincent had broken up with Danielle.
"You didn't even wait a day before you made a pass at him. Not even an hour?"
"We were just talking." she defended her actions, but she knew it was all falling on deaf ears.
Then the thing with the letter.
Marisa bowed her head in resignation. The day had been terrible. The turmoil, the fear that Danielle would find out. The embarrassment that she had written a love letter and the panic that all the graduates would read the lines.
"You're MK?" Danielle put one and one together and shook her head wildly. "Of course you are. Marisa Keach. I'm a complete idiot. You made fun of me behind my back. They were all laughing at me."
Marisa tried to ease the situation somehow, but her friend was too upset and angry to comprehend anything.
"Not at all. That was an embarrassing mishap, us walking across the yard at that point. Believe me, I would have liked to have sunk into the ground myself."
"Serves you right." came the curt reply. She wiped the tears from her eyes that had appeared with her anger.
Now she was bitter and no longer devastated. That was a good sign, wasn't it?

"How do you just deal with your conscience when you kiss him? Like I did him?"
Marisa fell silent, affected. She hadn't had to deal with these feelings yet. Especially not the blind jealousy that rose in her immediately. That was uncomfortable.
"You kissed?"
Danielle paused with her evil glare for a moment. Surprised. Then spitefully.
"We didn't do anything else. And more."
Marisa wished she'd never asked. She wished she had never listened to Vin and faced her friend. She shouldn't have chased after him, she should have let him go. She couldn't find the words. Felt miserable and alone. And couldn't talk to her best friend about it.
"I have to go now." she said sadly, getting up from their bed. "I just wanted you to know that I like him. And if he wants me to, then I want to go with him."
"You've been together a long time. That's what this is all about."
"We were just talking." she repeated again. But powerlessly. She wanted to get out of here, couldn't think beyond her bleeding heart right now.
"Don't lie to me anymore. I'm not blind after all. I saw the way he looked at you. In the schoolyard. All the time. And I told myself it wasn't true. You would never do something like that to me."
Marisa was getting smaller and smaller. She deserved all this hate, this misery.
"I will never forgive you for this."
And neither would she forgive herself.

~

Oh yes, a body to cry for. So perfectly rounded, in the places I will soon caress. While I thrust my cock stiffly into your cunt. Over and over again.
Yes, you are my chosen one. I will not be distracted from my goal. No matter what other deeds I must complete for now. You will soon be mine.
Luckily, I'll have myself by then. Oh yes, you horny, hot woman. Sit on me. Throw your long hair over your bare shoulders. Faster, move faster. Ah.

~

Day 6

Marisa and George were up early to hit the slopes. The blue one. She owed it to him. He had told her again in the evening how much he was looking forward to their first holiday together. Besides, he was so sorry that he was unfortunately not as good as her and he really tried to get better every day. She shouldn't blame him for maybe not telling the whole truth. He couldn't wait to spend the day by her side.

Marisa was the one to blame. She shouldn't have lied and hurt his feelings. How had she been so wrong? She wasn't really like that. She always said and did what was right. The last few days had only made her waver a little. Now she was fully behind her fiancé and the promise to spend time with him. She didn't want him to feel bad and sad. He was going to such lengths for her.

Marisa ran unsuspectingly down the steps, closely followed by George, when she landed literally in Maureen's arms.

In the naked arms of the blonde beauty. With wet, fresh-smelling hair. With the tiniest towel wrapped around her slender body.

Marisa's own breath caught in her throat. She looked stunning. Her self-satisfied smile confirmed that she too knew what she looked like at that moment. Her gaze landed on the person behind her. Her eyes sparkled.

And Marisa's gaze wandered to the person who was also coming from the direction of the bathroom. At least more clothed than his girlfriend. But her reaction surprised her

despite that. The deep stab in her heart totally unexpected and uncalled for.
And completely paralysing.
Vincent did not look away, held her gaze. But she could read nothing in it. She could not interpret his dark eyes.
She had to look away. And push away all emotions and questions. They had no place here. Were purely childish and unacceptable.
"Good morning." Maureen warbled cheerfully and her smile was adorable. She didn't mind at all that she was literally naked in front of them, and George's jaw almost dropped to the floor.
"Have you thought about borrowing the skates?" she asked innocently. As if now was the perfect moment to maintain a lengthy conversation.
George actually seemed surprised and contrite as he remembered their plans for today.
"Maureen, I ... " He hesitated. Torn with what he had promised his fiancée and what he saw before him. "Marisa and I -"
The other woman tilted her head a little and almost made a pout. Then she half-turned to the other, unsexy woman with her argument.
"I thought Marisa was assigned to the next group. You didn't want to get in her way."
George weighed his reaction carefully. He had actually said that.
Marisa felt guilty that he had worried so much.
"It's no problem if you already have plans for today. I'm sure Mitch has room for me."
Her fiancé hid his joy well if he felt it, and he gave her a light kiss on the cheek instead.
"You're the best."
Everyone smiled silently all around. With a confident and emphasising sway of her hips, Maureen walked past them, up to her room. An exciting sight that could turn anyone's head.

~

Mitchell was most pleased that she could join in. He had chosen a few runs on the red slope before they could hopefully move onto the black slope in the afternoon. She was most pleased that he chose her as a partner and that she could navigate with him.

They practised different skiing techniques and expended a lot of energy. It was exhausting to concentrate on everything and fight the cold. Overnight the temperatures had dropped a bit and her hands were becoming a problem. Whenever they had to wait at the various meeting points, she tried changing gloves, moving her fingertips and putting on thinner gloves as another layer. It didn't help much, she hardly had any feeling left in her fingers and she struggled with the sticks. She signalled to Mitch that she would wait for the other skiers and join them at the back.

With numb fingers, she managed to get her thermos out of her backpack and barely poured herself a cup. She scraped some snow loose and added it. Enough that she wouldn't burn her fingers, but not too much that the water was too cold.

Marisa watched the other skiers from the side and counted the various couples that passed her. There were still three to go...

She had maybe five minutes before she had to get ready to go again. Her fingertips felt better but were not quite warmed up yet. She was ready.

That was when the others arrived. Vin was among them. They all followed the rules, didn't leave alone. They recognised each other and saw her alone. Vin nodded to the other two and a moment later he strayed from the others and came towards her. He was fast enough that she could have stopped him. She was annoyed with herself for having had to stop. She hated it when she herself was the invalid.

And why the hell did he of all people have to be alone with her again?

"Are you alright?"

He stopped right in front of her, and took off his glasses. His face, on the other hand, red from the cold, from the sun. His eyes bright and as clear as the sky. What a contrast.

"Yes, I'm fine." She had no intention of showing him how she suffered from the cold today. She wasn't going to allow herself any weakness.

She poured the warm broth away again and set about hastily putting everything away so he wouldn't have to wait for her any longer.

Vin watched her and acted first. Repenting later.

Without hesitation, he took off his gloves too, stopping her from putting hers back on. He took her hands in his and squeezed them gently.

Marisa stared at him, trying to pull her hands away, but he wouldn't let her. The warmth of his hands felt good.

Far too good. It warmed her body not only there, but in other places too. Her breathing was irregular. Her heart was racing. What was wrong with her? Why did she have to react to him like this?

Him of all people!

Vin slid his skis a little closer, as far as he could without them both losing their balance. Marisa just watched, not reacting as he rubbed both her hands together in a crest and pulled them to his mouth. She didn't show how everything in her craved him as he gently breathed on her fingers. She felt sick, hot. She was vibrating uncontrollably. Damn.

"You just have to think hot thoughts." He whispered softly, meanwhile his efforts to revive her finger tips.

Everything else inside her was fully alive. A fire was burning that she had not felt for a long time. And she had to put it out immediately before it got out of control. She was engaged. Shit.

"Like the thought of Maureen and you in the shower together?" That had distracted her from the moment very well itself and she managed to withdraw her hands from his. Reluctantly though ... but she would never admit that to herself.

"If you like the idea."

"It leaves me completely cold." she countered immediately, as if she believed it herself.

He narrowed his eyes slightly at her answer. He tried to read in her eyes what she was actually feeling, but it wasn't working. He had no idea if she really meant it. It was killing him.

They were still close to each other. But her body language had changed. A few seconds ago, he had thought she felt the same desire as he did. Now he was convinced that she would claw his eyes out immediately if he even touched her by mistake.

"You prefer George's little passionless kisses on the cheek?"

Vincent's gaze was unreadable. Neutral, controlled. She didn't have the gift and raised her eyebrow in obvious anger.

"How dare you?"

What was he trying to say? What was wrong with her relationship with George? They were rather quiet about anything sexual. She wouldn't have it any other way.

Vincent gritted his teeth. If they were going to talk about it, let's talk about it properly.

"Do you love this man?"

She had had enough of his endless questions, of his doubting her and George.

"Fuck you."

She waved her sticks, they slipped from her numb fingers, and she bent over in annoyance. She struggled with the stupid thin things when she still couldn't pick them up. She would leave at any moment without sticks just to get away from him.

He ignored her offer. It was very inviting but inappropriate at that moment.

"Before you go down the black run, make sure you warm up in

the café and have a good meal."

"You don't have to worry about me." She said defiantly, frantically trying to put her gloves back on. It took far too long and became embarrassing.

But she finally had to give in and took a long look down the mountain. Vincent knew she was struggling with herself and remained silent. She wanted to ski, and she could only do that if she listened to her body.

And maybe it wasn't a bad idea to have her alone in the café. He had a question or two.

~

"How did you meet? When? Under what circumstances?"
The café was full of skiers and visitors as usual. They had just about found one of the smallest tables in the corner, where the windows gave little protection from the cold and the heating was miles away. At least they were sitting on comfortable cushions and had hot cocoa in front of them.
Marisa leaned back in her chair, uninterested. She had agreed to lunch, but was already regretting it dearly. She defensively folded her arms over her tight-fitting ski top. She had not intended to take off her snowsuit and felt rather exposed at that moment. One should always expect that after a hundred years one would suddenly find oneself sitting in front of one's attractive, hot ex-boyfriend again and become very aware of one's lack of smart clothes. She tucked her hands under her arms and tried to restore them with her own body heat.
What did he care how her relationship with George had started?
"Marisa?"
Pointing his gaze at her hands, he held them out to her. Like a small child, she instinctively followed his prompting and placed her hands in his. The warmth, the heat, his tender touches were well-intentioned. But immediately she felt that it had been a mistake to lean forward, to come closer to him and feel his skin. Her body betrayed her in a lightning second, her heart racing away. A thousand memories came up in one fell swoop. Not her tragic end this time. But her enchanting beginning.
She jerked her hands away from him and leaned back as far as she could. Vincent was glad about that.

Or maybe he wasn't.

Panicking to underplay her reaction, she gave up ignoring his questions. Maybe she would answer one or two pressing questions, and then he could finally leave her alone. Dinner had already dragged on for far too long. The others were already on the black piste. She glanced fleetingly at her mobile. Mitch had texted her the starting location. As soon as the onion in her fingers stopped, she was out of here.

"He showed up one day at the gym I go to. Tada! Our first meeting was in a sweaty gym, with twenty other people on a training bike. Satisfied?"

Vincent stored the information in the back of his mind. He was reassured that he hadn't somehow picked it up on the internet. And yet he was not at all satisfied and mentally sorted his further questions.

"How often do you go to the gym? Do you do it regularly?"

"Well, look at me. Do I look fit and toned enough for you?" and instantly regretted her defiant answer as his gaze actually moved slowly and seductively over her entire body. And then closed again.

"Why don't you just answer my question? Do you have a particular day or days that you go?"

"Every Tuesday and Saturday." She tilted her head and eyed the man in front of her. Did he spend his time in fitness training. His arms were muscular, his figure in good shape. Shit. Her mind was running amok.

"Why are you asking about this?" She cleared her throat slightly to shake off her wild thoughts.

"I don't trust him." he replied honestly. "I have a bad feeling about him."

Marisa laughed coldly, dismissing his concern immediately.

"I liked it so much better. Doesn't everyone dream of it just happening? Especially these days. I've met him in person. Would it fill you with more confidence if I had put myself online in the dating sites? Would it be better to expose all my personal details on the internet, for all the world to see?"

Vincent said nothing to that, still trying to categorise the situation.

"Was it love at first sight for you too?"

With you, yes.

Marisa hesitated. Her thoughts at that moment a little confused. She didn't want to think about it, didn't want him to question their current relationship. But this whole conversation had been a joke. She hadn't been able to concentrate. Simply because she finally wanted to get back on the slope. Just because of that.

"Why don't we talk about you and Maureen? Where did you pick her up?"

Yes, that was a good tactic. She was really interested in his answers, too.

He furrowed his eyebrows. He didn't want to be distracted from the subject. Something wasn't right here, and he needed to know more.

"That's not the same thing. That was pure lust. I don't bind myself."

"You don't bind yourself." she repeated his statement mockingly. As if she didn't know that. "You've never committed to anyone."

"And I never will."

Marisa felt her anger deep inside her. The regret, the disappointment, the heartbreak even after all these years.

"And that's where we differ. I don't want to live alone. I don't want to wake up one day as a crazy old woman with five cats. No. I want to spend my days, years, with someone."

She knew she didn't have to be so honest with him, but she was anyway.

"With George?" he asked again, as if he simply couldn't comprehend it. Marisa shook her head in disbelief. He had a crush on him. "When did you meet him at the gym? How long have you known him?"

"It doesn't matter at all. I've known *you* for 17 years and that doesn't mean we belong together any more than George and

I do. Can we finally stop talking about this and start driving? Accept it already that I'm going to marry George."

"You don't have to get so upset every time. Let's discuss it rationally for once."

For the first time he too seemed moved and irritated. He wanted to grab her by the arms and shake her.

Wake up! This man is not your future!

"So, he seeks you out at a gym where you go twice a week. He's what in his early 40s, 45 years old?" Vincent spoke as if to himself as he summed up the facts. Without considering what she was hearing or how she would interpret it. "Why does he want to be with you?"

That was enough. That bastard.

Marisa had finally heard enough, didn't care if her hands, her fingers were warm enough or not. She had to get out of here. Far, far away from him.

She stood up abruptly, but her gaze did not leave him. Her voice clear and distinct.

"Believe it or not, after you un - dumped me stone cold, I've had several relationships. Believe me there are men in this world who find me desirable enough and want to be with me without having hidden motives."

Marisa dumped him. Shocked and deeply offended.

She hadn't the slightest idea how damn desirable she was.

~

"I told her everything."
Vin had been waiting for her at the corner after the last lesson. Holidays at last, more time to meet. More opportunities to get to know each other better.
Marisa waited patiently for his answer. In her head she kept trying to sort out her thoughts and expectations. She wanted to approach the matter with a cool head, but her heart was fully gone. It was eager for him to finally make a start. She wanted him to hold her hand. Or for him to stroke her face again, like the last time. She wanted a kiss.
Didn't he want it?
He did not respond to her remark. Quite the opposite. They talked about all sorts of things, but not about how their relationship would continue. Or whether they had a relationship?
It was not to be misunderstood. Their conversations were deep and meaningful. And until now, she had never talked about the world with any boy or girl as she did with him. Her favourite things to discuss were the adults in her life. Teachers, parents. Vincent found it interesting to guess what was happening or had happened in their lives. They speculated how happy or satisfied they were. They tried to read thoughts, interpret facial expressions. And their imaginations so often made them laugh.
His close proximity was actually enough.
That day they laughed together, on the way home. In the cold, just before dark. Soon they would come out at the end of the path and arrive at the busy settlement where he would walk

away from her.

Marisa reacted quickly and from the heart. She took his hand in hers. His warm hand felt great, and she got tingles in her stomach. Even more so than usual when she even saw his laughing eyes.

But he instantly withdrew his hand from her. Marisa stopped, offended. She looked down at her winter boots, fighting back tears. She wasn't sad, she was pissed off. This anger pushed out these stupid tears that she would have liked to run away. After a few moments she regained her composure and looked at him angrily.

Vin had not expected this reaction. It changed something in him.

"I don't want to hurt you." He admitted now. Surprised himself by his words. His honesty. But those brown eyes were full of emotion, defiance and challenge. "I will hurt you."

Marisa tried to understand his words, but her teenage heart could not hear his warning. She wanted to believe that everything would be all right. She ignored the realisation that he had just broken up with Danielle and she was quite devastated. How many girls had there been before her?

She didn't think about any of that at that moment. Except that he hadn't wanted to hold her hand.

"Don't you want me?"

Vincent hesitated.

"You haven't the faintest idea."

~

"We haven't seen each other all day. Didn't you see my messages? I was hoping we could meet for lunch."
Marisa felt the guilt rising inside her. She had no excuse, had no excuse for not checking her phone often enough. And if she did, it was only to keep in touch with Mitch about her obsession with skiing.
And who had she had lunch with?
Shit.
And how had it ended?
Shithead!
He really should have left his comments in. She had been unable to think of anything else. Her enthusiasm of the departure had been in check. She had been so offended that he could even hint that no man would have any sexual interest in her at all. Like a sword to the heart. No wonder she hadn't felt any pleasure that afternoon. Maybe also because Mitch hadn't wanted to take on a black piste after all.
Misery, self-pity, anger.
And now guilt was added to the mix. Her fiancé had tried to see her. She had totally pushed him to the back, not thought about him at all. Had assumed all along that he was off somewhere having fun with the blonde Maureen.
Shit. Shit. Shit.
"I had trouble with the circulation in my hands today. I hadn't even been able to hold my phone for a long while." she explained honestly.
George looked at her quizzically.
"If that doesn't sound like an excuse."

Her look was incredulous. What?
He instantly regretted his cold comment and had to react.
"I was only joking." he added quickly and hastily took her in his arms so that she could not see his expression. He hugged her affectionately, but something was missing.
Marisa hesitantly raised her arms and hugged him too. For a split second she thought of Vincent instead of George and closed her eyes in disgust. There was no place for that here.
"I'm glad you're feeling better. Enough to play board games with me?"
She broke away from his embrace. She didn't feel at all like mingling with other people in the busy common hall. She was only too happy to just stay here and prepare for tomorrow.
"We can play here in the living room too."
But George looked at her disappointedly. This suggestion was unacceptable, didn't she know? And he didn't need to say anything else, and they made their way to the big alpine hut.
As they had thought, the room was full. At least not as full as the café had been at lunchtime today and there were several tables and seating for everyone. A few other skiers were already playing chess or rummy intensively. Just the thing for George. Marisa joined in the first round but found her fingers still tingling. She really hoped it would subside by tomorrow.
She excused herself to her fiancé and went to the bar to order a tea. Maybe it was just the cold she needed to chase away.
"Still having problems?"
Marisa pretended she hadn't heard him. He had a lot of nerve just showing up again like that, pretending he'd never, ever totally offended her. She picked up the cup and a bowl of peanuts.
"Did you say something?" she said coldly as she turned to him and then walked back to the other playmates just like that. Somewhere in the corner, George sat and had found a new play partner. Maureen.
Marisa sat down on the sofa in view and watched. The heat of the cup did her good.

"The cold shoulder again?" commented Vin, sitting further away from her. But not far enough. She could smell his aftershave all too well. He had showered and was now tormenting her with that irresistible smell.
The bastard. When was this torture going to stop?
"You're surprised, after your impertinent insinuation?"
Vincent now realised which way the wind was blowing. It was precisely because of the opposite that he couldn't stay the hell away from her.
"It's about George, not in general." he tried to explain himself, but it fell on deaf ears. His words weren't quite as clear either.
"From tomorrow onwards, we really should do everything we can to stop our paths crossing." Her announcement was bitter and clear. There was no compromise to be made here.
"Fine. I'll arrive a little later so you can ski with your beloved Mitch."
She nodded slightly. Mitchell. Wasn't he proof that some men found her attractive? After all, he always said so himself. Couldn't he accept that?
Marisa grabbed some nuts.
"Mitch. He doesn't harbour any dark motives either." She nibbled on her snack, very pleased with her comeback.
Her defiant reply, however, broke the strongly controlled camel's back.
Vincent leaned over to her. Not suspiciously close, but close enough that she could hear every word.
"I also want nothing more than to rip your clothes off and take you. With no motive. Just pure sex."
Vin got up to leave. He'd said too much, revealed too much, and was struggling with his hard-worked restraint.
Marisa swallowed, shocked, nervous. Aroused.
And the peanut stuck in her throat. Try as she might not to let on, she couldn't avoid a strong urge to cough. The tingling, the pain in her throat were unbearable, she had to defeat the peanut again. She would much rather digest his hot remark now than this nut.

Within seconds Vincent was back at her side, and so was George. One of them patted her on the back, another talked her down. The moment was full of comedy, certainly funny for others to watch. But she could have cried. It was extremely embarrassing and unpleasant.

Finally, everything was fine again. She could breathe again, just barely. And now?

The two men faced each other rather defensively. If looks could kill.

"I think Marisa wants me to take over now."

What was going on? She rubbed at her red, tear-filled eyes.

George helped her to stand up, which she thought was nice, but only to put his arm around her possessively. Tighter than usual. Not particularly affectionate. As a clear statement.

"You spend a lot of time with my fiancée." George's choice of words in the formal salutation was deliberate. It bothered him. More than he expected.

"You don't." countered Vincent equally coldly. With a brutal truth included.

Ouch. That had hit home.

That was the end of the evening. And the friendliness between the two was over.

Marisa, on the other hand, remained silent. So much had happened today. What she had to digest had been insulting, disappointing, cold, bitter.

And incredibly arousing.

Shit.

~

Did you see me today?
In all the excitement I had to lock myself in the toilet and get my lust under control. You had almost caught me, in my observations, in my intention. You smiled at me. I almost came in my thick snow pants. That would have been a mess. Luckily, the loo wasn't far. A little tenderness, urgent rubbing and it all settled down again. And then I could bear your closeness again. Your scent. So feminine. Your figure tantalisingly perfectly sculpted ... even in that stupid snow gear. Is that how you see me? Powerful and masculine.
I'm impatient. I don't want to wait anymore.

~

Day 7

Marisa had been dreaming. Intense dreams. Everything had seemed very real to her. She hadn't had such dreams and imaginings for a long time. And would not have them again in the future, but especially not with Vincent McDormant in the leading role.

She felt guilty, dirty and bitterly disappointed in herself. She was in a dilemma like never before. She was in a stable relationship, about to get married. She was ready to share her whole life with George. And she was dreaming of Vincent. How could she? It was unforgivable. It was wrong.

It wasn't her. She wasn't that kind of person, didn't want to be. It scared her. It made her feel guilty.

George looked at her silently. Could he read the guilt in her face?

"You look tired."

Marisa felt the blush rise to her face. Embarrassed, she ran her hand over her face to hide everything she regretted. The day was not getting any better. Out of her guilt, she spent the day with George and Maureen on the blue piste. She smiled politely, nodding cheerfully in approval, loathing every minute here with them. But then she remembered her dream. And her guilty conscience brought her back to the reality that she should have been nowhere else but here by her fiancé's side. Next to Maureen.

Her mobile vibrated in her breast pocket. Several messages

from Mitchell only reinforced her longing for freedom. The freedom of the mountains, of the snow. Nothing else.

It did her good that she hadn't even crossed paths with Vincent. It was better this way and exactly what she had wanted.

"We'll go to a movie night, together. I think that would do us both good. Spend some time together. Isn't that what you want?"

Marisa nodded in agreement. Her heart didn't share that desire today.

"Would you mind if I stayed here? I have a headache and I'm tired."

George looked at her. Hadn't he just made it perfectly clear that it would do their relationship good if they both went to movie night? What had she not understood?

"Weren't you going skiing alone tomorrow too? Shouldn't we get the most out of this evening?"

"Yeah, you're right. It's just that Mitchell suggested an interesting slope and I -"

"Deal. Let's go now and come back early."

Marisa smiled slightly.

The alpine hut had attracted all the visitors. Snow carts lined up outside the entrance, as did a couple of sledges. Marisa grinned at the sight. There was definitely nothing in the rules about not being allowed to sledge while drunk.

George prepared to get some of the popcorn and drinks while Marisa went to the bathroom. Out of the corner of his eye, he followed her walk and recognised the ski instructor from the other group coming from the same direction. This time not bundled up in a professional waterproof snowsuit. On the contrary, his clothes were a bit disarranged and he was busy running a cursory hand through his hair.

George was about to turn away when he saw an attractive lady in her mid-forties walk past. A very feminine figure, thick, full hair falling around her shoulders. Her stride provocative and confident. Such a woman knew that other men could not resist her. He wouldn't be an exception if he hadn't already been involved, of course.

His gaze immediately returned to the bar in front of him when Marisa came back. With a less elegant step, but nonetheless a seductive aura, because she herself didn't know how stunning she looked in those tight jeans and jumper. He smiled at her, hoping she hadn't noticed his stare at the other woman.

Finally they made their way into the large multi-purpose room. The mood in the large room was cheerful. Chairs and sofas were set up wherever there was space. Small groups of acquaintances sat here and there. Couples with underneath and a few single visitors.

Mitch was also in the corner, waving cheerfully at Marisa. By now he seemed less concerned about his clothes again and looked his immaculate self. His hair still a little tangled, but it suited him. His brown eyes friendly and inviting. If she didn't know better, she would suggest his openness and gestures were flirting. But of course that was not the case.

She took the moment to talk to him briefly while they showed a few more different trailers. The screen wasn't the biggest, and the speakers didn't quite drown out the excited chatter in the room. People arrived one by one, with full glasses in hand and small plastic bowls full of homemade popcorn. The rustling of the packets and the opening of the bottles slowly subsided.

As soon as the film would start, they could concentrate on the action.

Marisa laughed with Mitchell, which was good. He himself had been looking forward to the evening in particular, just to see this hit. He offered her his popcorn and as she could never resist the sweetness, she gladly accepted. When she turned to her fiancé, she recognised his disappointed look. Something was stirring inside her. She just couldn't say what it meant.

Her guilty conscience won out and she apologised to the handsome man. It was time to sit down with George. She stopped in her tracks as she watched Maureen and Vincent calmly settle down next to George on the sofa. He wasn't serious now! First big speeches about how they should spend time together; warning and disapproving looks and comments about their behaviour. Meanwhile, he looked deeply into the eyes of the blonde woman right next to him with a broad smile. *She* shouldn't forget, her ass.

As the film began, the room grew quiet and she had no choice but to join the others. She took another handful of his popcorn before sitting down next to George. At a distance. Her concentration was affected. This funny love story couldn't reach her mood. She heard the others laughing, felt everyone relax and enjoy each other's presence.

She didn't.

After a long while, she stood up and gestured to the toilets before hastily leaving the stuffy room. She grabbed her winter jacket and ran out into the freezing cold. It hit her hard in the face, she missed her hat, wished she had gloves, but for now she had to hang on. She pulled the jacket tight around her before making her way down the few steps, around the alpine hut. The snow growled under her feet, her warm breath filling the air. She found a couple of picnic benches behind the hut. With one movement, she pushed the snow off the table and sat on it.

And breathed in and out deeply.

George ... was her fiancé. She had agreed to marry him. But his unspoken expectations had surprised her in the last few days. It was all natural. They were in a resort, completely out of routine. No one could have known beforehand how well they would adapt to skiing. Maybe he actually felt sad that they had so little time together. Maybe he just didn't know how to handle the situation. Neither did she. And they just had to get over it themselves and work on it. No one had to be sad here.

Marisa stood up and made her way back the way she had come. Her footsteps clearly in sight.

Not only for her, but apparently for others as well. She stopped involuntarily when Vin appeared unexpectedly. She had to add this problem to her restlessness. All day she had avoided even thinking about him. Her dream, her unforgettable dream, was still on her conscience. And now, here in front of him, he seemed all the more real to her.

His blue eyes sparkled at her view. He too had not seen her during the day.

"You didn't feel like snuggling up to your fiancé?"

Marisa drew her eyebrows together. A great greeting. At least it gave her a chance to remain cold and distant. A follow-up to his comment yesterday would make her uncomfortable.

Wouldn't it? *Shit. Don't think about your dream.*

"No."

"You don't seem interested in him in that way."

"What?" she didn't know what he was about to bring up here. Or was this conversation riskier than she'd guessed? She had to keep her head and not talk herself into anything here.

She had heard enough and tried to walk past him.

He held her by the arm.

"I mean, when you and I... we were -"

"Stop it."

Marisa shook herself loose and made another effort to leave.

She didn't get far. She heard every word, felt his nearness. Her wall was crumbling. Her resistance wavering. His aftershave.

Damn it. Be strong.

"Do you love him?"

He made it easy for her. Fortunately.

With a jerk, she turned back towards him, narrowing the distance between them.

"Why don't we talk about you for a change?" Her anger and excitement burned in her lungs. She sputtered fire and distaste in her eyes as she looked directly at him and challenged.

"You arrived here with Maureen. Don't you want to snuggle up to her?"

Vincent struggled with her closeness. With her presence. It was more intense and arousing after a whole day of waiting and hoping.

"Technically, we didn't arrive *together*."
Marisa stared at him, trying to make sense of his words.
"You're not a couple at all?"
Vincent just shrugged his shoulders. Meaningless.
"That Johnny guy had put out a last-minute call for a couple of volunteers to take two rooms in a couple's mountain cabin. Maureen and I were a good match. Like I said, pure - "
"Yes, yes, I know." she interrupted him as he was already talking again about his attraction to the beautiful blonde woman. She had understood that. She couldn't keep up with that.
She didn't want to.
"You're still avoiding even feeling anything."
He was silent this time.
Too close to the truth?
"Again and again, just one night." she repeated in disgust, or just perplexed.
"Or two. Or a day here and there."
It sounded like he was making fun of her. In any case, he wasn't taking it seriously at all.
"How do you do it? How do you stay so detached?"
"Years of practice."
"But she sleeps in your bed. Or in the next room? How do you cope with that?"
Vincent ignored her question, lifted his gaze and held hers. Those brown eyes were driving him crazy.
"How are you coping with me sleeping here? Next door to you?"
This conversation was suddenly completely out of control, and he liked watching her search for a suitable answer.
Guilt, blush, loathing were about to set in when she recollected herself.
Oh, you wait! It takes two to do the tango...
Marisa hesitated for a small moment before lifting her head proudly and narrowing her eyes slightly seductively.
"So, you're offering one night." she repeated his words teasingly.

Bingo.

He swallowed dryly, suddenly the one who didn't know what to say.

"But no marriage proposal at the end?"

Somehow, she found this statement like a challenge. He had admitted that he at least wanted to sleep with her. Wasn't there the slightest possibility that she could make him develop feelings? He had at least liked her then, hadn't he?

"No, thanks. You and I, we are so far in the past. Forget my stupid comment yesterday. I didn't mean it."

Marisa sank deeper and deeper into the ground. She should be glad, should realise that her problem of guilt was hereby solved.

But his words stabbed deep into her soul. Of now and of then.

"I am not like you. I don't commit to marriage after a few weeks. Or months. Or ever."

With those words, he left her standing alone. Big regret as to why he had even followed her outside. What had he been thinking? What had he wanted to achieve? At least now they both knew where they stood. He had absolutely no interest in her. Not physically or mentally. He had proved that to everyone in no uncertain terms.

Marisa was glad. They didn't have that pure lust that he and Maureen had.

Thankfully. Not.

~

You love the attention of others. I can see it in you, how you seek every word, every touch from every man. How many men have you pleasured yourself with? Your experience and my unquenchable lust for you will be a perfect match. You will surrender to me. I push you powerfully against the wall, my hand between your legs. Ah, you're wet. You want it too. If not, I'll show you what you really want. Don't resist my rhythm. You'll like the way I fuck your brains out.

Day 8

A deal was a deal. Sometime and somehow, George had agreed that they would go their separate ways for the day. She hadn't quite wanted to show her joy as she still felt guilty. And ignored the urge to run out of the house early so she could ski every single minute too.

Hence her tardiness on the black run. What's more, it had taken longer to find and board the cable car than expected. But nothing stood in her way. Mitchell had given her the clear, he knew she was on her way.

Arriving at the meeting point, she could hardly wait to master the steep slope. She had taken a good look at the mountain from the ski chair in the cable car. A little navigation was part of the job. There were bound to be a few surprises on the way down. She was ready!

But not to encountering only Vincent and one other skier. Mitch or the rest of the group were nowhere to be seen. Shit.

Vincent recognised her figure from a distance and hesitated. He hadn't expected to see her here today. Their argument the previous evening had somehow ruined the mood. He needed distance, needed to be able to think straight before she would be in front of him again. Right now was too soon.

She felt the same way. Deliberately, she gave them a wide berth and stayed in the background.

Damn. What now?

She pulled her ski map out of her breast pocket and oriented herself to the signs and the slope.

"You can't go down the slope alone. It's too risky."
After all the hesitation and confusion, he had come up to remind her after all. She didn't even look up.
"Ski with us." he finally offered. He was sure his companion didn't mind, it wasn't as if they had known each other for long. He nodded in her direction. The woman waved her ski stick, her pigtails resting on her shoulders. Like a model on the runway. Hadn't he picked a pretty one for today. Of course, no surprise that she was not the flavour of the day. Didn't want it to be, of course!
"How generous of you." she said defiantly, not dreaming of accepting his invitation.
"MK - "
"Don't call me that." she warned him between her teeth. Her day had started so well and now she could have screamed again. "Don't leave her alone for so long or she'll be offended."
"Don't make those lousy comments."
Vin gritted his teeth in annoyance. He was torn. On one hand, he wanted to shake her and get her out of this defiant phase so that she would listen to him. But he did not dare to come even an inch closer to her. On the other hand, he didn't want to argue with her here any longer, looking into her brown eyes that spouted hatred and dislike at him with every syllable.
He hesitated, unsure what was best for everyone.
"I can't let her drive alone. She doesn't have enough experience like you do," he said desperately.
"No one asked you to." she countered immediately, putting her card away again and getting ready to go. "I don't have any problems tackling this descent on my own. I don't need you."
Without further ado, she sped off. A little faster than was appropriate, but the adrenaline was burning in her veins. Not only because of the thrilling descent with tight curves and misleading hairpin bends. It was unique and she felt alive. Oh no, adrenaline also at the thought that Vin had no problems enjoying herself and spending time with other women. After yesterday's conversation, it had become clear to her that Vin

didn't identify with Maureen in the slightest. This wasn't a relationship, this was a fling, pure sex. That was why he hadn't even mentioned how much time George spent with Maureen after all. As a boyfriend, it would drive him crazy, wouldn't it? Instead, he remained silent. Said nothing about the whole thing. It was so fucking obvious that her fiancé had his eye on the young beauty. It was embarrassing, it was humiliating. It was all shit.

Yes, the adrenaline from the anger was rising. She didn't want to see him, talk to him or think about him. She didn't want to know how easy it was for him to have a new woman by his side. Like a vicious circle, the thoughts wouldn't let her go. The two of them were guaranteed to have a great time. His laughter softened the hearts of all women. He was popular with everyone, not only because of his stunning looks and gorgeous eyes. But also because of his intelligence, his way of being able to converse properly. Not just superficial conversation. Much more. She missed that.

Shit.

Marisa stopped abruptly. She had been driving too fast, too inattentive. Because of him!

She tried to catch her breath, to relax her body. She had held her shoulders too tense, forced her legs to hold too much weight. This was not how she had wanted to complete her descent.

She breathed in and out deeply. And once more. She looked around her, the mountains, the white landscape, the trees, the drag lift, the cable car. She concentrated on what was in front of her. She wasn't thinking about yesterday, about her past. She wasn't thinking about tomorrow, about her future. She was here *now*. Now she was going to live. The snow fell softly on her snowsuit. She felt the little flakes land on her cold face, melt. She reached out her hand to catch the snowflakes herself. She looked closely at the ice crystals and found joy, in those intricate shapes. So tiny, so unique. So perfect.

A little later she took the map out of her jacket and set about finding her way again. Delayed but sure, she arrived in the valley after a few hours. Deepest fulfilment in her heart, in her soul. Free.

And what would top this moment. A sweet cocoa.

When Marisa returned with her hot drink, Mitchell stood before her. His posture different from usual. His face not warm and inviting.

He was annoyed.

Damn. The rules.

"Marisa. Please tell me you weren't driving alone. You know the rules, the regulations we all have to follow. Those rules are in place to keep you safe. So that we are all safe. We all have to abide by them, otherwise-"

"Sorry, there was a long line in the men's room."

Vincent appeared out of nowhere, put his arm kindly around Marisa and smiled ignorantly at Mitchell. "Did you tell him that this was the best run yet?"

His sanctimonious reply made Mitchell breathe a sigh of relief. "You had me worried for a moment. I was beginning to think I'd have to give you the red card. That would have been two long, dull days."

Everyone was laughing now, more or less. Mitchell looked around, mocking a few other skiers in the group. He tried to catch up with everyone and arranged for the next run. At a safe distance, she roughly removed his arm and stood well away from him.

Vincent looked her straight in the eye. Her cheeks slightly flushed from the sun and wind. A few strands of hair slipped out of her cap. Her hands clasped tightly around the hot cocoa. When he had seen her arrive, she had looked so happy. Now her expression turned to steely distaste.

"You're welcome." he replied just as coldly.

Marisa gritted her teeth.

"You didn't have to do that."

"Oh really? You wouldn't have minded being banned and unable to do anything for the next two days. It's not like George

is available between his appointments with Maureen."
Ouch. That had hit home.
"Did you hang out with your new girlfriend on the mountain?" She didn't want to hear any more. This man was driving her crazy. Did he have to keep teasing and irritating her? And make her nervous?
Vin shrugged his shoulders.
"I'll see her later."
Marisa just stared at him at his statement. It was that simple for him. How was that possible? How could you just play with other people, women, and feel nothing?
"For one night? Or two? How long do you think your longest relationship was with anyone." She teased, not paying attention to how she was upsetting him. "You dare judge my relationship, question it, when you have absolutely no idea what it means to be there for someone. To love someone."
Vincent approached her, threatening, aggressive, but he did nothing more than look at her. And how. Intense. Insistent.
His actions and movements completely under control. His eyes so icy cold it made her sick.
"You don't know what you're talking about. You don't know anything about my past. You just keep having these stupid girlish dreams in your head. As if something like true love existed. Wake up and be honest with yourself."
She swallowed dryly, hearing his words and knowing he was right. Never, ever would she admit that just now. Maybe tomorrow, with distance and when he wasn't near her. Her heart raced; her stomach tightened convulsively. He was so close in front of her.
Inches separated them. And yet miles.
"Six months is the limit."
With the words, he turned away from her and walked to the others.

~

"I love you!"

Marisa Keach beamed all over her face. At last, she had dared. At last, she had overcome her eternal shyness and said what she had felt for so long. She had wanted to confess it for days. Finally, it was her chance to be honest.

And to take her chance completely, she confidently put her arms around his neck. Something she had never dared to do before either. Something she had wanted to do for so long.

Now all he had to do was say the three words back and everything would fit perfectly. Then it would be like in her beloved novels.

But the reality was different.

Vin laughed out loud.

"MK. And what do you think I'm going to say back now? That I love you too?" He was still laughing. He roughly removed his arms from himself and turned away from her. Distance was needed. He tried to hide the anger in his eyes, but he feared that Marisa had already seen it.

Marisa took a step back herself, concerned. Her heart in ruins. Her head in total confusion. She had made a mistake. She could not undo it. Just as she could not turn off her feelings. She refused to cry here in front of him and concentrated hard on keeping an upright and confident posture.

He could not hurt her. No more than he had just done.

"These are girls' dreams. An old cliché that true love exists."

The young girl refused to believe him. She was only seventeen years old, he eighteen. As if he would know more about what existed and what didn't. If you didn't believe in it, you weren't open to it either. She had a big heart, big desire for true love. Maybe Vin wasn't the boy for her.

"Well, thank goodness we've got that cleared up, too," she brought out with difficulty. Her voice held out. Her posture taut. "Don't get back to me, okay? Thanks."

Marisa ran off. Tears on the surface.

Everything seemed so hopeless at that moment.

Hopeless and in love.

~

Mitchell did not take his eyes off his group. At the same time that Vincent had come to her rescue earlier, he had a funny feeling when he saw the two of them together later. Their body language suggested an awkward argument and he wanted to make sure that the two of them only went down the black run together when emotions did not interfere with their concentration.

They seemed to be staying away from each other. Good. By unspoken mutual consent, they each set off on the route with a different skier.

It was the last run for the day that Mitch had planned, one that was going to be tough. At various points, they would text at each other. But otherwise, he gave them the independence to tackle the mountain themselves. At the end of the day, he expected big smiles and pride.

As long as they all arrived safely at the bottom.

Marisa loved the descent, found deepest fulfilment in it. The black slope had a gradient of more than 40 per cent in some places, which made it all that much more exciting. She moved with the switchbacks, bouncing her hips with practice. She had a good pace going, braking and adapting to the jumbled edges. Not far from the valley came the final but most beautiful challenges. She had heard from Mitch that they had also built a small ski-jump towards the end of the slope. She signalled to her ski partner to wait, and she would try the risky jump. The other nodded in agreement and waited a few metres behind her until it was his turn.

Marisa roughly calculated how fast she should approach and

how she would soothe the landing. Full of confidence, she took a run-up. Nervous and excited at the same time. Could she master this? Was she good enough? Too late.

Marisa bent her knees and flew. It only took less than three seconds and she landed again, safely and gracefully on the snow. Elated and proud. Still with a laugh on her face, she turned to her ski partner so he knew it was safe to plan his jump.

Ouch.

Before she could get to it, the other skier rammed into her without braking. Both landed hard metres away in the snow. Marisa felt pain everywhere, but especially in her foot where he had driven straight into her ankle before they had slid painfully on together. The ice-cold, hard snow rubbed against her face. It felt like it was tearing her whole face open. As soon as they came to a stop, she tried to pick herself up again to see if everything was still on her. It all hurt. The man half on top of her, beside her wailed.

That idiot hadn't waited long enough for her to get far enough out of the way. He crashed into her full force after his jump.

After a few minutes of trying in vain to get out of his legs and body, she gave up. She laid her head in the snow, annoyed and angry, and had to think. Save strength and talk herself out of how much her face was burning.

"Shit. Marisa. Shit."

She was actually relieved to hear *his* voice for once. She was glad to feel him beside her. She closed her eyes in reassurance as soon as he piled into the snow beside her to relieve her of the dilemma.

Impatiently and rather roughly, he helped the other skier to his feet. He looked a little silly, but had no serious injuries other than embarrassment. He moved lightly on his feet and his face was not scratched in any way.

There was hope for her face. Maybe it was the bitter cold that was getting to her after all. But at that moment she could not really hear her mind and closed her eyes again. When the

man saw her lying so helplessly in front of him, he panicked. Vincent, however, stopped him from lunging at Marisa and driving everyone wild. Controlled and deliberate, he spoke to the skier, distracting him from Marisa's condition. He talked about his injuries and pain and got him to calm down. He then called his partner over and ordered them both to take the safest and quickest route to the valley. He gave clear instructions to inform Mitchell exactly what had happened and where they were. Under no circumstances were they to lose sight of each other and take risks. It was not far from the valley, being safe was a priority. He himself would take care of Marisa.
Wow. He did a fine job of that.
At last he was by her side again. She felt him more than she saw him. Even in the middle of the snow, deep in his snowsuit, she could smell his aftershave. Should she really be thinking about that now? How hard she had hit her head, for she could not control her emotions at all.
Vincent helped her sit up so she was no longer at the mercy of the cold snow.
"What were you trying to prove again? Why can't you be careful?"
In a flash she came out of her deluded state again.
"Let go of me. I can do this alone."
In her defiance, she pushed his hand away and stood up abruptly. The sharp, unexpected pain in her ankle made her lose her balance and she landed hard on the snow, with Vincent beside her.
Shit.
"I can see how you can do it on your own."
"Go away. I can't take your arrogance and stupid comments right now at all."
She pulled off her gloves angrily to touch her aching cheek with her fingers. She felt the side very carefully, afraid to feel blood and open wounds. It was not so. A weight fell from her heart.

Vincent watched her movements and recognised the pain that plagued her.

"Fine. Just do as I say." he suggested instead and was met with a condescending look. "Can you stand?"

Marisa didn't move an inch. She was far too angry to just do as he asked.

"No. First of all, I want to make it clear that I am not at fault here. *He* skied into *me*."

Vin looked at her quizzically. She had to be freezing, suffering, after all. Still, it was more important for her to explain first what exactly had gone on.

"You took the plunge?"

This time she smiled in reply. With her mind on the moment of the jump. Unique excitement. Euphoria. And it surprised him to such an extent that it left him speechless. His heart was racing. Something he hadn't felt in a long time stirred inside him. He could only smile back. Just as he had done then.

Silence followed. Glances, deep into each other's souls.

This time, when he reached out his hand to her, she took it. He pulled her to her feet, subconsciously noticing how she drew in her breath sharply in pain. But he did not take his eyes off her. He should be concentrating on getting her to safety, on examining her injuries. But he could not move. Stood still and close in front of her. Inches away from her. He heard her mouth open slightly, the hot air escaping him. Her breath came haltingly. Her gaze questioning. He came a little closer. Stopped. Slowly he lifted his hand and stroked his fingers over her bruised cheek. It burned like fire where he touched her. She trembled at this tenderness. Was lost. She did not dare to breathe, to move. Was under his spell.

George.

All at once she remembered her fiancé. Of her promise. And of why she had to avoid Vincent.

He saw the change in her eyes, felt the panic. He stepped back. He'd much rather have done anything else, but he had enough self-control that he wouldn't take what he wanted.

"Fortunately, we both know how this would end."
His words hurt her more than her ankle. She didn't know what to say back. Didn't have a chance to sort out her thoughts. She remained silent.
Dawn loomed ahead of them. She had no choice but to lean on him and walk the rest of the mountain, wearily and haltingly. The silence was crueller than the pain.
Mitchell and a couple of first responders soon approached her and took over the rest. Vincent stayed in the background and took their equipment to the first aid stand.
It was only a sprained ankle. It was just a bruised hip and bruised cheek. Nothing that wouldn't heal.
But much more had gone to pieces in the last few hours than these superficial wounds.
Marisa was back in reality. The grey, miserable reality. She fought against the thousand emotions that were just hitting her. She tried to block out the guilt. It was no use. She found herself in the throes of her reproaches and hatreds. And she knew it was justified. She wasn't worthy of being George's girlfriend. She disgusted herself. She had no self-worth.
And he hadn't even kissed her yet.

~

He even refused a hug. Holding hands had also been out of the question. What had they actually connected? Nothing. So according to that, they hadn't been a couple at all. So theoretically they hadn't broken up. He had never been her boyfriend. And despite all this, all these feelings of guilt towards her best friend. The sleepless nights where she had felt so bad about betraying her friend.

And he hadn't kissed her once! She was suffering because of him. Because of a few weeks of secret meetings in the woods, at the toboggan hill, at the Christmas market. Because of a few conversations about her future.

Damn it. Why was she so deeply devastated when all he had done was ruin their friendship and she had lost all respect for herself.

Despite everything, her hopes for a reconciliation with her friend remained. Ron had also invited her to a party at his flat. They weren't that well acquainted, but he was Danielle's brother. Did that mean she had forgiven her? Could they talk about how Vin had dumped them both? Only too gladly would she talk to someone about it, get the hurt, the disappointment off her chest. And she missed her best friend so much.

Marisa deliberately showed up a little later than the other guests. Most of the boys and girls were from the upper class, with whom she didn't have much to do. A few of her classmates were there, and she was looking forward to their company. It went relatively well. The music was loud, the chips salty and tempting. A few alcoholic drinks were offered, although some of them should perhaps hold back a little.

She was lucky and found Danielle alone in the kitchen.
"Danielle?"
If looks could kill... A reconciliation was probably far from on the table. Danielle hadn't forgiven her.
"Ron invited you. It wasn't my wish."
"Do you want me to leave again?"
Danielle said nothing back and walked back into the living room.
Marisa had a decision to make. Should she stay? After all, she wasn't giving up. She would stay and maybe she could talk to her again later.
Determined to win her best friend back, she went back into the living room and froze. In the corner with the high school graduates, Vin was standing with her back to her.
Shit.
She immediately felt sick and dizzy. The one beer was heavy in her stomach, and she wished she hadn't had anything to drink... or much, much more.
When had he shown up? Was he aware that she would be here too?
Shit. Shit. Shit.
She took refuge in another corner to talk to her classmates. This all worked well so far, until someone suggested playing some games. The small, safe circles dissolved and they all joined in the middle.
When Marisa looked up, she met his gaze. And could read nothing in it. Her mate Andrew didn't notice her panic and pulled her down to the floor with him. Vin looked away.
Charades wasn't so bad. A bit embarrassing for some, but at least they didn't all have to make fools of themselves. Only those who were already a bit more into it or desperate to impress someone. Danielle was completely in her element. With jealousy in her stomach, Marisa had noticed how her friend hadn't taken her eyes off Vin all evening. In fact, she had sat right next to him. And he had remained seated. That hurt.
But then came the devastating game. Truth or dare.

If only she had gone home earlier. The evening was already fucked, she felt miserable and insulted. And now this on top of that.

The first few rounds were excruciating. She nearly jumped out of her skin with each spin of the bottle and then jumped up in relief when it wasn't her turn. The incursions of 'dare' were still relatively lame.

Finish your glass.

Do a headstand.

Show your bra.

And then...

...the neck of the bottle landed on Danielle. And her eyes sparkled open.

Kiss one of the boys.

Marisa held her breath. She knew. She knew what she was going to do. And yet she couldn't bear it. Danielle took his face in her hands and gave him a kiss. Him. Vin.

It was over.

She wanted to run away. Wanted to cry out loud. He hadn't kissed her *once*. And now this.

She was devastated. And her friend was enjoying it.

The others noticed nothing. They played on. The questions and actions became wilder. The bottleneck landed on her. She chose truth. She didn't care about anything.

Danielle immediately jumped in with a question, the alcohol in her veins and hatred for her former friend driving her forward.

"How many boys have you kissed?" She giggled spitefully.

Marisa frowned. All the boys in her class and Grade 12 listened intently.

"None." she answered honestly, and Danielle almost spat out all her beer again. She laughed out loud, looking from Vincent to Marisa and from Marisa back to him. And laughed on and on.

No one really knew why she was so mean to her friend. Marisa, however, had it coming.

After a few more rounds, Vincent was not spared when the

bottle finally spun out in front of him. He too chose truth.
Danielle hastily considered what question to ask, but the others were quicker.
"Do you want to go with Danielle again?" The girls giggled excitedly.
Vincent did not respond to the advances of her beside him. Her hand on his leg, for example, left him cold.
"No. I want to be with MK."
And with that, he had spoken the truth. In front of everyone. Not that most would even remember it the next morning. But Marisa had heard it clearly. So had Danielle, who withdrew her hand in a huff and didn't utter a word. She could have said so much, in that moment. She could have revealed who MK actually was. But for some reason, she didn't.
The other guys laughed at his remark, pulled him up. Tapped him encouragingly on the shoulder. All this time he hadn't taken his eyes off her.
With the shock over, Marisa lowered her head and smiled for the first time that evening.
Vin saw it too.
Hours later, the teenagers were lying left and right in the living room on sofas and armchairs, on the floor and chairs. How one could sleep in such a position was uncertain, but young people managed.
Early in the morning it was time to get out of the sleeping positions before the parents came home again. Marisa half sat up, totally groggy from the party and still surprised by his concession. She leaned her head against the sofa and watched the quiet bustle as one by one people rose and stretched. Not much was said.
Until suddenly, in the other corner of the living room, the boys burst out laughing. It was so loud and sudden that Marisa got up to see what was going on. The guys were standing bent over the sofa, laughing wryly. Marisa pushed past them and froze.
In front of her stood Vincent, bare-chested. And it took her breath away. Never before had she seen someone half-naked in

front of her, and then Vin to boot. The person she raved about endlessly. The blood immediately rose to her cheeks.
"Watch out, she's about to attack you. You know she hasn't kissed anyone yet!"
They laughed up again and patted him on the shoulder.
"But you only have eyes for your Em Kay."
And then she saw, the real reason they had brought him up and why he was standing here so naked. The fools had written the letters MK on his left breast in the night with a permanent marker. With a heart around it.
That had delighted them greatly, to have played such a trick on him. It would take days for him to scrub that stupidity off himself again.
For the second time, she smiled at this bizarre situation before heading home, knowing he would be in touch soon.
Maybe with his T-shirt still off.

~

Still day 8 ... after the accident

George showed great care when she came limping back from the black run. He helped her to get comfortable. He kissed her gently on the forehead.
And Marisa sickened at the guilt she felt. His closeness didn't trigger the same desire that Vincent did with just a look. And that realisation almost killed her.
She was glad to be able to stay in the mountain hut to rest her ankle. She was glad she didn't have to see anyone. Like Vincent, for example. She was glad that her memories of the previous hours, of the deep desire, were fading. The more time she spent with her fiancé, the more she felt again the security and peace she so appreciated about him. She was looking for a steady, secure future and George would give her that. She didn't need a hot fire every time he accidentally touched her. She didn't expect numbing passion when he was inches away from her. She was too old for that. That had been taken care of. A few little kisses here and there was all she needed. Sex was also far too overrated. Neither of them felt the urge. It was not the most important thing about their relationship. When they were married, on their wedding night, George would turn to her. He didn't seem to be in any hurry about that. But they had discussed how many children she would like after all. Then there would be no way around it.
Towards the end of the evening and the initial worries, George seemed a little agitated and unbalanced. He looked at his mobile phone several times. Until he finally spoke out what

was on his mind.

"I've had such a long day in the cold snow." he began now. "So have you, of course. Erm, well I had thought with your foot too... erm, well I think we should go to the sauna. The warmth will help your ankle and we can all warm up properly from all those long days outside."

Marisa frowned for a moment. Her initial reaction was to disagree with him but didn't. Never did. Out of guilt.

"The temperatures have dropped quite a bit in the last few days."

"Yes, exactly. We should use the facilities here as much as we can."

She nodded in agreement.

"Mary, darling. How's your foot? Can you tread?"

She tried good-naturedly to show him that it was possible. She did not, however, show the pain she was feeling. That was enough for George, and he jumped up cheerfully.

"Would you like your swimming costume or bikini? And some towels?"

Full of drive and impatience, he gathered all the things together. He lovingly helped her out onto the snow cart and they were on their way to the sauna. Because he wanted it so much. Because she felt guilty.

Because Maureen would be there.

In the changing room, Marisa sat down on the bench and took a deep breath. Her ankle didn't hurt that much anymore. The pulsing had stopped a long time ago and the painkillers were totally helping. She should move her foot and keep it active, just like the first aider had said. It was good that she was active. George was right, the warmth would do them good. The last week in the fresh snowy air had made them cold.

Marisa wrapped the towel around her chest and made her way slowly but powerfully. She hesitated for a moment before entering the heated wooden booth.

The steam was overwhelming as she entered. She had forgotten how high the temperatures were in these rooms. Her body struggled with the change of climate. After a short while she got used to it and she carefully walked over to the benches. Taking deep breaths and slowly relaxing, she lay down on her towel and tried to get used to the heat. She couldn't stay lying down for long when no position was comfortable enough. Just as she straightened up, and she was about to put her towel on, Maureen came into the sauna.

Wearing a bikini that only scantily covered her feminine parts. At least she had one on, Marisa thought. She might as well not have. Her hair pinned up in a knot made her thin neck look that much slimmer and more seductive. Wow. She was ravishingly beautiful.

Maureen barely noticed the plain woman in front of her, with her black swimming costume and messy hair, and made her way to the bench near George. Graceful and deliberate, she lay down on her towel. Even Marisa was mesmerised by her body. She herself had had enough of the heat and would meet George at the bar later. As she took her eyes off the model and turned towards the door, she bumped into a male chest. Out of surprise and embarrassment, she stepped carelessly on her bad ankle and winced unexpectedly.

Instinctively, Vincent grabbed her upper arms to give her balance and save her from greater embarrassment. Her hands automatically reached up and landed flat on his chest.

His naked, hot chest.

Marisa's breath caught and she wished he had let her fall.

He wished the same. And then again, he didn't.

Jerkily she stepped away from him, far enough that it didn't give the wrong impression as they stood here by the door.

Beads of sweat clustered on her forehead, some running down her temple, along her neck, between her breasts. There was no comparison between her and Maureen. Like night and day.

And yet he found her a thousand times more beguiling. Irresistible. Seductive as a siren.

As soon as she finally came to, she limped a little away from him. It wasn't enough. She was still standing in front of him.

But he did not force himself to act rashly.

Marisa didn't see what it took for him not to yank her into his arms on the spot and kiss her to the ground. She did not see how his eyes darkened at the sight of her, because she awakened a desire in him that he could not contain.

She saw him move away from her and not try to approach her. For which she was infinitely grateful to him.

A young woman cleared her throat behind them, saying that she wanted to pass them. Did they have to stop right in front of the door? They turned towards each other. Too close again.

"What are you doing on your feet? You should go easy on your ankle." His dismissive remark helped him take his mind off her sweaty body.

He tore his gaze away from her to shield himself. His gaze landed on her injury, and he drew in a sharp breath. The swelling was obvious, dark spots slowly appearing. He had had no idea how badly she had sprained her foot.

"On the advice of the first aider, I should keep the ankle moving well."

It was funny how they stood here in front of each other in the heat, talking. The metre distance between them was perfect. They were not attracted to each other at all anymore.

Not at all.

"You're not planning on skiing tomorrow, are you?" he admonished her. He hid behind cold words.

"My foot doesn't fit in my shoe." she countered, annoyed.

Marisa had not yet thought about the consequences of the sprained foot. She lifted her towel to wipe her face lightly. Immediately she realised that she was now standing in front of him without protection. Hastily and nervously, like a teenager, she wrapped the towel around herself again.

Another person now wanted to leave the sauna, so they stepped out of the way, a little closer together again. It didn't help. They could not escape the attraction, the situation.

Try as they might.

"Let's go sledding."

Marisa stared into his face, then her gaze landed on his chest.
His bare, fine chest.
This time strong and powerful of a grown man.
Without a permanent pen.
"You want to be with MK." she murmured softly, a teasing smile on her lips.
"You haven't the faintest idea."

~

Today it was so hot. So hot. And you - so naked. So fucking seductive as you walked your curves, your tight cunt past me. I was struggling. Really struggling not to push you down on the hot sauna bench and fuck your brains out on the spot. Nothing had happened to you, but in my head, that's where it was going on. It was wild and unique. You resisted a little at first. But my hand around your neck helped. You liked it in the end, I felt the resistance weaken. Your sweat mixed with mine. My fresh, sticky seed inside you, on you, between your breasts. Ah.

~

Day 9

Guilty.

Marisa had woken up with a smile. She had felt great anticipation, of a day on the mountain. With Vincent.

Then she saw the man next to her.

And she recalled her misplaced feelings. She realised immediately that there was no way she could spend the day with Vincent. Alone, tobogganing. Having fun.

But especially not with that strange tingling in her stomach when she even thought back to their hot conversation. There was no way she would expose herself to a situation that could jeopardise her relationship with George in the slightest.

With a sense of action and regret, she stood up. Disappointed but not surprised, she felt the pain in her ankle when she rested her weight on it. But it didn't stop her from making a day of it with George.

Yes, of course she wouldn't mind if they spent the day on the blue slope. Yes, she can put her foot in the ski boots without any problems. No, it doesn't hurt much.

Marisa gritted her teeth and set off with him. She ignored the surprised look on Vincent's face when he saw her ready to go for a day on the slopes.

"We'll be on the blue piste if anything comes up," George explained with a cool look in his eyes.

Vin just shrugged his shoulders. He couldn't have cared less what they were up to. And Maureen to boot. She was never far from George. Did Marisa not care either? How could she be so

blind and not see what George was up to with the other?
But he just had to let that rest. It was none of his business. What bothered him, though, and made him angry, was the pained look on her face when they left.
He should leave it alone. He shouldn't interfere or worry. She was old enough to know for herself when to rest. He would be cursed if he helped her out here.

~

Marisa plopped down exhausted on the seat in the café. Little beads of sweat were on her forehead. Her back hurt, not to mention her ankle. She had wanted to keep up, had wanted to spend the day with George. Unfortunately it meant she had spent too much time on her feet and to compensate for the pain she must have been standing funny somehow. No wonder her bruised hip was now complaining too. The last few steps to the café had been very tedious.
After the long lunch, she had slowly warmed up again. All the standing had not only weakened her limbs but also made her feel cold. Gradually she felt better. The pulsing at her ankle, however, became stronger the less the rest of her body hurt. George and Maureen had gone back to their group alone. Later she would seek him out again.
With longing and regret, she looked at her phone to see where Mitch and his group were. Not at all to see what their respective skiers were up to. Innocent curiosity. They were all ... here.
Marisa looked up just as she recognised Mitchell in the doorway. She waved at him, joy in her eyes. He immediately rushed towards her, a twinkle in his eye to find her alone. He sat down with her.
"But skiing? Are you coming to the slopes?" His brown hair lay a little tangled around his head, but this did not detract at all from his good standing.
On the contrary, Marisa noticed a woman walking straight past their table just to get his attention. Her gaze was clearly fixed on him, inviting and open.
Mitch smiled back before turning to his coffee and his

conversation.

Marisa would only be too happy to accept. She carefully tried to turn her foot. Maybe a miracle had happened, and now it didn't hurt. So much.

Unfortunately not.

"Tomorrow, hopefully. I think I'll have to rest the ankle for today after all."

"Sensible plan. You can check out the area a bit." he suggested helpfully. He pulled out his very used map and showed her a few places she was sure to like. "This mountain here, unfortunately, we never go up as a group. There are different ways of going up the mountain and also going down. Both cable cars, and toboggan runs. Perfect for less active visitors."

Marisa took a picture of his map and loved his idea. A little later he made his way back to his group while Marisa wrote a note to her fiancé.

What an appropriate adventure could await us! x
Would you like to come with me? x
When will you be ready to leave? x
Where are you?
Hello?

Marisa switched off her mobile phone. He obviously had no reception or the possibility to write at the moment. She didn't want to wait any longer, so she set off on her own to the mountain. As promised, everything was good and easy to reach.

And what a magnificent sight this mountain brought her. The snow-covered peak towered far up into the clouds. Its surfaces covered with the finest snow and fir trees sprouted in various spots. And in the midst of it all, colourful bustle. The busy cable cars, the various mountain huts where one could rest, warm up and refresh oneself. Other huts offered equipment suitable for every kind of skiing holiday. A paradise for many visitors. There were so many people here and she felt part of the party.

She checked her mobile phone again. To no avail.

"He's not coming."
Marisa literally flinched. His voice came out of nowhere, as if from her thoughts. A voice she would recognise anywhere.
She turned slowly to face him. Vincent was actually standing in front of her, in his snowsuit. She felt sick, cold, hot.
"What are you doing here? How?"
"Mitch." He gave as a curt reply. He didn't look particularly excited, just at that moment. So why was he here then?
"Why?"
Vincent hesitated with his answer.
"Someone has to look out for you. Knowing you, you were just about to borrow some skis and tackle that mountain. Carefully, of course."
Marisa looked away from the mountain hut where she had been standing. In fact, the thought had crossed her mind that she could have at least tried the blue run.
"How kind of you." she retorted, annoyed, and tried to walk away from him. She gritted her teeth firmly with each uneven step. He helpfully put his arm under hers for support, which she immediately refused and she moved further away from him.
His presence was unbearable. She didn't know what she was struggling with more.
Don't show him how much of a torture this is for you.
Vincent could have burst with rage. Why did she have to be so damn stubborn? After all, it was only well-intentioned. No other ulterior motives. At least not at that moment.
"Where do we go first?" he asked instead as he followed her. He saw her tense face, recognised how she was suffering.
"We?" she interrupted him. "Nowhere. George is on his way here and meanwhile I'll ride the cable car up the mountain alone, at my leisure. There I'll decide on the most suitable descent."
They both knew that was a lie. She still hadn't heard from him, but she would definitely not announce that now. She just had to get some distance. Her body did treacherous things in his

presence. For a split second earlier, she had been happy to see him here.

Shit.

They got quite a distance before she didn't know which direction to take. The queue to the cable car had to be here somewhere. Where were the other visitors?

"You're so fickle. Not in the mood for me today?"

She stared at him in shock. What had he said?

"Me - in the sauna. That doesn't mean anything."

"I know that too. But at least we don't have to be at each other's throats every time we see each other."

Her mind was going crazy. She didn't want it to. But their past hung between them, and the pain, the disappointment kept winning.

And her boundless panic that she was far from immune to his attraction.

Shit. Damn.

"I'm here on holiday. I'm taking a break." she finally began in exasperation. "I'm away from my work, away from responsibility, so I don't have to keep making decisions and fathoming all sorts of things."

"What do you have to fathom?"

Vincent looked at her confused. She seemed more upset than usual. In turmoil with herself.

Until she was finally honest.

"Whether you really want to sleep with me or just haunt me?"

They both stopped in their tracks and looked directly at each other. Not at all what he had expected as an answer. Not at all what she had wanted to admit.

Vin took a step towards her. His gaze was on her lips, on her slightly open mouth. He felt her reaction, the tremor in her body. He felt it too. Just two, three inches and he could feel her again, touch her, seduce her. Her eyes dark, alert, ... uncertain.

Panic rose in her. What had she said? What impression did he have of her now?

He immediately saw the moment when all her guilt hit her.

Guilt, fear, remorse. He pulled back with the greatest of effort. It required so much strength and patience from him, it soon killed him.

Marisa's emotions were going crazy. His movements, his closeness drove her mad. With an ice-cold shock, she realised that he was only making fun of her here. Every time he came close to her, it was just a game to him. Every time he pulled away immediately when it was unavoidable, the next step would be intimate. The next step was irreversible. Of course, he had no interest in her. She wasn't his type, never had been. She was no Maureen, and not worthy of an affair.

She clenched her hands into fists and looked at him angrily. He had turned her head. Yet all this time she had been the only one who had lusted after him. All this sexual attraction came only from her. How else was it possible for him to resist all these moments?

She was such a complete idiot. Such a bad girlfriend. Fiancée!

Her anger at herself was stronger than her anger at him.

"And that makes you angry? Are you so unhappy with George that you have to cheat?"

All colour drained from her face at his clarification. That was what it had sounded like. She had asked him if he would sleep with her.

Fuck.

"No." she replied clearly and icily. "I have no intention of cheating. Especially not with you."

Vincent breathed slowly. Annoyed. Bitter.

"So, what's the problem?"

"I don't want to be further broken by having to see you here either. And being reminded. Being cornered."

Her eyes said more than her words. Pain was written all over her face.

Hopeless.

At least no longer in love.

~

Quietly, the snow trickled on. The landscape covered. The chimneys were smoking.

With each step, the fresh snow crackled under her feet. A sound that brought her joy. Childish joy that it should also snow at Christmas.

She wanted to run, to race. But she kept up her serene pace. She didn't want to show him how impatient she was to see what their meeting today would bring.

She finally arrived at the secluded playground. At the end of the blocks of new buildings, at the edge of the residential area with small hills that united the various rows of tall apartment blocks. Shortly after, we came to a field that bordered a small forest. Another place that would look heavenly white that afternoon. Maybe Vin wanted to take her for a winter walk. That would be totally romantic.

Don't be ridiculous. As if he'd ever shown any romantic interest in her or them until now.

And yet she was incredibly excited to see him. After the party at Ron's, he had contacted her. And she had accepted.

He was standing on the hill. Alone, of course. Everyone else was already in their warm rooms, in front of the television. It was already dark, but the snow lit up the area.

"Hi."

"Hi."

Her joy too great for her to control her nerves. He looked so sweet, so adorably sweet. And he was here with her.

And she just smiled at him.

He was lost then.

They spent the rest of the afternoon into the early evening in the snow. On his sled, to be exact. It was the most fun she had had in a long time. And the most exhausting, too. They raced up the hill and whizzed back down much faster. They pulled and pushed. Rolled and slid. Until their clothes were wet through to their skin. Their gloves full of snow crystals. Their hair, peeking out from under their hats, was totally caked with little clumps of snow. They both looked like wild Eskimos.

Marisa never wanted this adventure to end. But she too slowly felt the cold spreading through her, she could barely feel her feet. She hugged herself for a while, but it was no use. It was time to go home.

"I have to go in." she finally said, ready to say goodbye. Sometime then during the holidays he would surely get back to her and they could spend the day together. Maybe talk about what had happened.

Or maybe not. It was not important.

"I'll take you."

Marisa was surprised at his offer, but of course didn't refuse. Their flat wasn't too far away, and the silence between them wasn't awkward.

"Can I put the sledge in your basement? For tomorrow."

And there was that smile again, lighting up her whole face. Or at least the parts that weren't covered by snow and hair.

"Sure." Her joy was immense. She opened the front door and ran down the few steps to the basement. Each step left little piles of snow behind. Her hair dripped with the sudden warmth of the house. The storeroom was close by, available to all the residents in this entrance. The sled was dripping as much as they were. Small puddles appeared everywhere. Surely it would all be dry by tomorrow and no one would complain.

Marisa pulled off her hat and gloves and ran them roughly through her frozen hair. She turned to face him before turning the light off again.

"What's wrong?" She looked at him worriedly.

His gaze dark, unmoving. Intense on her. She couldn't interpret what he was thinking or wanting right now. She stopped, confused.

"MK." he whispered softly, stepping up to her. Without hurrying, without taking his eyes off her.

She froze in place. He tenderly stroked a few wet strands from her face, careful enough not to accidentally touch her skin. She swallowed nervously, the tingling in her stomach unbearable.

His kiss was gentle, warm and loving. Tentative. Her reaction like an explosion. She almost fell to her knees, but he framed her face with his hands and deepened the kiss.

Her pulse raced away, her hands clutching at his forearms. It took only a lightning second for her to know how she should and could react. She returned his kiss, his desire. Felt emotions that were completely new to her and never thought she could ever feel so intensely, so driven.

It was here in the basement, with wet hair and sodden clothes, that her relationship with Vincent McDormant really began. That date, that time, that minute, she would carry in her heart forever.

As would the end.

~

Marisa sat in the café at the top of the mountain, looking out over the valley, over the neighbouring mountains. She was lost in her thoughts, her memories. The good ones and the bad ones. Not all the moments of their six-month relationship had been bad. Quite the opposite. Of course, it was much harder for her to find him here. He was and always would be her first great love. No matter how it had ended, she couldn't change or deny that.

Did she feel more drawn to him because of it? Was that why her head was constantly brooding over what he thought of her? Did he still think about those innocent times? Two teenagers who didn't fit together in the end.

Let it go, dear head. Enjoy the moment. Be attentive to the now.

One last glance at her phone, an indifferent shrug of her shoulders and she headed for the toboggan run.

Make the best of it. Self is the woman.

Sledging was great! Fast, humpy and exciting! It didn't matter to her that she was sometimes the only visitor sledding alone. It did her soul good.

After the fourth run, her swollen ankle slowly made itself known and she dropped weakened into the snow to catch her breath.

"Did you hurt yourself more?"

She closed her eyes and just laughed resignedly. If she couldn't get rid of him, he should at least make himself useful. Vincent looked down at her. He had been wrestling with himself all this time whether to follow her up the hill. Whether he should go and see her in the café. Or whether he should help her up the slope.

He had remained strong. He had stayed away from her. He had done what she had asked him to do.

And then she had collapsed in the snow. Of course, he had had to react. Now he saw her in front of him, laughing and almost crying at the same time. She was all right, had not needed his help.

Marisa looked up, into ice-cold blue eyes. A dream. A nightmare.

"If you have a pain pill with you, you can stay."

A little later she was sitting on the sledge, her ankle raised and gentle as Vincent pulled her easily up the hill without any problems. The first time, at least, it was easy for him. The next few times were slower. But the descents were worth the effort each time.

They were just both no longer 17 and 18. Their lungs and muscles needed more endurance, which they hadn't had for a long time.

One last run down the mountain, one last hump and jump. A successful landing and the end of the day. Exhausted and carefree, this time they both let themselves fall into the snow. Once again their legs and arms would not make it up the mountain.

Their faces stretched towards the sky, they tried to enjoy this moment as long as possible. Soon they would land back in reality, painfully.

"Almost as good as our first time." she said innocently. Her eyes shone.

Vincent straightened up and looked at her quizzically.

"Our first time?" he teased her with her words.

The blush immediately leapt into her cold cheeks. Her ears glowed. She sat within seconds, shaking her head in panic. How had she got herself into this awkward position?

"Tobogganing. First time tobogganing, of course."

He said nothing to that. His eyes dark. As always, she failed to read anything in them. He had a talent for hiding all his emotions behind that icy stare.

"Who reminds who of what?" he finally said and stood up abruptly. After her previous rant about how his mere presence only stirred up bad feelings in her, she had just done what she so loathed after all.

Hypocrites.

And what a memory it was. Tobogganing. The first kiss. He was thinking of the exact same moment as she was right now. Could see the moment right in front of him, relive it. His body reached out longingly for her.

Marisa stood up too, the joy and sparkle gone from her eyes. Regret suited her less.

"We should go." She set about grabbing the sledge to drop it off at the mountain hut. After a few steps, she turned back to him.

A mistake.

Vincent hadn't moved an inch.

"No." he said quietly and he moved slowly but surely towards her. "Not yet."

His kiss was cold, hard and frighteningly erotic. She had no chance to fight him off, had not seen the moment coming. Or had she? She pressed her hands weakly against his chest, but Vincent thought nothing of withdrawing from her.

She felt his warm fingers around her neck, his thumbs against her face. She tried to think, to act, not to feel. But everything inside her screamed in response to his questions.

Yes, I want you too. Hold me. Touch me. Take me.

Her whole body responded to him, to his passion as her own unbridled desire burst from her. His lips, his tongue teased her deeply. She moaned softly as he deepened the kiss. She let herself fall.

Her mobile phone rang.

As if burned, she jumped back, out of his arms. Out of desire, into deep misery.

The ringing grew louder.

The pure lust that had ruled her body a moment ago turned into hopeless regret. Her face filled with anguish and regret.

Guilt was a powerful feeling.

As if in a trance, she pulled the mobile phone out of her pocket and looked blindly at the number. Her breath caught in her throat.

George.

Her fiancé.

"MK -"

Marisa just looked at him, then walked away without another word.

~

Evening Day 9

After escaping from the mountain back to their alpine hut, George had had the grandiose idea of playing some board games. Marisa had agreed, was not given to private conversation at that moment. She took advantage of his interest in playing to read a book in the corner. But try as she might, she could not concentrate on the plot. Her whole head was spinning, she felt dizzy, sick.

Guilt had so many qualities.

One could have guilt. She had that too.

One could be guilty. So was she.

One could bear guilt. She couldn't.

Marisa had never felt so bad. She was unable to eat or drink. She couldn't control her self-destructive thoughts.

That kiss should never, ever, have happened. How had it come to this? How had she allowed herself to lose control so badly? There was no excuse. No excuse for her behaviour.

She never wanted to see Vincent again. It was all his fault. No, her own fault. Fucking guilt. She would never look him in the eye again, or stay in his presence, or think of him.

He had awakened the worst feelings in her.

Vincent stepped into the great hall.

And the best.

Marisa turned abruptly as the sight of him reminded her exactly how she had reacted to him. She felt her cheeks glowing. Cursed her body, which had not listened to a word from her mind and reacted to him totally uncontrollably. Still.

And again, and again.
Shit. Shit. Shit.
A jumble of emotions. Guilt. Lust. Guilt. Desire. Guilt. Remorse. Misery. Fear. Curiosity. Guilt. Guilt. Guilt.
Marisa stared blindly at the page in her book. She knew he was near her. Smelled his aftershave even before she heard his voice. At least he had had the good sense not to sit next to her. Instead, he sat on the sofa behind her. Two protective walls between them, that should be enough.
"Do you have a minute?"
"From the side? Don't we look all the more suspicious that way?"
Vincent smirked at her comment. At least she was talking to him.
"We might as well continue our conversation from earlier."
Yes.
"No." She replied louder than necessary.
"There is no excuse."
That's exactly what I said to myself.
"I'm sorry you feel bad. But I'm not sorry for kissing you."
Neither am I.
She was silent. Her heart had said more than she was willing to admit.

~

"Who kissed who?"
Marisa swallowed dryly. This conversation was unbearable. But the thought of not telling him about it and continuing their relationship despite the circumstances was more unbearable. He had to know the truth. It would hurt him, disappoint him. Eventually he would be able to forgive her.
George looked at her intently. His eyes dark, his posture taut. So far, he had taken the news well. Really well, actually.
"He me."
But I wanted him too.

"Kissed right?"
And how.
"Yes."
She blocked out any memories of the kiss, but his specific questions didn't help.
George hesitated, deliberating. His face closed.
"Okay.... It's okay. You didn't want this to happen."
Yes, I did want it to.
"He surprised you and you stopped him. It didn't mean anything."
I didn't stop him. It meant something to me.
George stepped up to her and took her lovingly in his arms. He hugged her to him, a little tighter than usual and for a long time.
Marisa wasn't sure if he would cry or try to overcome his jealousy. But nothing came. No tears, no sorrow, no anger.
Only understanding.
Peace and security. Just as she had always wanted. A steady relationship. A thing to rely on.
After a while, he let go of her and walked slowly towards his bed.
"I can ask Johnny if he has another room available for me."
"No, there's no need. I don't want you to go." And continue to have fun with him.
And that settled it. No other questions, no demands, conditions. Nothing.

~

Marisa had confusing dreams. Over and over again she tried to push her bad thoughts away. But it was no use at all. She tried to wake up from her sleep, tried to bring herself back to consciousness. She did not manage it. Her guilty conscience dragged her down deeper and deeper.
You useless, unfaithful slut.
I'll keep you in my sights.
I kissed her.
Really kissed her.
I didn't want to stop.
Next time, I won't stop.
It won't mean a thing.
Marisa was torn.
What is happening right now? Were these Vincent's thoughts? Did he think so condescendingly of me. Kissed you, not me? Who was he talking about? I didn't want to stop either. Next time? I can't let that happen. I'm not an unfaithful slut. I don't want to kiss you again, not if it just leaves you cold. Weren't you just playing with me? Were you just testing me to see how faithful I was? I didn't make a pass at you, didn't get your hopes up. Did I?
What did she want?
Or who?
Her trembling body tossed restlessly. Her brain would not let her rest, and yet she was not allowed to get away from this misery. She always remained on the surface to reality and yet could not escape.
She saw herself lying on the bed. George behind her. Her back

turned to him, he gently stroked her arms, up and down, up and down. She felt the touches as if she were wide awake. She felt the confusion, the urge to turn away from him. But saw how she leaned into him instead, to please him.
And over and over again, that song.
Mary, Mary, do you act against it,
What are you doing to us
But I forgive you, Mary You and I belong together
Mary, Mary, my Mary What are you thinking of doing about it?
We'll be married in six weeks and then everything will be fine. It was just a slip, a moment of weakness. I have those moments too.
Mary, Mary, don't ever act against it again.
But we'll stay together. We need each other. There are so few good people in this world.
Mary, Mary, I won't let you go so easily. I'm so glad I found you.

~

Being engaged actually means fucking regularly still. The hot desire is still new and unexplored. Those early days, the first time, are the sweetest and most satisfying.
What are you doing with someone else? Dirty, unscrupulous slut. Already taken, but still looking for more. Do you smell him? His cock. You cunt. Unfaithful cunt. I didn't even consider you at first, now I have to divide my attention between you and her as well. I can do that. I think of you as I let myself go into the arms of the hot woman. She wants it too. She can't change her mind anymore. I'm ready for anything.

~

Day 10

The next day couldn't start soon enough. Marisa got up with the first rays of sunshine. She hurried to the bathroom, where she locked herself in for longer than usual. She turned the shower on hot, burning her skin as if in punishment. The pain was to distract her from her inner turmoil.
Last night had reminded her what a good man George was. How could she have hurt him like that?
Unforgivable.
Irrevocable.
It was obvious she was going to spend the day with George. Not once had she even thought to look at her phone to find out where Mitch was. She stayed with her fiancé, with her future. Even when George was out for a few hours to sort something out for the next few days, she didn't give in to the temptation to contact the others in her group. Especially not Vin.
George wasn't gone for long. Afterwards, it was a nice, relaxing day. She appreciated the silence while they both read their books. She accepted, his bad mood becoming more apparent with each hour of togetherness. She couldn't blame him. She had ruined the day, the holiday, their relationship.
"We can leave if you'd rather. Spend the rest of the holiday at home where we're comfortable."
He looked at her bitterly.
"I have no intention of changing my plans because of you."
She accepted it. Yesterday he hadn't been angry. Today, at least, he was showing more emotion. That was normal.

"On the contrary. Starting tomorrow, we'll continue exactly as before. Then you can prove to me that you won't risk our relationship again. You stay with your beloved ski instructor and pull yourself together."
Marisa nodded slightly.
It was his right to have such expectations. It was normal. She deserved that cold tone.
And she had no problem pulling herself together.

~

"Get a grip. We're in the middle of town."
Vincent pushed her off him. His lips still wet from her naughty kiss.
Marisa hadn't been able to stand it any longer, and as soon as they'd rounded the corner from the marketplace, she'd pressed him against the wall of the house and assaulted him with her lips. Her kiss had been teasingly hot. His reaction instantaneous. She felt a deep desire deep inside her and hoped he felt the same. His breath hitched. A sign that he was facing his desire too. She was all the more surprised by his refusal.
Why had the shot backfired? She would have liked to sink into the floor when he pushed her roughly away from him and admonished her coldly.
Her heart broke. Her self-confidence even more so.
She was damned if she was going to show him her heartbreak and fought her tears with anger. It worked.
"Are we still playing hide and seek? Let's keep doing exactly what we were doing before. After all, it could jeopardise our relationship if we show ourselves together in public."
She stomped off angrily. The last bit of snow on the alley made her angry exit a little more difficult. She wasn't making as much progress as she had planned. This fucking mud sucked. She slipped and struggled to keep her balance.
Once back in the marketplace, she stopped. Now what?
"MK, stop."
She didn't turn to face him. She had to keep as much anger and annoyance as she could. Seeing him in the bright light and his sweet blue eyes in front of her would only make her weak.

He had to come to her.

He grabbed her arm and stopped her from running further away. She had less grip than usual with the wet snow, and she gave up trying to struggle.

"I didn't mean it."

"Get a grip? That was pretty clear what you wanted. Or not." she snapped back. Still offended. And she had known it. Her anger was wavering.

"Or even." he said, annoyed, and pulled her close to him. Here in the marketplace, where anyone and everyone could walk past them. "If you can't pull yourself together, I can do it even less."

Vin kissed her forehead, then her temple. Her neck. She closed her eyes. His tenderness so overwhelmingly beautiful. Her pulse beat up to her throat.

"Yes, I don't want to show us in public." He brought out with difficulty. Marisa only half heard what he said. "I want to be alone with you if you kiss me like you did earlier."

Everything inside her contracted at the thought of being alone with him. But how? When? Her parents were always home, his too.

"But that will have to wait a while. You shouldn't rush this thing."

What?

~

How long do I have to wait? I want you now. I'll come to you in the mountain hut. I watch you sleeping comfortably in the warm bed. I satisfy myself over and over again at the sight of you alone. Do you feel my presence? Is that why you toss and turn in your wild dreams? I forgive you at the moment of my climax for hurting me.

~

Day 11

Nothing had changed on the piste. The new snow had fallen minimally. The cable cars were just as full as before. The skiers in their group looked hardly changed.
And yet something seemed off. Or was it all in her imagination?
Was it her guilty conscience clouding all her senses?
Rightly so.
Marisa joined their group expectantly. She smiled kindly at Mitchell, hoping for normal events. The young man, however, was a bit lost with his plans today, seemed a bit indecisive. Rapidly changing his group split. Originally Marisa had been supposed to leave with him. Now she was paired with Vincent. She was about to start to complain when her mobile buzzed.
Marisa jerked slightly and looked at the message. It was from George.
Have a nice day. X
When she looked up again, she saw Mitch had looked at her phone in the same way. In a flash he turned back to his group and explained the route. She was even more annoyed that she had missed complaining. She had not yet glanced in Vincent's direction. She didn't know what she would see. An arrogant smile to say that he had known from the start that she was easy. Or an icy cold look to say how disappointed he was in her. A third variation floated fleetingly through her mind at the moment. A look of desire for her. Just as she had seen it that day.

Which would she prefer?
She blocked out all her thoughts and questions. She didn't need to dwell on it yet. The run up to today's slope was long. She stayed far enough away from him. She sought refuge with her usually easy-going ski instructor. But even now he seemed nervous. After a few minutes, she gave up trying to talk to him. She concentrated on the now. The mountains, the snow, the beauty of this landscape. She felt at home here. She had always felt at home here. She had to tie herself to this feeling. Little by little, many of her bad thoughts fell away from her. She was ready to ski and feel alive for a few hours.
Mitch checked again with his group to make sure they all knew the piste number and where they would meet. His gaze nervously fixed on Marisa one last time. She smiled encouragingly at him. And then he was gone, as were most of the other skiers.
Marisa was ready, looking at Vincent, who seemed equally ready to go. They hadn't exchanged a word since that moment on the sofa. Since he hadn't apologised for the kiss.
And she hadn't blamed him.
She smiled weakly and drove off. This track was unique. The curves long and branching. The snow almost untracked and slippery. There were little challenges that she was happy to take on. It offered her opportunities to use her skiing technique well and safely. Her ankle hardly weighed down; her hip was doing great. She felt free.
After a good hour, she looked for a quiet place to stop for a moment. She pulled out her mobile phone and took a photo of the landscape, of what calmed her. Maybe later she could look at that photo then and remember that day. Not the rest. Just this contemplation.
Marisa was still looking out at the landscape, her piste map in her hand, unheeded. She heard Vincent driving up to her. Felt his nearness. Her tingling in her stomach was treacherous and inappropriate. Fortunately, no one could see her body's immediate reaction to him.

"Are you alright? Standing here in the snow, almost freezing to death. Enjoying the silence.... Unless you wanted to ... "
Vincent made insinuations that made the blush instantly shoot up her cheek. Luckily they were already bright red from the freezing cold.
"No." she replied immediately. Then less vehemently. "I mean yes."
He stared at her. She stared back.
"But no. No." she added. Before they both fell over in shock.
He tried to read her. He just couldn't. Over the years he had made it a habit, and a successful one, to recognise other people. Their gestures, their movements, their words. But he couldn't do it with Marisa. He cleared his throat loudly to distract himself from his thoughts and fantasies.
"Which way?" he finally asked. His voice neutral, not cold, not friendly. Just like Vincent McDormant.
"I'm not sure." Her words were out before she could stop them. Shit.
Vincent fell silent. He looked at the woman in front of him, who stood completely motionless and uncharacteristically calm. Usually she had a snippy reply on her lips. Otherwise she looked at him full of anger and dislike. Now she looked ... blank. Lost. Uncertain.
Was she talking about the piste or their relationship? Was she giving him a chance to discuss it here? Or did she want more?
"What does the map say, the weather?"
Marisa shrugged.
"I don't want to listen to that."
"And your heart?"
To that even less.
She looked into Vincent's eyes, those sweet blue eyes. The ones she had once loved so much. And had since become such a bane.
"That says I'm thirty-four years old and should be slow to keep up." He didn't respond to her honest words, to the change of subject. He had guessed she had something to add. But her

views were surprising. "I should finally be married so I can have a say, make new friends. Have children. The things a woman is expected to do. Hey, I also threw up until I was six months pregnant and my stretch marks still haven't faded. So I can finally be part of the conversation."

She stopped abruptly. What had gotten into her that she was revealing so much to him? What did it have to sound like! Like a mid-life crisis.

Finally be part of the conversation.

Vincent had nothing to say. He didn't want to go into what was tormenting her. He knew only one way to protect himself from these emotions.

"Are you marrying him just for his sperm? MK, what the hell? You can find a hundred other men for that. Not George. I have a bad feeling about him."

Marisa sent him a dirty look. Of all the things she had just confessed to him, he had focused on that.

Did he have to put it like that?

And then get to the heart of the matter as well?

Damn.

"I'm not discussing this with you."

"This is crazy, Marisa. If he knew we ki -"

She looked at him emotionlessly. Strongly and decisively.

"I told him. I was ready to leave him. I gave him the choice. He wouldn't let me go."

Mary, Mary, why are you acting against us?

Vincent wanted to find relief in her words. Had to put reluctance and coldness into his reaction. Not disappointment.

"Most certainly, don't leave him for me. It would only be a short fling. A quick fuck. An act of pure lust, nothing more. You're right, don't break off your engagement over this. It's not worth it."

Marisa drew in a deep breath at his cold words.

That ass. Why did he have to put her down when she was already down?

Vincent drove off without waiting for her.

Her mobile phone was texting at that moment. Like fate.
I'm standing by your side. X
Marisa looked around jerkily, suddenly feeling as if he were watching her from behind a tree. She saw nothing but her beloved firs and bushes. The shiny snow. The beautiful landscape.
Her wonted calm wavered.

~

"Do you have to talk to me like that? You're not among friends anymore."

She hadn't liked his kiss. His vulgar choice of words even less. He smelled of alcohol and cigarette smoke.

"Does something about the word fuck bother you?"

Vincent had been in a bad mood ever since he had come back from a long weekend with the boys. The two days must have gone wrong somehow if he couldn't even look at them properly. His mood was weird. His behaviour jerky.

Marisa stood in his way so he could no longer pace back and forth in her room.

"Vin, what happened?"

He ran an annoyed hand through his blond hair.

"It's just an act of pure lust now. Fucking. That's what you've wanted all along, isn't it?"

She stared at him in shock. What the hell had gotten into him?

"Not at all. Maybe you should go back. Sleep it off."

"Or maybe we should just get it over with. All this stress with you and your declarations of love could be saved then. Just fuck."

She couldn't follow this conversation. She had dared to tell him her feelings once. That had been weeks ago. Since then, she hadn't spoken up about it again. She definitely hadn't written any love letters either. How had she been able to annoy him? What stress had he felt?

That stupid boy. Broke her heart into a thousand pieces and kicked her while she was down.

"It doesn't mean anything. Nothing. It's just sex. Don't even talk yourself into it. It doesn't mean anything."

She felt sick at his statement, at his coldness. A horrible thought rose up and wouldn't let her go.

"Were there girls at the party?" she asked, concerned. Didn't even want to know the answer.

"More than enough." He admitted. His expression tortured.

She wanted to throw up and get down on her knees. What had happened? Try as she might to be strong, she could find no words. Her breath caught; her heart stumbled. Her whole ideal world lay in ruins before her.

"Go away." she asked him softly.

Vin looked at her again, thinking he was doing the right thing, and left her room.

~

For the first time, George suggested they not eat with the others, and they shared a smaller table alone. His warm hand rested on hers and he asked her kindly about her day on the slopes.
"Did he behave?" His smile did not match his words. His voice cold.
Marisa looked at him in shock, had immediately regained herself and smiled back.
"Yes.... Yes, he ...." was her screwed up reply. What was she supposed to say? Apart from his deviant view on a short-term affair between him and her.
"Sorry. I didn't mean that. I'm glad you had a good day."
She nodded slightly. When her phone buzzed, she lifted it unsuspectingly.
The blood drained from her face. Her breath stopped.
George looked at her questioningly.
"Are you alright?"
Marisa switched off her phone and nodded just slightly.
"I just need to go to the bathroom real quick."
She just about managed to run there before adrenaline pulled at her knees and she collapsed shivering on the toilet bowl.
Carefully, she pulled her phone back out of her jeans to read her message again. Maybe she had misinterpreted it. Maybe she hadn't looked properly. It was all a joke.
She opened the message.
She saw herself, right next to Vin. Very close to him. With the sweetest smile on her lips.
Along with the words.
You dirty bitch. When I catch you, I'm going to fuck that smile off

your face.

~

You are sad. You are in a bad mood. Have you just started your period? Is that why you can't smile? Or are you trying to drive me away? No, I'm sure I'm not. I'm the fuck of your life. I don't mind a little bleeding. Don't worry, hot chick. I can shower off all the traces of you afterwards. I'm getting closer to you, day by day. Can you feel my eyes on you? Do you feel how I want to rip the clothes off your body? If I let you, would you take the lead and ride me to climax? Maybe after our first, second time. If you don't want to run anymore, then you can make me explode without my effort.

~

Day 12

Marisa didn't tell anyone about it. She tried not to think about it.
What could it possibly mean? Some guy took a picture of her and added a few primitive words. Nothing more. No need to panic. She wasn't alone during the day, no one could hurt her. And when? She was always around people. Why was that? Someone was having fun with her here. Had someone seen her kissing Vincent, even though she was already involved with George?
Who? Maureen? Would she be up to something like that? She knew her far too little to say yes or no. Who else would have reason to send this to her and threaten her? ...... George? He had had the opportunity to break up with her, after all. Besides, he had been sitting at the table with her when she had received the message. It definitely wasn't him.
…….. Vincent? Had he been in one of those cursed moods again, where he couldn't face his emotions and instead lashed out with impossible words. She couldn't imagine that. All this meant too little to him. She meant too little to him. Besides, he was clearly in the picture. Right in front of her, inches away. She could literally feel his breath on her face and ….
Her heart was beating too fast.
All right, she had thought about it quite a bit after all.
She hoped that the day on the slopes would give her enough distraction.
Finally, she arrived at the group. The others excited because

they had heard about the snowstorm in the weather forecast. They had to keep an eye on the weather. It was supposed to storm soon and bring a bunch of fresh snow. The white clouds in the sky underlined the warning.
"Marisa, Vincent."
"Or can I go with you today?" she interrupted immediately this time. The photo in mind. The last conversation too.
Mitchell looked like he wasn't feeling well today. His skin pale, his eyes as if haunted. He shook his head quickly.
"Tomorrow. Maybe." And with that he didn't let himself be talked into it. Otherwise he had always been anxious to leave with her. What bothered him about it today?
Marisa saw him join another skier. She smiled slightly and was immediately relieved. He had his eye on someone else. Now it all made sense.
However, that didn't help her herself. She had little desire to talk to Vin today. He looked as happy as she was to have to spend the day with her.
Fortunately, there were only a few stops on the piste, so little opportunity to have to talk. They made it to the starting point without exchanging a syllable. That's how it went.
"Shall I go first?"
"As you wish."
Marisa gritted her teeth in annoyance. That had been a simple question. He didn't need to waste energy on dislike for it.
"This could be a great day." she only murmured.
"You wanted to change ski partners."
"Because you're in a bad mood." she countered directly, and an icy glint flashed just as coldly from her eyes at him. All she wanted to do was ski. Why couldn't she pursue her passion more without fighting like children first?
"You're putting me in a bad mood."
She opened her mouth in a huff and immediately shut it again. *He must have gone mad!*
"Me you? You're getting at me because I don't want an affair, I want a marriage." She had summed up his argument a little

better than he had yesterday. It sounded relatively harmless. Still hurt, though.

"I can't believe you're not breaking up with him. This is never, ever going to work out."

"What do you care? Why should it bother you of all people anyway?"

Iron silence.

Marisa looked down the hill. Regretted this argument. The time they wasted over and over again, never coming to a resolution. She waited for him to see it on his own. Nothing happened.

Can't we call a truce? This is my only holiday for the whole year. I wanted to enjoy it."

"What about the honeymoon?"

He was incorrigible. He still had to make her white-knuckle.

"Are you finally going to let it go?" Her eyes sent a thousand tiny arrows in his direction as a warning. He ignored each one.

"What about the honeymoon?" he repeated insistently. He couldn't ignore the subject. He had to discuss it with her. Otherwise his thoughts would jump in other directions.

"I don't want to talk about *that*."

Vincent could have shaken her. Wanted to somehow get her to open her eyes and her mind and let this foolishness go.

"Why not? You asked for a truce. Let's talk about it calmly and simply."

Marisa shook her head. He wouldn't give up. He was unable to comprehend why she should marry George.

"And if we don't?"

She instantly regretted her question. His gaze darkened, his closeness suddenly so unmistakable. Had they been so close all this time? Had she been moving closer and closer all this time?

"That's the only issue keeping me from ripping your clothes off."

She wanted to come at him with a sly reply. Wanted to admonish him that he should finally put her relationship with George to rest. But this offer reminded her of their kiss. Of their reaction. Of the pure lust they had both felt. Longing to experience it again.

And slowly slid away from him.

"No." she said softly. But her eyes sang the opposite. "I want more."

"For fuck's sake. I don't want to marry you. But neither do I want you to marry him. Wake up already."

Marisa ignored his words. Ignored the deep stab in her heart. She had heard that before. And yet it hurt just as much now as it had then.

"This is the last time we're going skiing together. Find someone else to put down all the time." she countered instead. Before she left, she gave him another angry look. "Find someone else to hit on."

~

He didn't just leave her alone like that. Oh no, he came back immediately the next day. Less drunk, but all the more restless. Marisa had hardly slept all night, just cried and regretted. And missed him so much. But she would never admit that now. Seeing him in front of her was a challenge she didn't seem up to yet.
She wanted to walk past him, down the steps, into the library, just as she had planned. He held her by the arm. She tried to shake him off, he let go and stood right in front of her instead.
"I fucked up." he admitted. It didn't hurt any less to hear it today, as it had the previous day.
She just looked at him. In that moment, she hated his sweet blue eyes. Why did they have to be so perfect? Oh, and his blond, short hair. So shaggy and soft.
It was all so unfair.
"I didn't cheat." he said, almost shaken, as if that had been the sin. He lowered his head, shook it, ran his hands over his face before looking up wearily.
Marisa was a mess, but her heart was instantly ready to forgive him and forget all the heartache and tears.
"I don't want to marry you. But neither do I want to be without you." he said suddenly. The truth hurt and healed at the same time. "I keep trying to think of reasons why I want to go with someone else. I listen to the guys who say I'm boring."
He stopped, realising he wasn't making any sense at all.
"I plan activities with them because it keeps me from ripping your clothes off."
With a resignation he seemed to regret, he rested his forehead

against hers, grabbed her hands and squeezed gently.

"I hurt you. I wanted to avoid it. But I can't stay away from you. If you really want it, I will be with you."

She received his tentative kiss openly and with revealed feelings. She let herself be pressed against the letterboxes of all the residents of her apartment block and fell a hundred times deeper.

"Tell me now that this is all too much for you. You don't want this." he whispered between his greedy kisses.

"I want this. I want it all." This time she put her hands around his face and kissed him back.

There was no other way out for her but to let this relationship take its course.

She knew more than anything at that moment that he would break it. Over and over again. But she put up with that. She wanted more.

When the pain came, she would get through it.

~

The second photo also came at an inopportune time. After that long, stressful day with Vincent, she had finally managed to relax on her bed. She let the conversation play over and over in her head. It brought her nothing but confused thoughts and emotions. Guilt, memories, hopes, desires. She had to force herself to shut her mind off. She remembered the photo she had taken of the beautiful, constant landscape. Breathing deeply in and out, she looked at it intently and felt the tension, the stress, fall away from her.

George was just in the shower and the sound of the water running soothed her soul.

At that moment, a new message jumped onto her screen.

The photo first. Her heart was pounding up to her throat. She looked around anxiously, hastily getting up to check all the windows and doors were locked. The curtains drawn. She noticed in her haste back to her room that lights were on in both the other bedrooms. Subconsciously, she noted that Maureen no longer shared a bedroom with Vincent. Or a bed.

After the initial shock and fear, sheer anger and defiance came up. Determined not to let it get her down, Marisa looked closely at the photo. When was this? At what point had she actually been so close to Vincent? She hadn't even noticed. What's more, she had never taken his expression for granted like that before.

That's the only subject that keeps me from ripping your clothes off.
The words rang in her ears. As in the picture, her cheeks began to glow.

Shit.

Whoever took these photos had nailed the moment. Her infidelity was obvious. It was written all over her face. She liked Vincent's attention. She liked that he wanted her. For sex, at least. To fuck once.

Fuck.

The words that came after ran cold down her spine. All the colour gone from her face after all.

You incorrigible whore. If you can't learn from your mistakes, I'll have to show you how to painfully repent.

~

Him? What do you want with him? Blond hair, blue eyes. Yes, I can understand that. But can he do you? Can he satisfy you for hours? I don't think so. You look lost. No joy, no release. I can show you a new world of orgasms. Give me a chance. Come closer to me. Look at me again. Smile. Ah, yes, I know what you need. Not him, not any other. First me, then you'll never need another cock. I'm ready for you. I've practised curbing my desire, so I don't explode inside you on the spot. Practice makes perfect, I've had enough pleasure with myself. Now it can start.

~

Day 13

George deserved more. Marisa made up her mind to finally push the bad thoughts far away. She wanted to be with him. She wanted their relationship to have a future.
She would do everything she could to make sure he would be happy with her. She would not give him another reason to regret anything. She no longer wanted to hear that stupid, haunting song in her subconscious.
Mary, Mary -
What are you doing for us! she quickly changed the words. It sounded much better that way.
Her day on the slopes would be positive, no more melancholy or temptation to dwell on her past. There was no point in that. There would be no more tell-tale photos. She was the best of friends from now on, as before.
Therefore, it had been her idea that she would spend the day with George again. She was having a great time. She wasn't bored and didn't miss the adrenaline rushes at all. She didn't keep thinking about her group and how steep the descent would be today.
Marisa was completely satisfied. George smiled lovingly at her face as they sat together in the dining room in the alpine hut and now made their way to the common room. The other guests had also enjoyed a delicious dinner and were now making their way into the large, warm room to relax and warm up their limbs after a busy day. To their surprise, there was a winter disco tonight. The DJ was setting up all his music. The

chairs and seats had all been moved to one side or away to create a makeshift dance floor.

Her attention was fully on her fiancé. Until she saw the others. Mitchell was also finally returning from a long day on the black run, followed by the other skiers in his group. Marisa felt her heart tugging in their direction. She wanted to hear all they had achieved today, where they had been.

"Go on, go and catch up with Mitch. I can see the longing in your eyes."

George stroked her cheek gently. His kind words did good. He himself wanted to talk to some other skiers. Maureen had just arrived over there.

Together they made their way to the bar. Mitch looked briefly in their direction, a quick nod and then turned away from them. Marisa frowned in amazement, but immediately she was talking to her friends and George sneaked in among the others, greeting Mitch in a friendly way and making his rounds. Until he finally arrived where he had been drawn.

Out of the corner of her eye, she saw him too. She had no interest in talking to him. She didn't want to hear how he had survived the day without her. There was no way she was going to join him. She took her chance to order herself a drink.

"You were right. I had a much better time skiing without you."

Ouch. That lousy son of a bitch.

"Good for you."

Just then, a young woman walked past him, winking.

"Thanks for a great experience today." Her voice sweet and suggestive, she stroked his arm familiarly and kept walking. But first she sought direct eye contact.

Vincent had no problem doing the same to her. His interest and pleasure written all over his face.

Marisa refused to turn to him and show him that she had been following all this closely. And it hadn't bothered her at all. From now on she concentrated only on the bartender in front of her.

"What can I offer you?"

"Why don't you surprise me?"
Vincent changed his plan and stayed a while longer. She hadn't responded, which had bothered him more than he'd expected. The young man immediately had a gleam in his eye as he responded to her question. He wiped his hands on his tea towel in a jiffy before he set about gathering all his ingredients. His hair pulled tightly into a ponytail, he moved elegantly and well-practised as he mixed it together.
She laughed back in a friendly manner. Inwardly, she was just waiting for Vincent to finally leave. But he didn't.
It was going to be a long evening for everyone. A little alcohol might help out.
"Do you like it sweet and intense?" His blue eyes played with hers. He had an attractive woman in front of him. He was obviously going to make the most of it. Who knows maybe, she would be waiting for him at the bar at the end of the evening?
He also completely ignored the man next to her who was watching the spectacle, unimpressed.
"I'm going to be sick."
Marisa refused to be swayed. She had no time for him.
"I like it sweet and sour."
The guy in front of him loved his task, not taking his eyes off Marisa for a second as he served it.
"Green Temptation." His blue eyes shone invitingly. Marisa smiled back at him and accepted the intriguing drink.
Then she turned to Vin, raised her glass with a seductive smile on her lips and nibbled lightly on her straw. "Here's to resisting every temptation."
And with that, she made her way to her fiancé. The disco could begin.
After the delicious drink and no sign of her ex-boyfriend, she relaxed a little. The mood was relaxed, the people fun. Everyone danced their own style, the music seduced even the grumpiest visitor.
Marisa spotted her ski instructor standing in the back corner, his mobile phone in his hand, fully occupied texting someone.

He didn't seem to be listening to the music, not quite in the mood. Maybe she could help a little and talk to him alone. He looked a little lost, less neat and sexy than usual. She had imagined that such an evening was the event for him to enjoy himself with other skiers. This was what he lived for, after all. He hadn't noticed her. His eyes radiated pure panic as he looked up. He straightened up tightly and put his phone away.
"Do you resent me for not being there today?"
Mitch laughed nervously and shook his head slightly.
"Not at all. The group missed you, though." he said kindly, as he always did. "Especially your partner Vincent."
He took a sip of his beer and looked intently at her over the rim of his glass at his remark. She looked back in wonder and shrugged.
"He's distracted himself well enough, I think."
Mitch nodded. Her reaction was neutral, uninterested. He took advantage of these rare moments when he had her to himself. He had always had a weak spot for her. This woman had no idea what power she could have over other men. Unfortunately, he had never seen a chance for himself. Now it was far too late. She was engaged.
"Yasmine just arrived this week. She wasn't quite up to your standard, I'm afraid." he told her. "No one is as good as you."
Marisa laughed out. She leaned towards him a little, finding the alcohol had weakened her inhibitions somewhat. Encouragingly or flirtingly, she didn't really know at that moment, she put a hand on his shoulders.
"As if."
"You're right. I'm pretty good too."
What in the world was he just talking at her about? It didn't fucking matter.
They both laughed, Mitch grabbing her wrist kindly. They drank and chatted. At least he didn't look so rushed anymore. She managed to coax him into a dance before finally excusing herself to go and see George. It had been a while since she had seen him. Vin was standing by the fireplace with Yasmine,

but she hadn't looked for him. It chilled her to see the other woman moving far too close to him. She flicked her long red hair provocatively off her shoulder, her smile gorgeous and unambiguous. She was ready for anything.
This is making me want to vomit, she thought mockingly, repeating his own words from earlier. She chuckled lightly to herself.
She shouldn't drink anything else and yet she found herself at the bar.
Her favourite bar tender was pleased to see her again, this time interested in talking to her for longer. She was in no hurry and listened with interest. When he was not behind the bar in the winter months, he taught young women how to fight wild waves and water. He was a surf instructor on the French coast. His days, weeks were more exciting, like their whole lives together.
He served her the next drink, colourful and decorated with fruit. She loved the little parasol on top.
Simon knew how to make tourists happy. That was obvious. She laughed openly at him.
At last, she spotted George, who was just stepping back into the room. She walked briskly up to him and gave him a little kiss on the cheek. He seemed to have been outside for a while, his face was icy cold, and he smelled of snow. He smiled at her, but the warmth did not seem to reach his eyes. She ignored her observation. It didn't mean anything.
"Dance?"
She faced him cheerfully. His gaze on her drink.
"Really? Aren't we a little old for that, darling?" He tried to sound rather than his remark. She just shrugged.
"No way. We have to practise for our wedding dance after all."
When he still made no move to join her, she danced off on her own. She joined the others on the small dance floor, her mocktail in hand.
George did not take his eyes off her. He ordered himself a vodka or two and watched her intently from the side. Her

movements carefree, matching the music. She was laughing with the other skiers in her group, feeling incredibly relaxed.
Without stopping swinging and singing, she pulled her mobile phone out of her pocket and glanced at the message just in passing. And froze.
As if struck by lightning, she didn't move an inch. Fear written across her face. Then hidden again.
Marisa put her mobile phone away again, put her glass on one of the tables and left the dance floor.
George stood up, concerned, when he saw her in front of him. Her face pale.
"Mary?"
"I just need some air." she said curtly.
He nodded understandably.
"You've been enjoying too many cocktails.... Darling."
She hesitated and looked at him for a while longer. Should she tell him what she had been sent? Should she tell him that someone was watching her? She stood before him undecided.
He would listen to her, comfort her. He might be able to help her from the technical side. But would he understand the photos that were sent to her? Tolerate them? Interpret them as insignificant?
Marisa turned away from him, grabbed her jacket and ran out into the open.
Her head was spinning. Her stomach did the same. But she knew it wasn't the alcohol. A sweet and sour cocktail had not made her drunk. She could take more than a whisky.
No. That reaction was because of the photo. The fact that there was someone who wanted to harass her with her single, insignificant slip.
To what end? Each time the photos showed only a moment of a long, distant, aversive conversation between her and Vin. She had to hand it to this psychopath that he really did snap away in the split seconds when they were close to each other. Otherwise, there was only hatred and dislike in their eyes, wasn't there?

She ran her hands over her face. Several strands had come loose from her knot. She had to look relatively wild and unattractive, with no particular shine or make-up. But she didn't care about that at the moment. She had other problems. Marisa paced restlessly back and forth in the snow. She hardly noticed how the snow fell quietly from the sky, leaving a light layer on her hair. She had to sort out her thoughts, get her fear and panic under control.

This guy, this weirdo, was here. Here at this disco. To be precise, he had photographed her and Vin at the bar. The only moment today that they had spoken together. The one smile she had given him and hadn't even meant. Yes, it looked seductive. Yes, it gave the impression that she was flirting with him right now. But it hadn't bloody been like that. Hadn't he been able to see the anger that had been on her lips before and after?

Crap.

Keep thinking!

He had just sent it now. Who was that? One of her ski group? Someone she spent time with day in and day out? Someone she had laughed and joked with? In all those days, they had got to know each other pretty well. Not once had she got a bad feeling from one or the other. That was why the psychopaths were so successful in their methods. One had no idea they lived among us. What was his next step? What did he want to achieve? Was she safe? Maybe she shouldn't be out here alone -

Marisa literally jumped out of her skin when she heard footsteps behind her. A shrill scream under her hand just suppressed so that all the men didn't come running out of the alpine hut immediately, embarrassing her to the bone.

"Fuck, Vin. Fucking hell." She leaned forward as gravity soon threw her into the snow. "What the hell?"

She had her hands clutched to her stomach to control her adrenaline. She had regained her breath. But she was shaking all over. If she didn't pull herself together now, she would throw up at his feet. That would be unforgivable and she would

have to leave immediately.
Vin looked annoyed at the woman in front of him. He wanted to help her, didn't know how. She pushed his helping hand roughly away from her, and stepped far away from him.
"Yeah right. What the hell, MK?"
She shot him a warning look. Why did he have to keep using her unloved pet name? It drove her crazy that he kept using it to remind her of her turbulent past.
"You ran out of the hall all of a sudden. Like you'd seen a ghost!"
Marisa swallowed dryly. Slowly her body had calmed down again. She had herself under control again. Only unfortunately, she now had a new problem in front of her. Vincent McDormant was standing in front of her in the snow. The little flakes of snow landed in his tangled blond hair. He looked stunningly sexy, the dim light on his face. His inquiring eyes fixed on her. A dream of a man.
Don't get distracted. Get control of yourself.
Fucking alcohol.
'I wasn't feeling well,' she gave as an excuse. Believable enough.
"Bullshit. That's not why you suddenly turned pale as a ghost."
Marisa hadn't known her reaction had been so obvious. Who else had seen it? The guy who was responsible for the whole thing? Well then, he had certainly been pleased. She had played right into his hands.
Shit.
Vincent watched her turmoil, how she struggled with her thoughts. How she tried to appear neutral, dismissive. But he saw the nervousness behind her eyes. He recognised the fear that had made her want to throw up soon.
"I wanted five minutes alone." she changed her tactics. Perhaps with some kindness and vague explanations, he would believe her and let the subject rest. "There's nothing worse than throwing up in front of everyone."
Without thinking about it, she took some snow in her hand and rubbed it cooling over her forehead and cheeks. The cutting cold did her good, brought clarity.

She thought of how cold he must be. He hadn't grabbed a jacket, just stood in front of her in his jeans and jumper. In fact, he seemed to have really run after her right away.
But not her fiancé.
Be quiet, you silly heart.
She needed more than a little snow on her face. She needed to get out of here. Maybe someone was lurking behind the trees, taking pictures.
She was getting scared.
Vincent just watched her. Her cheeks were red, she had been very cheerful and sociable all evening. It could be that she had drunk too much. But he had only seen her go to the bar once. Most of the time she had been talking to Mitch or the other skiers or dancing light-heartedly. He could stand some of that snow himself at the thought of how much she had beguiled him with her dancing. All evening long.
He gritted his teeth in annoyance as he realised for himself how he had been unconsciously watching her all evening. Shit.
"You like it sweet and sour?" he repeated her words now. He knew exactly what he was addressing. "You want to be able to resist any temptation?"
He didn't come any closer to her. Oh no. But what he was doing to her here was much worse.
The snow actually felt good in his hand, between his fingers. He put a block of snow against his neck, in his collar.
Marisa just stared at him. His movements so sexy, his gaze fixed on her so hot.
"I can do that too." she said so weakly he could barely hear.
Her mind completely distracted by her other worries and promises to be a good friend.
Fuck.
Vin ran his fingers through his hair, lifting his head just a tiny bit. Challenging. Attracting.
"You mermaid."
She didn't dare breathe, trembled with desire. He did not come closer to her, did not tempt her. The distance between them

so great, and yet non-existent. She swallowed, looked at his mouth, his lips. And bit down on her own, aroused.
"Mary? Mary?"
Marisa awoke as if from a trance. She shook off her thoughts, her lust.
Mary, Mary, why are you acting against us?
Vincent did not move an inch, did not speak a word. Only saw all emotion replaced with guilt and remorse. Her eyes showed deep misery.
Her mobile vibrated in her pocket. She knew what that text meant. The whole game started again, and she had nowhere to hide. Everything came crashing down on her all at once.
Marisa ran towards the alpine hut, into George's arms. Only later did she read the second message. She was damned.
I spy with my little eye and that is ... your ex-fiancé.

~

Why had she drunk so much? She had let herself be tempted by the stupid sangria. The sweet taste, the delicious orange slices. Yuck, just at that moment she never wanted to touch lemon fruit again.
But at least she had Vin by her side. Swaying, they both left the bar, arm in arm, and made their way back to his flat. His parents had agreed to let her stay over.
Their first night together. In his bed.
Arriving at the front door, he pulled her into his arms. His kisses sweet and provocative. Marisa put her arms around his neck and returned his lust. It took them half an eternity to climb up to the sixth floor. Over and over, he seduced her with his tongue, driving her mad.
"How do you like it?" he breathed in her ear.
She giggled at the tingling of her belly. She was on fire, every touch driving her nearly insane.
And the world spun ceaselessly.
"Sweet and sour." she brought out. He kissed her neck, sucking in her skin gently, tickling her with his tongue. "Just like you. Sometimes you're sweet, sometimes you're sour."
Vin accepted it. At that moment, he wasn't going to argue. In that moment, nothing else mattered but Marisa Keach. His MK.
The thin key wouldn't quite fit into the keyhole when they finally stood outside his flat door. Marisa clung to his shoulder and laughed softly.
"Do you see one or two of them?"
Eventually they were in his flat, in his room, on his bed.
And the spinning got worse.

How she had managed to run to the bathroom without throwing up at his feet, she didn't know later. But the moment had been embarrassing enough. The dizziness even more so. She had to hold on to the toilet bowl so she wouldn't fall over in his bathroom.

She cursed the sangria, cursed her inexperience with alcohol. She cursed herself. She had screwed everything up. She had been looking forward to this first night for so long, had been dying to finally make love to him. Wanted it done at last. But no. She had to get drunk on the weakest alcohol of all.

She could never leave that bathroom again. He would never want to get close to her again. He would never love her.

Marisa stared up from the floor, blinded by tears, as Vin entered. His eyes concerned, not blaming. He closed the door behind him. Then he took some toilet paper, moistened it with cold water and put it to her forehead, her cheek, the back of her neck.

The cool wetness felt good. His care did her good. Her world was slowly becoming whole again.

"This is not how I imagined our first night together."

"I was nervous. I thought some alcohol. .... I couldn't resist the temptation."

"Neither could I." he laughed, holding the cloth over his head just the same. He obviously wasn't feeling much better either.

"And you know what other temptation I can't resist?"

Marisa shook her head, instantly regretting the quick movement.

Vin kissed her gently on the lips. Only briefly. And yet much more significant.

"This one."

Marisa could quite badly distinguish the tingling in her stomach and the inner arousal from her condition. She regretted every single sip. Every minute here on the floor was so devastating. She wanted to respond to him, wanted to get closer to him. But she didn't trust her body.

It was a long time before she finally lay in his bed, her stomach

a little calmer, her head still. As long as she didn't move.
It was the worst night of her life.

~

Your hips. Your breasts. Your ass. Especially when you've taken off your thick snowsuit and are revealing yourself. Ah, then I get horny. You move like a woman who knows how to make a man climax. You twist, bend, sway your assets to the rhythm of the music, you don't see me standing in the corner. Lascivious. Stiff. But I see you. On top of me, naked, your round breasts bouncing up and down in time with your movements. You throw your head back passionately as you cry out with an earth-shattering orgasm. You will scream my name. Only mine, no matter who you fucked before. You will never think of another fuck afterwards. Or want to.

~

Day 14

Marisa needed a distraction.
Yes, she wanted to marry George.
Yes, she wanted to be a good fiancée to him.
No, she didn't want to sit in the café for another day when she could be trying the steepest slope ever.
Today she wanted to feel the icy wind on her face. Today she wanted to be free.
George didn't mind.
No problem, darling.
I'll wait for you at the café, Mary.
You know I trust you.
Today, her fiancé did not miss the opportunity to accompany her to the meeting point. He stayed by her side until most of the skiers had arrived. His gaze warm, smiling. His eyes cool.
Vincent just nodded at them uninterestedly, Mitch stared coldly in their direction. The good humour he had shared with her yesterday seemed to have vanished again. He addressed his group, again repeating the rules and routes for today. He split the group, not daring to look at Marisa and George.
"Joe, Casper. Yasmine, Vincent. Marisa, with me."
She was most pleased.
Finally, it was time to say goodbye. George made a big fuss of kissing her lips. Rather unusual for him. He never usually liked to show so much tenderness in public. But she would not complain. It wasn't uncomfortable for her. Just surprising. A tiny bit uncomfortable.

"Hey Mitch, you alright?" she finally greeted him after George pulled away. "Thanks for choosing me as your partner. The two best."

The glow on her face broke his heart.

He barely nodded, setting about putting on his gloves and getting ready for the day.

She frowned. Why was he being so weird to her again?

"Mitch?"

He checked his mobile phone and she saw him gritting his teeth angrily because of whatever he had just read. With an aggressive movement, he pocketed it again and turned around. "Sorry. I drank too much yesterday. I'm not the best company today." He wasn't sure she'd buy that. But she only smiled more.

"You and me both."

In the cable car, she finally took a deep breath. The day could begin.

It was amazing how hours felt like minutes. How physical exertion didn't matter and you found more and more strength and energy within you to take on the next descent.

The edges were quite confusing this time. It took patience and restraint. It was no wonder that they met other skiers who found this descent a little more difficult.

Her heart sank when she recognised Vincent and his new partner, Yasmine, ahead of her. They were both standing bent over the map right next to each other. They seemed to be getting on very well, skiing rather out of their minds.

Mitchell stopped for them, as a responsible ski instructor should. Marisa was annoyed. She didn't want to see the two of them close up, making big eyes at each other and patting each other unabashedly. She preferred his affair with Maureen a hundred times better at that moment.

"Everything all right with the navigation?"

Vin looked up in surprise. His eyes sparkled as their gazes met. Her heart leapt into high gear. She wanted to do the same to him. Then the moment was over in a flash.

Yasmine laughed hypocritically and pretended it was no problem that she didn't understand the markings on the map correctly.

How the hell had she managed to end up in their group? She must have had more experience skiing than she was letting on. Yasmine tilted her head slowly and appropriately if it was helpful. She thought it was nice of Vincent to try and explain all these little symbols to her.

How sweet of him.

Marisa wanted to throw up. Her face stiffened. Jealousy didn't agree with her.

I am not jealous! she immediately contradicted herself. What was going through her head!

As if. Vincent could do whatever he wanted. She herself had suggested it to him. So that she could concentrate on her relationship with George. She didn't want his attention on her at all. She didn't want to get into inappropriate situations again where she wanted to jump into his arms.

Shit.

"We'll be fine."

I bet.

"I've had enough experience."

With what, exactly?

"Don't wait up."

You want to take your time.

"You go ahead, we'll follow."

You want to be alone with her.

Marisa didn't need to be asked twice. She drove off without checking the map. Only later did she think how stupid she must have looked running away.

Mary, Mary, what do you do every time?

You want to stay with me, don't you?

She did not see him again for the rest of the day. Which was just as well, of course. She hadn't wanted to see him. Not with her, above all things. She had an exciting day on the slopes without him. She didn't need a long conversation defending her relationship with George. Everything that was important had been said.

Mitchell looked impatiently at his watch. Then at his mobile phone. Again at his watch.

With the complicated departures today and the new members, however, he didn't want to underestimate the departures. He was sure they would make it back down the mountain safely and without any problems. They had gained enough experience and practiced skiing techniques that it was theoretically possible.

What worried him most were the weather warnings flashing on his mobile phone. He made the hard decision to cancel the rest of the descent and contacted his group with the new meeting point at the cable car, for a quicker and safer exit.

One by one they all trickled in. He sent the first few to the café for something hot to drink. They shouldn't catch cold on the mountain. Sure enough, as if on cue, the weather changed and the wind picked up.

Marisa insisted on helping him with the calling. She stayed by his side, despite the stark cold on her cheeks and nose. Her hands struggled, she could feel her fingertips going numb. There were only two left.

Vin and Yasmine. What was stopping them?

She didn't want to think about it.

George.

Think of George.

Mitch was deeply relieved when everyone had now arrived safely and with little delay. Despite the disappointment of a shortened day of skiing, everyone was in good spirits and completely agreed that it was time to get to the valley. With the wind and snow came more announcements over loudspeakers that the cable cars would not be in operation even if there was a snowstorm. When they all arrived at the cable car, each cabin was filled to the maximum weight with skiers and equipment. To say there was a lack of space would have been an understatement.

Marisa stood at the very back in one of the corners and watched as another fourteen or fifteen skiers got on and stood nose to nose. As luck would have it, Vin joined them. And Yasmine.

Oh, did they finally have the chance to get closer. What joy.

She couldn't watch, trying to fight her anger, her discomfort. She looked out at the mountains as the doors closed and the cabin floated downhill like magic. A little later, the next cabin was also packed, and would depart. In a few minutes they were on safe ground.

Marisa's breath caught as she suddenly felt him in front of her. She wanted to be angry, wanted to admonish him for it. But she said nothing. Instead, she kept her gaze off him, fixed on the mountains.

But all her senses knew that he was standing right in front of her. He smelled so good, like snow and cold. She knew his hair was a wild mess after a long day under his helmet and cap.

The wind made the cable car sway, a few of the passengers exhaled loudly, slight anxiety began to spread. An uneasy murmur began.

Vincent reached up for the holder that was above her head, next to her hand. There were only inches separating them. Every now and then the wind brought movement into the cabin. Every now and then his snowsuit brushed her belly. Their fingers accidentally touched. She let them. And looked up at him.

Oh, if looks could betray one, it was the moment. It struck her deep inside, like a bolt of lightning. Her knees weak, her whole body tense. But well cramped. Defenceless.

Vin hadn't expected to be so affected by her gaze alone. He swallowed. Weightless.

"I'll remove myself as soon as I can." he said coldly, trying to get his thoughts under control. This cramped cabin tested his willpower. The warmth of her hand next to his burned his skin in that small spot like fire.

"Stay." she whispered instead. Deeply shocked by her blunt answer, instantly repentant. And full of lust again.

Mary, Mary, how dare you act against us?

He had heard her and understood her, however softly the word had been.

His face against her neck, his hot breath on her skin. She felt him. Desired him. Leaned towards him unnoticed.

"I will not touch you until you allow me."

Pure lust.

"I will not kiss you until you open to me."

Pure agony.

"I will not make love to you until you push this guilt away from you."

Pure confusion.

Which was worse? The guilt or the deep, unsatisfied desire?

Mary, Mary - you unfaithful bitch.

Marisa closed her eyes in agony and turned her head slightly away from him. The song, that vile song was getting louder and louder in her head. She was on the verge of covering her ears but dared not let go of her holder. And what for? What would Vin think of her? She would look completely mad. And she couldn't explain it. How could she tell him that she constantly felt she was being watched? Hearing voices in her head, at night, while she slept? As she summed it all up for herself like this, she was no longer sure how real it all was. Had she gone mad? Were all these events just in her imagination? In her dreams?

Vincent misunderstood her reaction and instantly shut himself off. Should she just put George first, should she kid herself that their relationship could go well. Eventually she would realise that he was not the man for her. And then it would be too late. She would be married, with a child and alone. Or was that all she really wanted? A child to love and to hold?

Vincent cursed the swaying of this cable car. Unexpectedly, he put a protective hand around her waist. Completely innocent yet arousing. He hated the unbearable position they were in right now. He just wanted to get out of here. Away from her and her stupid notions of a settled future. He moved away from her.

The cable car had arrived safely in the valley. They hadn't crashed.

Only Marisa herself plunged into an endless chaos of emotions.

~

Her nervousness got worse. Every time she met with him, she expected them to sleep together.
Her first time. She was so excited about it that she could hardly sleep and eat. What would it be like? What would it feel like? Would they get completely naked? And what the hell was she going to do with her hands? She also wondered if it would hurt....
Marisa fought the urge to take a sip of beer after all, as she stopped briefly with him at the snack bar. She was shaking inside with excitement and nerves whenever he so much as looked at her and smiled. She felt much worse when he kissed her just like that, in public.
And how!
There was no question about what he wanted. But when?
She refrained from grabbing the beer. She never wanted to touch a drop of alcohol again. On the contrary, she still felt embarrassed to the bone about what had happened *that* night.
"You're shaking." he remarked, with his face still millimetres from her mouth. His kiss had been hot. Teasing. Teasing. Unfair. "Are you cold?"
Marisa shook her head just slightly and rested her head against his forehead.
"No. I'm just nervous." Her honest answer was all too sweet.
Vincent took her cold hands in his. They stood close to each other, at a tall plastic table with hot fries in the bowl on top. She had no appetite for *that*.
"We'll manage all right. I have enough experience. Don't keep waiting for the moment. It just happens."

I bet. ..... With what, exactly? You want to take your time. You don't want to be alone with me. JUST WHEN IS IT GOING TO HAPPEN?
Another little kiss on her forehead and they went on their way again. Apart from his closeness, she loved their long walks in the woods, in the fields. Talking for hours, listening. She found this time with him the most enjoyable. It helped her relax, think of other things. Usually.
But today her thoughts were in pure confusion. His nearness pure agony. The warm hand in hers ignited pure lust.
"Have you had many girlfriends?"
His comments at the snack stall came up again. She had to ask after all.
Vincent laughed at her cautious question. How long had she been waiting to ask him that?
"No."
"Really?" She didn't believe a word he said. Had he forgotten how they had met?
"No, girlfriends none."
"But you have ... but you're not anymore..." A blush rose to her face. She didn't know exactly how to express herself. In any case, she expected an honest answer. This uncertainty was eating her up inside. How many other girls did she have to keep up with? How many girls would he compare her to? What if she wasn't half as good as them?
She felt sick.
He stopped in the middle of the forest and looked her in the eye, a smirk on his lips. She didn't like him making fun of her at all.
"This is all irreversible. So why worry about it?"
He would never understand the reason.
Vincent kissed her gently.
"I'm going to touch you when you're hardly expecting it." he whispered in her ear.
Every caress from him was unexpected.
"I'll kiss you so hard you won't be able to think."
Like right now?

"I will not make love to you until you push these many thoughts away from you."
Ouch. That could be a long time coming.

~

Even without photos, the messages had bite. Perhaps even more force than with a picture. Threatening. Calculating. Mean.
How was your day, dearest slut?
Hours on the road with your crush. You disgust me.
Did you think about your fiancé for a second?
Why so shy? Aren't you going to answer me?
Shall I visit you in your bedroom later?

~

Day 15

Marisa looked tiredly out of the windows in the alpine hut. She had been tossing and turning all night. She felt as if she had not slept for a minute. The voice in her head had not rested.
The weather had worsened. A lot of fresh snow had fallen, the wind was blowing hard.
The mood in the large room was mixed. Several guests were using the day to catch up on other winter activities. Others were disappointed not to be able to spend the day on the slopes today.
The question was whether she wanted to spend the day sitting in the corner doing nothing or whether she could at least enjoy the snow a little.
"Mitch had mentioned that there were some interesting cross-country trails nearby. We could try those out?"
"You want to go out in this weather, darling? It's freezing with the wind. And it's only getting worse."
George squeezed her hand placatingly and turned back to his newspaper. For him, that settled the issue.
He was right, after all.
"That's right. Maybe tomorrow?"
George looked up. She was restless, nervous and unhappy. What could he do about it?
"Is it really so bad to spend a day by my side?" His comment was meant sweetly, a little teasing but on the whole a joke.
Marisa smiled slightly. Guilt spread through her entire body. And ate her up inside.

The day was pleasant, quiet.
Boring.
Marisa gave George a kiss on the cheek before excusing herself to get some fresh air. He looked up only briefly, his attention now on the chess game with another guest. On her way out, she saw Maureen arrive. The beautiful blonde looked around the large room to see if she knew anyone. Without even noticing Marisa, the young woman walked straight up to George. She put her dainty hand on his shoulder before swinging her perfect curls to the side and smiling at him.
What now? Marisa's mood wavered. Guilt forgotten, confusion set in. As if she had seen nothing, she turned around on the spot and ran out into the snow. Around the corner she found a group of other visitors amusing themselves by building a snowman. Among them were her acquaintances from the ski group, somewhere she had also taunted Mitchell. Yasmine, however, did not, as far as she could see.
It just seemed like the best idea to her.
With a delighted laugh on her face, she joined them and helped with the snow globes.
She would recognise his voice among a hundred people.
Shit.
Their meetings were unexpected. And each time, both parties were completely unprepared for these situations. Too late to turn around. Too late to run away.
Vin said nothing, his eyes cold and dismissive. She did the same to him.
She had no idea how big they wanted this snow brigade to be, it was at least two different bases. A snowman and his wife? She followed Roger and Felix's instructions. Little by little the snow piles took a good shape. Sculpting was not so easy. Luckily there was enough snow to replace the various body parts as soon as they fell off unhindered. The others laughed with the addition of the round, feminine curves. As nature would have it, they were not symmetrical. The snowman had more to suffer.

"So, Marisa, when's the big day?" asked Felix as he worked his gloved arms into the central sphere.

Marisa handed him some snow, a useless act. She didn't like this change of subject at all. She knew exactly how Vincent was just following the conversation with rapt attention.

"Erm... in less than two months." she replied fleetingly.

"How did George propose to you?" came a feminine voice from behind the snow woman. Steph? Stephanie?

"Oh, no one wants to hear that. I don't want to bore you."

She really wasn't going to tell this story in front of everyone. Especially not with Vincent in the audience.

"Come on! We've got a long day ahead of us!"

Mitch grinned mischievously at her and gung against her arm. He seemed a little more relaxed today. No more hangover? Vincent's gaze was unmoving and fixed directly on her.

"We were out to dinner, and he asked me what I wanted to do for the rest of my life."

"Roses? Candlelight? Music?"

"It really wasn't a romantic affair like in a book. More practical, at our age."

Everyone laughed at her last comment and thankfully that was the end of the subject. The others now began to talk about their own relationships and affairs, the two couples already had a much more interesting story of their proposal.

Marisa stayed in the background. Didn't want to hear how messy and banal her relationship was in comparison. She had always had problems with having to compare herself to others. This wasn't helping her.

"Are you beginning to realise you're making a mistake?"

Vincent had joined her unheard. Without even really helping with the snow globes, he crouched down beside her. Out of earshot of the others. Out of sight, too, hopefully.

Marisa shot him a dirty look.

"Are you going to start that again?" she hissed in annoyance, her eyes sparking fire. "There's nothing more to discuss here. I'm here on holiday. I made my decision, I said yes. I'm not here

to be questioned all the time or for you to doubt me."
She pushed the snowball back into the ground angrily and rose.
Vincent grabbed her arm and pulled her back down. The discussion was far from over.
"I don't doubt you; I doubt your reckless decisions. Don't you want more? You of all people should want more."
She shook herself free of his grip. His nearness made her all fuzzy.
"I'm finally satisfied with my life as it is. And I will be content with my life. Why do you want to tamper with my arrangements?"
He didn't know how he would get her to open her eyes.
"At least wait another year before you marry him." He conceded as a suggestion.
"For what?"
"To get to know him better."
"I know him well enough."
Vincent pressed his lips tightly together. Her insinuations had been clear, and he didn't like the idea one bit.
"That you know what his sexual preferences are and how to satisfy him doesn't mean you know him."
Marisa's breath caught. After all, he had no idea about her sex life. If only he knew that George wanted to wait until the wedding night to make love to her. He was in no hurry, just as Vincent had been then. They were so much alike!
"He must have had a past. What did he do before you? Why does he want to marry you within a few weeks?"
She didn't think she heard right.
"You're disgusting."
She stood up abruptly and had to leave. He, wanting to stop her, rose as well. He didn't get to say or do anything. Her anger was boiling over. Her anger uncontrollable.
"If only I had listened to my mind and ignored you the first day and pretended I didn't know you. Then I would have been spared all these stupid insinuations."

Fortunately, the others didn't seem to have noticed their heated argument and were still happily building their snow family. They were beginning to take real shape, the logs from the firewood helping, just like the carrots someone had provided. What had she missed out on when she'd had a pointless fight with Vincent?

Mitch was checking something on his phone when he saw her coming. He looked at her in dismay.

"Are you alright?"

"Isn't there something we can do? This afternoon?"

He pulled out his phone again and calculated the weather forecast. He looked regretfully at the woman in front of him, who at that moment wanted nothing more than to get away from this place. She wanted to get out into the snow, feel the cold breeze in her hair and draw the freezing cold deep into her lungs.

"It looks bad. Cross-country skiing would be the -"

"Perfect. Let's get going."

"Not so fast. I have to sort it all out and prepare the group and so on. Maybe they don't feel like it either. Besides, we need the right equipment for it. By the time all this is sorted out, it's already afternoon. Not much time to go for a long run before it gets dark, especially in this weather. Tomorrow we can get it all organised."

Marisa looked saddened in the latter's eyes. It made sense. It was already too late.

She couldn't bear an afternoon in the peace and warmth. It gave her too much time to think about everything. And she didn't want to do that for reasons. Resigned, she walked towards the entrance. Hesitated. Waited.

"I'll go cross-country skiing with you. If you can put up with me obnoxious person."

Vincent stopped at the bottom of the stairs. He allowed her great distance. Himself too.

Their conversation was still on his mind. Despite all his training, years of experience, he could not get through to her.

It was driving him mad.

"What?" she wasn't thrilled with his proposal. But not averse to it either. "Why would you go cross-country skiing with me? We can't spend five minutes together without being at each other's throats."

"Or ..."

He let the words hang unspoken in the air. They both knew what he was alluding to.

That bastard.

Sexy, gorgeous bastard who offered to let her enjoy the afternoon over the snow.

"No more arguments." he promised neutrally. At least for the next few hours.

Marisa felt cornered. She wanted out, she wanted to be active. She didn't want this with Vin, she didn't want to disappoint George. She didn't want to jeopardise their relationship.

Nor would she. It was a matter of a few hours cross-country skiing. There was hardly time for frolicking in the snow and cheating.

"I'll let George know."

~

"Do you want to get married at some point?"
They were on their way home from the cinema, where he had been persuaded to watch a romantic comedy with her.
Vin gave a short laugh. What was going through her head? The film had motivated her too much.
"No." he said, as if it would never be the case for him, of course.
Marisa hugged herself into his arm. Not noticing his answer.
"As if you could decide that now. Who knows, maybe I'll be your wife?"
Her eyes shone at her suggestion. She smiled at him sanctimoniously.
She didn't really believe that, he thought affectedly.
"How would you propose to me?" she teased him further. The conversation was becoming awkward for him. "Roses? Candlelight? Music?"
"None of that. Our life is not a movie, or a love story. If it were, it would just be a practical affair. Nothing more."
She giggled at his answer. And already it wasn't a 'no' anymore. So, she had a chance after all.
"So marriage is in the cards after all." she said cheerfully.
"You've known me five weeks. At least wait another year before you get involved."
"What for?"
"You should know the person. Everyone has secrets, dark thoughts. An affecting past."
Marisa wasn't really listening to him. She didn't care at all. She was just satisfied to hear that marriage was not out of the question.

"Oooh, dark thoughts. Is that what you call it?"
Her smile was sweet, she was sweet. But on this night, it was unbearable.
"You don't even know if we're sexually compatible. That's why."
She stared at him, offended.
"Just because I don't know if I'm going to sexually satisfy you yet, I can't marry you?"
Vin stopped in the middle of the pavement and ran his hands over his face. He shook his head in annoyance. His brow furrowed.
"This conversation makes no sense at all, MK. I don't want to get married. I just want to sleep with you. That's all."
Shit. That had come out wrong.
This time she had listened to him properly. Her sweet smile faded in one fell swoop.
"You're disgusting."
Marisa turned back and walked home alone and broken-hearted.

~

Wonderful. The landscape, the view, the air.
Refreshing. Awakening. Healing.
And incredibly exhausting.
Marisa had forgotten how tiring this kind of skiing was. Especially with the cold fresh snow. She had underestimated how hard she would have to fight the new snow crystals to make any progress at all. The employee in the rental shop had warned her that the weather conditions were not favourable, but he gave the cross-country skiers an extra portion of wax and Marisa and Vincent set off. After half an hour, they had finally broken in and both got off the mark more quickly. The great resistance made them tired. At the same time, Marisa had to concentrate on skiing, which kept her from thinking about other things.
Vincent took over the navigation and picked out some of the most beautiful routes she had ever seen. Even when the view was foggy, she recognised the beauty of the area here. They skied side by side in silence by mutual consent. Marisa liked this kind of skiing, she didn't always have to rush down the mountains at top speed and run the risk of breaking her neck and leg every time.
Vincent stopped and consulted the map. The snow swirled around him excitedly.
"We should turn back. It took much longer to walk this short distance than I calculated. We won't make it back before dark otherwise."
Marisa leaned towards him to see the markings on the map. The little snowflakes kept landing on it, covering the paths.

"This route leads towards another valley. Maybe another 20 kilometres? We could get a bus from there?"
Vincent tried to read all the remarks and calculate the ups and downs. It was risky. Under normal circumstances it would be doable, but in this weather.
"We should turn back." he repeated anxiously. He didn't like this wind and limited visibility.
Marisa looked behind her and then ahead again.
"It took two hours to get here just the same. We'll make it the rest of the way. We'll just have to keep at it a bit."
He let himself be persuaded to keep running. For the first hour they were well on pace. But dusk hit them earlier than expected. The ups and downs had been deeper, consuming more time than expected.
By late afternoon, they were still in the middle of trees and mountains, far from a village or any civilisation. It was getting harder to see which direction they were running. The map showed no shortcut all around.
Marisa fought exhaustion and hoped they were still on the right track. Vincent turned to her periodically to make sure she was not lost. His pace had slackened a little too, every now and then he paused to check the map. He didn't say a word, but she knew they could have been back in the warm by now. She regretted her decision to keep walking instead of turning back. Now they were in a mess. Her stomach growled; her head grumbled. A hot cocoa would be a godsend right now. With every further metre she felt her hands and feet less and less.
Spending all night in the dark, freezing mountains didn't sound thrilling.
"There, look."
Lost in her own murky thoughts, she had stopped looking ahead. Relieved, she recognised smoke coming from a chimney in the distance. And a little further away, more smoke. A few small properties scattered everywhere lay ahead of them. They couldn't believe their luck.
Vincent aimed at the houses with the last of his strength.

Despite knocking several times and the smoke from the chimney, no one opened the door. Slightly apprehensive, they again made their way to the next property, and then the next. It felt like half an eternity until they arrived. It had only been a few hundred metres, but they had been more exhausted from the last stretch. They were worried that it wouldn't open here either. The next houses were another hundreds of metres away. At that moment they might as well have been in space. They wouldn't make it there tonight.

A light came on. She breathed a sigh of relief. An old man, in his worn pyjamas opened the door. He had already been asleep and Marisa felt her guilty conscience rising. At the same time, she no longer felt her body and it didn't help. She had to disturb this poor man.

At the sight of them, he just smiled. Marisa was glad.

"Come in, come in."

With stiff limbs and tired joints, they entered. One by one they took off their snowsuits, hats, gloves, thick socks. Where they lay, they left thick drops of water. Marisa would set about cleaning everything up again. The warmth that came to her from the house came not a second too soon.

"Are you lost?" The man spoke in a broken German, enough though to make himself understood to them. He let them step into his living room, where the remains of a small fire were still flickering. His gaze landed amusedly on Marisa's face and figure. He stood up to her. "Get warm. Hot."

Vincent watched this with a quizzical feeling. The latter's hospitality surpassed itself in that he reached for her hands and rubbed them together in his.

"Do you have a room where we can stay tonight?" he interrupted that moment.

Marisa immediately regained her composure and pulled her hands away. She smiled kindly, not wanting it to seem rude.

"A room? Or two? I have three, four." He was very hospitable. Apparently, he lived alone in a large family home.

"One -"

"Two. Thank you." Marisa jumped in immediately, relieved not to have to share a room with Vincent. Or a bed, even.
That would never have ended well.
The man smiled contentedly, far too contentedly, in Vincent's suspicious opinion. He showed them where the rooms were. On the first floor he had a small room with a bed, where he pointed Vincent. Then, timidly but deliberately, he put his hand on Marisa's back and led her down the corridor to the last room. This room had a double bed and an adjoining bathroom. Marisa felt like she was in a boarding house.
"My daughter. Child."
Marisa thanked him kindly. The man nodded to her again before moving away from the room. She breathed a sigh of relief and looked into Vin's challenging eyes.
"Two rooms?" he asked in a suppressed voice. After all, the man didn't need to overhear how creepy he thought this whole thing was. "We shouldn't sleep separately."
She looked at him, annoyed. She was cold, tired and exhausted. Did he have to start an argument right now.
"You're not sleeping here with me."
"As old as the man may be, I don't have a good feeling about him. Who knows what he's imagining right now."
"That's exactly what you said about George," she retorted, raising an eyebrow.
Here he goes again with the same line.
"And I'm usually right."
His eyes looked as tired as she felt. Dark circles under his eyes made their presence felt.
"You don't trust anyone either, do you? Now I don't even take it personally that you have a problem with George. You obviously have a problem with men."
Vin furrowed his eyebrows in annoyance. He would have been only too happy to disagree. But unfortunately he had met more than his fair share of people in life who were really up to no good. And today this man was a fine example of that.
How could she be so naïve as to feel at home here in a complete

stranger's house?
He was too tired to argue with her.
"As you wish. Scream loudly so I can come to your rescue."
Marisa shut the door behind him. She took her mobile phone out of her pocket. The reception was poor, but it was enough to see that she had missed eleven calls. I wonder if her other messages had arrived during the day. She had let everyone know where they were and that they would be late.
Hastily she wrote another message to George and Mitchell to tell them they were safely in accommodation. Hopefully they would arrive.
She used the adjoining bathroom to take a hot shower. She was cold to the bone, her fingertips and toes pinching and twinging unbearably. The hot water helped immensely.
As Marisa stepped out of the shower, an eerie feeling of being watched came over her. A feeling she couldn't shake. It was ridiculous, she thought. She was in the bathroom, how could anyone be watching her. There was no one here.
Open the door and go to your soft, warm bed. Rest your bruised nerves.
Marisa did not manage to open the door. She stood there for half an eternity as if frozen, wrapped in a towel. Only when she heard her mobile vibrating in the other room did she jerk the door open and go into the room.
Her heart was beating up to her throat, her body was trembling.
See, nobody here. All safe. You stupid cow, let his words get to you.
Marisa grabbed her phone to read George's text message.
She dropped it as if burnt.
Shit.
Without waiting any longer, she grabbed all her things and mobile phone and ran out of the room. As quietly as possible, yet insistently, she knocked on Vincent's door. And again.
Shit. Was this the right door? He hadn't fallen asleep yet, had he?
Please, please open the door.

He did. And standing in front of him was Marisa Keach in a towel, her hair up in a knot, little drops of water on her neck, on her chest.

Shit.

Marisa didn't see his eyes darken. Instead, she walked right past him and could breathe again.

Vincent closed the door but didn't dare turn to her immediately.

"You drove me crazy with your mistrust," she said defensively when he finally looked at her. Instantly she realised how she was standing here in front of him. She swallowed. She tightened her grip on her towel. Had she lost her mind?

Shit.

He didn't say a word. All the effort of the day was taking its toll on his self-control. Or rather, lack of self-control.

"Can I stay?" she asked cautiously. Everything in her was tense, her eyes wide, she looked as if she had seen a ghost.

As if he could send her away again.

"At least your room had a double bed." he joked at last as they both looked at the small bed.

She swallowed dryly. Nervous. Panic in her eyes. She ran her hands over her face in agitation, pulling the towel tighter against her.

"I'll sleep on the floor." he finally said, trying to take the weight off her shoulders. He saw her drop her shoulders in relief and slowly colour returned to her face. He wanted to know what had happened, why she had been so beside herself. He wanted to offer her a strong shoulder, to take her in his arms and comfort her, whatever was making her sad.

But he also wanted to tear the towel off her body and press her against the bed and make love all night.

So, he stayed away from her. For a few minutes he went back to the other room to get some blankets and pillows so that the night wasn't quite so unbearable. In the meantime, Marisa had dressed fully again and hid under the covers.

"Do you want to talk about it?" he asked softly.

All the emotions of the day rushing at her that she could barely hold on to her temper and almost broke down crying.

She just shook her head slightly.

She wanted to tell him everything, wanted to know what he thought of these anonymous messages. She wanted to hear him give her good hope for the future. Wanted him to wish her only the best.

But she also wanted him to take her in his arms and kiss her as intimately as before. She wanted to feel him, move with him and not regret a second of it.

So she remained silent and used the bedspread to hide her turmoil.

~

It echoed loudly in her head, in her dreams.
Mary, Mary, you sanctimonious bitch.
"Not Mary." she murmured softly.
She tried to turn, to get away from the song. But her legs were so stiff from all the cross-country running that she couldn't escape. As soon as the last sounds of the song had died away, she took a deep breath.
Her peace did not last long. Again, she turned around, holding her hands in front of her face. Didn't want to see the news, didn't want to read it.
You disgusting person.
Did you really just get lost?
"Yes, believe me."
Where are you spending the night?
Are you shagging yet?
"No. No."
Think of me tonight.
"No, please don't." Her voice sounded desperate.
Vincent sensed her restlessness, her nightmare. He couldn't see her suffering. He had to do something.
With the utmost need and strength, he carefully lay down in bed with her, leaning his strong body against her back. She felt ice cold, even with her clothes over her skin she hadn't warmed up a bit. His arms found their way around her restless body and he held her close. His face in her neck, in her hair. He breathed in her scent deeply.
"MK." he murmured in her ear.
Soon her movements stopped and the loud voices were silent.

Marisa finally fell asleep, safe in the subconscious knowledge. Vincent stroked her cheek gently. Her skin so soft, so warm. Her body temperature had equalised again. Her breathing steady and soothing. There was no reason for him to stay in her bed any longer. He had helped her because that was what one did. It had no deeper meaning than that he had felt sorry for her. Now he could get comfortable again on the blankets on the hard floor. He would never get to rest otherwise, with her rolling so close to him. Her scent so beguiling. He just needed - Vincent got up and spent the rest of the night on the cold carpet.

~

Not another tear was he worth.
Damn him. How many times had he dragged her down, offended her, insulted her - just broken her?
It was over and done with.
Only her stupid dreams she couldn't control. She tossed and turned for hours. Couldn't sleep, couldn't dream, couldn't relax. She couldn't stop thinking about him.
Him, that cold, arrogant, unfeeling boy with the sweetest blue eyes.
When would she finally get over him? How long would this pain last? When would this deep longing to be near him subside?
He wasn't worth it. Just not worth it.
All he wanted was to fuck.
How she hated that word. How she hated her own innocence. If she'd already had a hundred boyfriends, they would have done it long ago. And all this tension would have been over long ago. He would have got what he craved so much.
He would have, her mind added the mustard. If he'd really gone for it, she would have jumped into bed with him twenty times by now. Every time he kissed her, she was wild for him. All he needed was -
Stop it now. It's over.
Out of my dreams, out of my thoughts.
Into my bed.
Shit.

~

I was a little distracted. Another one had crept into my dreams. I tasted her, fucked her into unconsciousness. I had no other choice. You made it so hard for me to appreciate your body. So slutty, so open. Yet so inviting and hot. I wouldn't say no. I'm all over it again. I'll follow you wherever you are. I'm there too. I watch you and hold myself tightly and caressingly.

~

Day 16

Just as strange as the night before, the morning was also in the friendly man's house. He offered them breakfast, which looked like it was his only piece of bread and the last sip of milk.

Marisa felt bad accepting it, but the old man wouldn't let them leave unless they had eaten something. She marked his house on her map and wrote down the address. As soon as she was able, she would pray Johnny to send him money.

Vincent planned silently to himself. He hadn't said a word since they had got up. Hadn't he slept well on the thin blankets? Certainly not. It had all been her fault. First she hadn't wanted to turn back and then she had asked for two rooms. He would have had his own bed if she hadn't run out of her room like a crazy woman and forced herself on him. After all this confusion and stress, she was surprised at how well she had slept in the end. I'm sure her exhaustion had something to do with it. Not her company.

"Can I help?" she asked kindly, moving closer to him. His gaze cold and not welcoming.

"So you can send us miles in the wrong direction again?"

Marisa drew her eyebrows together in wonder. She hadn't expected such a dismissive answer. After all, she hadn't guessed how bad the weather would end up being, and the ups and downs. She remained silent. Suddenly on the verge of tears. Maybe she hadn't slept well after all, if a little remark like his made her cry.

She got up and helped the old man clean up. Vincent banged

his fist on the table. Why did he have to come at her like that? He had seen her tears come. What had got into him? Had he forgotten last night, how she had tossed and turned in his arms in bed for hours, haunted by nasty guilt all the way to sleep? She hadn't slept well at first either. It was only when he - Therein lay the problem. He hadn't forgotten that night. Not a second of it. And how he wanted so much more from her than just to hold her.
Shit.
Finally, he rose as well. His back stiffened and his legs hurt more than usual.
By the time he found her at the front door, she had calmed down and banished the tears.
"MK."
She didn't want to be called that; he knew. And yet he kept doing it and it hurt.
"Let's go." she replied instead.
"I didn't mean to tackle you. I - "
"Fine. Let's go." she repeated impatiently. If he wanted to talk about it now, she couldn't promise not to cry on it.
"No, you wait until I've talked it out." He gripped her arm. His voice annoyed. "I shouldn't have blamed you. I chose the first route that got us into this miserable situation. No matter which way we'd have chosen, we wouldn't have made it back safely. Sorry."
Marisa looked up at him. His blue eyes so cold today, so clear and distinct.
"And I haven't slept much." He finally added. Having her standing in front of him like that was pure torture.
"I'm sorry about that too. I might as well have slept on the floor. The hard floor, the cold floorboards. It - "
"It didn't keep me up all night." he interrupted her train of thought, and his closeness was suddenly much clearer. His voice so angry and directed right at her. She widened her eyes in shock as she thought they had been talking in their sleep. Maybe she had been talking about her rotten psycho type. Had

she not lain still? Had she shouted?

"Did I say or do anything?"

Vincent just shook his head, his eyes on her warm, flushed face. What was behind these nightmares? What was she trying to hide? Why the hell couldn't he get her to confide in him?

"You and me in a room. That's what kept me awake." He whispered in her ear. Her whole body responded to his closeness, his words, his hot breath on her face.

In one stroke she had forgotten her nightmares. In one stroke she was on fire.

She trembled, not daring to move. His lips so close to her skin, yet so far from her mouth.

She could turn just an inch and their lips would touch. She only needed to stir, and she could give free rein to her lust. He invited it, he told her that he wanted nothing more than her. But that had never been the hurdle. He was sexually attracted to her. Feelings, however, were out of the question. A quick fuck and then it was on to the next. Like Maureen and then Yasmine and now Marisa.

Oh yes, and not to forget George. George, her fiancé should be on her mind here too. And with another beat, her emotions were no longer jumbled. They were crystal clear. Guilty.

So she bowed her head.

So he stepped away from her.

And they made their way back to the valley with an uncomfortable silence between them.

~

Mitch was glad to see them. After all the excitement of the two of them being lost in the bad weather, it had caused some criticism. The many messages Marisa had sent throughout the afternoon had been received ... but had done a poor job of easing the panic.
George looked a little tired as well. Or just annoyed?
In all the short weeks she had known him, he had never appeared anything other than calm and understanding. Everything always went smoothly. They had never had any disagreements or arguments. It was the perfect relationship. And boring.
Today it was different. Today he was animated.
"You spent the night with my fiancée?" George walked challengingly towards Vincent. The latter was as surprised as everyone else in the ski group when the loud voice rang out. "What the hell do you keep doing with Mary? Can't you finally keep your distance?"
Marisa looked shocked at her fiancé. Mixed emotions jumped to the surface. Guilt most of all. He had suffered, he didn't like this situation. She had hurt him. She felt terrible.
"We're going skiing together. That's all." countered Vin calmly and matter-of-factly.
"You know very well that's not all." said George more quietly and omnisciently. His eyes full of anger and distaste. "You're by her side all the time."
"Not by their own choice. Our ski instructor makes the decisions."
Mitch was about to demonstrate, but George shot him a

warning look, causing him not to make a sound. This was not about him defending himself. His problem was solely with Vincent.

And his honest and innocent answers only drove George more up the wall. He looked angrily at Vincent, then at Mitch, then back at Vincent.

"George. Nothing happened. We couldn't turn back in the bad weather." Or rather, she hadn't wanted to turn back.

She put her hand on his arm soothingly, but he shook her off again.

"I'll see you at the mountain hut. Don't get stuck again."

With these words he angrily stomped off. One by one, the other skiers went about their business.

Mitch checked his mobile phone, gritted his teeth and put it in his pocket, annoyed. Everyone seemed a little annoyed and slightly irritated today. He looked impatiently at his watch.

"Marisa, we're doing a red run this afternoon to make sure we get back in one piece. Are you coming? Vincent?"

She wanted to ski so badly, whatever happened, that was why she was here. But first she had to save her relationship. Everything else would have to wait.

"Not anymore today. Tomorrow, hopefully."

Vincent eyed her from the side. Her regret was obvious, her eyes sad. Of course, she wanted to spend the day with George. That was perfectly clear to him. And yet he didn't want to let her go.

"I was beginning to think I'd catch one." he joked, watching her gather her things. The cross-country skiers had already dropped them off. All she had to do was go to the minibus and follow him.

She just looked at him quizzically. Had no comeback.

"You're not really going to run after him, are you?"

"Should I spend the afternoon with you instead? That would be a great idea for my relationship. You obviously have no idea how a relationship works."

"That's right. I have no experience with relationships. And

don't need one."

She should leave. She should go and see her fiancé right now and apologise. But no, here she was, arguing with her ex-boyfriend. When was she going to learn?

"I can see that. One look, one dinner and sex. That's all."

"Dinner? Like I'm going to give them the time of day to poke around in my life and try to change me. One look, one word and just sex."

Marisa couldn't believe what she was hearing here. And unfortunately, not for the first time.

"You really don't understand why I'm going to my fiancé now, do you?"

"With you and George, no. I can't comprehend it."

She didn't understand what he was trying to say. Her own emotions in the way of even being able to think clearly.

"Imagine if we were in a relationship and I did that to you. Wouldn't that hurt you immensely? Wouldn't you want to talk to me about it and clear everything up? I owe him that. I've done such a fuck up. I have to go."

"I repeat myself, with you and George, no." He stood in front of her so she couldn't ignore him. "You talk about love and understanding all the time. Why do you, you of all people, settle for less than what you've been looking for all your life?"

"That's where you're very wrong. I want to be with George. I want to marry him."

He narrowed his eyes. Her choice of words very careful. Very general and weak. Why didn't she talk of love and desire? Why didn't it sparkle in her eyes when she spoke of him?

"Really? Then why do you react to me whenever I accidentally touch you? Why does your body calm down in the middle of the night when I hold it? Don't tell me again that you are happy with him."

She had no answer. Had to digest his accusations first. He had held her? In the middle of the night? Last night? That's why she'd felt like she'd slept well.

"You have doubts. You want more. And George knows it too."

She gritted her teeth angrily until she couldn't. She didn't want to hear another word. Couldn't stand his ideas.

"Go ahead and keep it up. Let's start there, like 17 years ago, so you can kick me even though I'm already down. Instead of accepting that other people prefer to live in pairs rather than alone, you have to keep putting a flea in my ear. Nothing has changed, you only think about yourself, how you can ruin my relationship so you can fuck." She put her warm hand on his face, inwardly seeking the strength to let all the anger and dislike reflect in her eyes. "Thank God you didn't come back then. I would have, without hesitation, taken you back into my heart. That would have done me in."

She turned from him and walked back to the mountain hut. She was trembling. She had played too much with fire. Had reminded herself too much of the fateful days of her first love.

~

She could have gone into town. Strolling in the stationery shop for a few minutes and passing the time would have been easy. She would have liked that. She could have walked home. She didn't live far from the grammar school. Twenty minutes there and back again. She would have made it back in time for her next lesson and got some fresh air.

But no. Instead, she had thought to spend her free period in the designated classroom. She had wanted to repeat something for the next check.

A mistake. The mistake of her life in hindsight.

Marisa was sitting in the very back corner when Vin had the same idea of spending his free period here. He was in his final year of school, his A-Level exams were starting soon. He had a lot to catch up on and understand. It was all he needed.

He deliberately chose a table furthest away from her and sat with his back to her. This only made her angrier. After all these long days since their failed conversation, she had managed to think of him with anger and resentment. The first four days had been pure torture, so many tears, so much pain. Now, on the sixth day, things were going really well by comparison. Only at night did she sometimes still feel sadness and longing. But now it was anger she felt. He did not even think it necessary to greet her. Her heart broke again. How could this be? Had it not already shattered into a thousand pieces?

"I won't apologise." he said coldly, not waiting for her to agree for him to sit down in front of her.

She looked up, stunned, into his sweet blue eyes and was lost. Shit. Damn.

Her heart yearned for him as never before. She was happy that he was talking to her. She could have cried just because she had him in front of her again.

Marisa looked intently at her notes and remained silent.

"Marisa, don't act like you need to repeat English! You know more vocabulary than your teacher." He reached for her sheets and turned them over. How did he know that?

She looked up again.

"You really don't understand why I don't want to talk to you, do you?"

"If it concerns you, no. I have no idea what's going on."

"Then why are you talking to me?"

"I have to repeat myself. I have no idea what's going on with me, if it concerns you."

Marisa nibbled lightly on her pencil. She looked at him shyly. And waited.

Vin swallowed dryly. The mere sight of her was driving him crazy.

"Would you settle for so little, even though you're so desperate for your happy ending like in a romance novel?"

"Is it perhaps more than just a look, a kiss and sex?"

"So, are you my girlfriend again?"

"You're avoiding my question," she countered instead. A question she wanted an answer to only too badly.

"No, I'm just not answering it. There's a difference."

Vin waited a moment longer. His patience didn't last long.

"And to my question?"

After a long while.

"Maybe."

Marisa smiled slightly and looked again at the sheets in front of her, even if they were covered. His presence was enough for her. Hopeful. He, however, did not like her reticence at all. He looked around briefly to see who was in the classroom. Obviously no one important as he reached for her hand. With regret, she immediately withdrew it.

His precautions to ensure that no one would see them together had hurt her. She had had enough of playing hide and seek.

"No, I'm not your girlfriend anymore." she said coldly instead. Her heart felt and longed for the complete opposite. But her mind won out at that moment. It was either all or nothing.

"MK?"

His face showed shock and anger. He looked at her intensely from the side. After a few short minutes, she had gathered all her strength and courage to face his blue eyes.

"You once said to me that I should finally push away my guilt. I have. I want to walk hand in hand with you through school. I want to hang out with you and your friends. I don't want to be your secret anymore."

She couldn't breathe with tension. Her whole body so tense that everything hurt. She held her pencil so tightly that her white knuckles stood out.

Vin hesitated. Then he stood up abruptly and looked down at her.

"Come with me."

Marisa didn't know what he was up to. And yet she followed him out of the classroom, past the reception, out the back exit and into the schoolyard, which was surrounded by both sides of the high school. The building stood in a U-shape around them. Classrooms all over the three floors. In the middle of the courtyard, he stopped and turned to her.

"If you really don't care what anyone thinks or says behind your back, then here I am." he said challengingly. "Kiss me."

Marisa wasn't sure what he had expected. Had he thought that her request was not serious? Had he assumed that she would never in a million years face his friends? Or was he damn sure she would never show herself with her boyfriend in front of her best friend Danielle?

No matter what had been going on inside him, his eyes lost the mischievous gleam as she walked towards him. He forgot to smile as she stopped right in front of him. And he no longer knew how to breathe when she put her hands around his face and kissed. Without shame, without remorse. Full of lust. She put her arms around his neck to deepen their kiss. He held her tightly so that he did not sink to the floor.

Neither of them had expected this reaction. Neither of them could stop again.

It was only when the hour bell rang that they broke free from their hot embrace.

"Marisa."

"Vin."

Luckily, she hadn't gone to town or run home then. Luckily, he had also stepped into the same classroom during the free period.

Without hesitation, she had taken him back into her heart.

And only bitterly regretted it much later.

~

George had calmed down when she spoke to him.
George had listened quietly as she told him where they had ended up.
George didn't say another bad word about the fact that she had spent the night with another man in a strange house.
Marisa said nothing about the fact that they had only shared a bedroom. And as she now also knew, one bed. She had not yet come to terms with that herself. It wouldn't be a good idea to confess that to him now.
Marisa took all the blame for not having spent the many days of her holiday by his side. She acknowledged that such a thing was unacceptable. She agreed that she had made a mockery of their relationship in front of the other skiers. Everyone had laughed at him, and it had bothered him.
She did not ask where he had spent the night.
Precise as clockwork came the photo, followed by the news.
The photo captured the moment when she had put her hand on his chest for ten seconds during their argument. During an argument. What you couldn't see here. She had her back to the weirdo who was still watching her. Why? To what end was he threatening her?
Four more days, that's all she had to endure all these challenges. Then she was back in her own world, with her feet on solid ground. Professionally successful, independent. Soon married. Then she could finally put all the stress and pain with Vincent away.
You've got the hang of it.
You're the expert when it comes to infidelity.
Do you have pictures of your night with him?

SUSANN SVOBODA

You will regret this betrayal.
When I'm alone with you, I'll make the passion flow from your veins.

~

Day 17

"Of course you're skiing today."
"I have no problem with you seeing Mitchell."
"I'm not angry with you at all about yesterday, darling."
Marisa allowed herself to be persuaded to spend the day apart. It wasn't possible to disagree; George had insisted that they didn't sit in the mountain hut. Even so, she really wouldn't have minded today. Her limbs ached even before she stood up on her skis. Her head was pounding, and her breath came in short gasps. After all those long, unprotected hours in the freezing cold, she had caught a chill.
As Mitchell was about to split them into small groups, she ended up back with Vincent. She looked up wearily, pleading with her eyes for him to reverse his decision. The man, her acquaintance, someone she had respected and liked for years, hesitated at her broken look. He seemed to be struggling with himself. She grew impatient and annoyed. With whom did he prefer to make the descent? What other woman was there to discover here?
Her irritability had no limits when she was ill.
He had been there yesterday, after all, and had heard how much it bothered George that she was always with Vincent.
Shit.
No one was happy about this split. Vincent wasn't jumping for joy in the air either.
Her mobile vibrated. She turned away from everyone before reading the message.

It was only George.
Thank God.
Have a good day, Mary.
Guilt hit her right in the heart. She felt cornered again.
"I'm going to sit this one out," she decided on the spur of the moment.
"What?" Vin furrowed his eyebrows in confusion. As if he didn't know exactly why she had to make that decision.
"Why? We have one of the most difficult descents ahead of us today. You don't want to miss it." Mitch was not about to let her go. He literally pushed her towards the others in the direction of the cable car.
"I'm not feeling so well."
"What's wrong?"
"The adrenaline will take your mind off it. If you just sit around at home, you'll feel much worse."
He ignored the other man's question and kept trying to get her to come along.
Marisa looked up the hill. Felt the headache lurking in the back of her mind. And gave in.
He was right. If she stayed alone all day, she would have too much time to think and remember.
Mitchell hadn't promised too much. She loved every moment of the descent. The fresh snow made the slope a little unpredictable, but that was exactly what inspired her to do her best. She could finally try out her skiing technique and see what she could do. She didn't mind landing on her bottom several times. The challenge was to concentrate fully on the downhill and she did. Even with Vincent right behind her. Their paths barely crossed. They had no opportunity to argue or discuss. They stayed in each other's background, like a safety net.
Ouch.
That had certainly hurt.
Marisa broke off her course and headed straight for Vincent, who had landed hard in the snow. For the first time, she

realised in the back of her mind. While she had often had to taste the frozen water, he had always stayed safely on his feet until now. This fall had looked all the worse for it.

Marisa approached her ex-boyfriend and before she knew what was happening to her, her left snowshoe also slipped from under her feet. Despite a futile attempt to keep her balance, she too crashed painfully onto her side. Right next to Vin.

Ouch in any case.

Marisa immediately got back on her feet so as not to give the wrong impression. Her ankle complained slightly, but nothing had actually happened. She looked carefully at the snow near her and spotted the various patches of slippery ice.

This could have turned out worse.

"Are you hurt?"

Vin rose without difficulty and patted the snow off his suit.

"Just pride."

She laughed at his remark.

"First time?"

Her face was covered by all the gear, all he could see was her mouth smiling adorably at him. But he knew her brown eyes behind the sunglasses were glaring straight at him. It made it all the more unbearable.

"Are you laughing at me now?"

"Not at all. I'm just glad you're human too."

And how. No human could resist that desire.

Marisa recognised his silence, knew his eyes were just stripping her to the skin. She felt the heat rising inside her. Or was she running a fever?

She cleared her throat sheepishly to break the spell. And also, because there was a sudden tickle in her throat. It gave her a little tickle to cough.

It was also a way of distracting him from his hot thoughts.

Her eyes watered from the exertion and she took off her glasses.

And there were the thoughts again.

He took off his sunglasses too. And stepped up to her.
"Vin?"
He exhaled deeply. Annoyance and disappointment hit. What the hell had gotten into him? What was he trying to achieve with this manoeuvre? Was she finally ready?
"You shouldn't call me that either... like you did then. Unless you're ready to follow your desire," he warned her.
"I'm engaged," she countered weakly. But his nearness brought her to her knees. She was barely breathing. Her heart heavy. And moved away from him a little. Immediately he changed the way he had responded to her. Immediately he went back to questioning their relationship, her decision to refuse him. He could take her rejection very badly.
"Have you met his family before?"
Marisa shook her head in annoyance.
"Do you have something like a list of questions in your head? Do you have to quiz me on every single one of them?"
"You're avoiding my question." he remarked coldly.
"No. I'm not answering your question. There's a difference."
Vin nodded his head challengingly.
"Is it because you don't know her? Did you just realise you've never met any of his family or friends?"
Marisa didn't want to admit to that, even though it was the truth. It didn't matter. And yet it was gnawing at her at the moment.
"And I had thought you were on the verge of kissing me." She lifted her chin seductively. Her mouth so teasing. "Instead, all you're thinking about is George again. Are you just realising that you might be jealous of him?"
Vincent grabbed her arm and pulled her roughly towards him. His eyes full of anger and fire. How dare she? Why did she have to play with fire?
His lips so close to her face it drove her crazy. His breath was like little feathery kisses on her lips. Each one so delightfully sweet and arousing.
Take me, it cried out inside her. She was deeply shocked. Or

actually she wasn't.

"Yes, I think of George all the time. How he takes your clothes off ... kisses your neck ... your breasts. The way you move under him." His eyes made love to her at that moment and she couldn't get out of his spell. She was close to letting herself go. She wanted to let herself fall and just feel what he was describing. But with him. Only with him. "And you say his name when you come. Or will you think of me then?"

All at once she was awake, in reality. Full of fear instead of excitement. Marisa felt an icy chill run down her spine when he asked her that.

"What?"

Hadn't she heard a question like that before? Did he have something to do with the photos and the sick messages?

She turned away from him with a jerk, seeking distance and a chance to think. She felt sick and her body trembled from the shock. Was this possible? What did he have to gain from it? And how would he be able to take photos of himself and then write such lousy messages to go with them?

Marisa looked around. Carefully and attentively, she looked in all directions. Where was the guy who took the photos? She could have bet that she would relive this moment in picture format later. But was Vincent behind it?

No.

Yes, he wanted to torment her, constantly put their relationship down, but no, not behind her back. He never minced his words. He didn't need to mentally drag her down as well. No, she didn't think Vin had anything to do with it. His question had been genuine.

But the moment had passed. Fortunately....

Who knows how she would have answered if her panic hadn't immediately ruined the moment.

Vincent cursed himself over his words, his actions. This had gone too far. And not really his style at all. It was time for the holiday to end. He had to get back to his world, work, help others. The time here with her was just driving him crazy. He would have to sleep with a hundred women to get her out of his mind again.

"That had been unforgivable." he finally said. "You -"

"Let's move on." She had no interest in hearing again how she drove him crazy. He had proved that point several times already. Just then she wanted to get away from this place, back into the valley. She suddenly felt eerie.

The wind blew up howling.

~

"Have you slept together yet?"
Marisa looked up from her textbook in surprise. Her former best friend had sat down next to her in bio class. Since when had that happened? She had been busy digesting all these different circumstances. Danielle was talking to her again, but her question made her uncomfortable.
The teacher hadn't noticed the whispering and continued with the lesson. Marisa continued to try and write notes, there was an inspection coming up next week. The other, however, had no intention of letting this subject rest.
"Are you too good to talk to me now?"
"Shh. We should be careful. During the break?" she offered placatingly.
"Marisa, do you have the answer to my question?"
She shook her head awkwardly and looked down at her piece of paper, struck.
As soon as the lesson was over, all the students made their way out of the lab and out into the courtyard. Marisa felt little rush. Her first conversation with Danielle had not started well. She was worried about it.
"So?"
They stood in a secluded corner. Everyone else was busy talking about the latest show and getting a quick cut in. She, on the other hand, was standing uncomfortably in the cold and no longer hungry.
"What did you want to know?"
"Whether you're sleeping with him?" Her eyes still cold and dismissive. Her voice full of impatience.

Marisa was torn. She wanted so much to have her old friend back. And talking to someone about her worries and fears would be worth its weight in gold. But she didn't seem herself. Her behaviour was forced and still not friendly.

"Why do you want to talk about it?" she said hypocritically. 'Of course it was the top topic among all the girls. When did you have your first time? How long did you wait? Did you come? ... Did it hurt?

"I'm just curious. After your play in the middle of the yard yesterday. It looked hot. So, did he finally get you too? I have to say, the fact that you two are still together surprised me. Usually he's only interested in a girl for a couple of weeks. You can ask anyone here."

It wasn't about becoming friends again. On the contrary, she wanted to really hurt her. Really hack away at her self-confidence so that Marisa wouldn't believe in herself and Vin. Just a few weeks? They'd actually gotten past that, if you didn't count the miserable times apart. Was he still interested in her because they hadn't had sex yet?

Yes, of course he was. He'd made that perfectly clear.

And you forgave him for it. Deal with it.

"And I had thought you were on the verge of apologising to me for kissing my boyfriend at the party."

"Me apologise to you?" The other laughed icily. "Don't be ridiculous."

"Instead, you're thinking about me and Vin again. Are you just realising that you might be jealous of me because he's still interested in me and not you?"

Danielle stared at her coldly. She hadn't expected that argument. Her eyes filled with anger and defiance. How dare she?

"Yes I think about Vincent all the time. How he kissed me and took my clothes off piece by piece."

"Stop it." she stopped her friend immediately. Couldn't stand the comparisons. She had jealousy and pain written all over her face. She tried to walk away, but Danielle wouldn't let up.

"So you haven't done it yet after all? I bet you don't have the guts. Or maybe he doesn't find you attractive after all. It's quite simple, when me and Vin - "
Marisa was blinded by tears and self-doubt. She ran out of earshot and sight of the others. The jealousy was unbearable. The fear that she was right, much worse.

~

She felt truly unwell.
"We'll go to the alpine hut for a while. Maybe a sauna, or a game of cards will do you good."
He stroked her back good-naturedly before gathering his things.
Marisa did not agree. What would do her good was hot tea and her bed.
"You do want to spend the evening with me, don't you?"
George smiled in her direction. He would not tolerate excuses or any other suggestion. She had disappointed him too many times already, now was not the time to turn him down.
The cold air on her heated face did her good. She sat down in a corner and pulled her book out of her bag. A hot tea by her side. Just what she'd wanted to do, only in her own mountain cabin, without the other guests.
Without having to see Vin. And Maureen. Whose face lit up when she saw them both sitting in the corner.
Her gaze lingered on him as she recognised him limping painfully to a table. Had the fall on the ice been more disastrous than he had admitted after all? She immediately looked away as he turned in her direction.
"Are you sure you don't want to go to the sauna?"
George leaned lovingly over his fiancée, his hand possessively on her shoulder. She nodded slightly.
"You go ahead. I'll wait for you here."
He kissed her gently and then he was on his way to the dressing room. Maureen and Vin followed him shortly after.

She waved to him again, like a good unsuspecting woman. Something stirred inside her at the sight of her fiancé next to the beautiful blonde. She pushed the bad thoughts far away from her. Vincent was also in the sauna. He would tell her if she should worry.

Wouldn't he?

Her head throbbed more and more. She made her way to the bar to ask for some aspirin. On her way she saw Mitchell in the corner. He had just come back from the bathroom, his clothes still a mess. And his hair a mess. And behind him, an older woman.

Marisa smiled and was about to look away when she noticed Mitch grabbing his back and contorting his face in pain. She beckoned him towards her.

"Too many rigorous movements?" she teased him and took her aspirin.

Mitch laughed when he knew exactly what she was alluding to. And she was almost right.

"No, not from that. I sprained my ankle on the slopes today."

She stopped. And had an idea.

"Yeah, that happened to us too. Vin slipped on the black ice too. Maybe you were in the same spot? About a hundred metres from piste point 14, did you see us there?"

He looked like he was in more pain than he wanted to indicate. His face contorted, little beads of sweat on his forehead.

"No. No, I wasn't there. Why do you ask?"

Marisa didn't answer him. She still had the feeling that they had been watching her on the mountain. She had hoped that perhaps he had noticed someone taking pictures. Unfortunately, that didn't seem to be the case. She was disappointed.

"I - " She couldn't tell him what was going through her head. She stroked her forehead wearily. Resignedly. "I was just hoping you hadn't seen my case."

Her joking distraction worked, and he laughed along with her. But the joy was not in his eyes. His back was still giving him trouble and he apologised to her. She wished him a speedy recovery so that he could be back on the slopes actively tomorrow.

He agreed with her.

"We have to keep an eye on the weather. They had predicted a heavy snowstorm. Who knows if we'll even be allowed in the mountains tomorrow."

~

Was she a coward? Had she not yet dared to sleep with him?
No, she wasn't. On the contrary, she would have thrown herself into his arms a hundred times already if he didn't find an excuse every time why today wasn't the right time.
But the whole thing made her a little nervous. The first time to show herself to another person, to give herself away completely and become vulnerable.
Vin had so much experience in that area. It scared and worried her.
"MK, why are you crying here in the corner?"
She wiped her eyes as if caught.
"I'm not," she said defiantly. She stood proudly and confidently in front of him. She didn't want him to know how much this whole affair was breaking her. It was all about sex, after all.
Vin remained silent. He had seen how she had talked to Danielle. Had also seen how this former girlfriend had driven his girlfriend away. Face lowered. Danielle had looked after her, laughing.
He didn't like seeing her so sad at all.
"That's good. No matter what Danielle talked you into, you know what's true." he said awkwardly. "Do you?"
She looked at him questioningly. What?
"She was talking about you and her again. In details. I couldn't hear it."
"Jealousy doesn't suit you."
She glared at him. There was no time to joke right now. She tried to walk past him, but he held her by the arm and kissed her. Just like that, here at break time, in front of all the other

students, big and small. She had to get used to it.
"You're not running away from me again." he whispered to her. He did not increase the distance, instead he gently touched her face. His fingers burned on her skin. "We've already wasted far too much time sulking and arguing about things that don't matter."
She rested her forehead against his. He was right, after all. But at the same moment, she knew her dilemma wouldn't just go away. Not until she finally dared to take the next step. If he would let her. It was like a vicious circle.
"O.K." she replied simply. Lost her heart. He always said just the right things, at just the right moment. He knew her too well.
"Danielle suits jealousy even less." he finally added. "The few days we spent together, we didn't have deep conversations or trips to the woods. We didn't taste sangria until we dropped or play in the snow for hours. We didn't just walk side by side because we understand each other without words."
The doorbell rang. A restlessness surrounded them, but Vin did not move an inch.
With the noise of excited and annoyed teenagers complaining loudly about having to go back to class, he finished his comparison. She was struggling to hear him properly.
"And we didn't sleep together."

~

The photo was sent in the middle of the night.
Marisa woke up immediately. A cold shiver ran down her spine. She refused to read her message. She didn't want to look at the photo.
And she tried to ignore it. But sleep was no longer an option.
In the early hours of the morning, she took her mobile phone and locked herself in the bathroom.
She recognised her own snow-covered ski suit and her cold face. Her chin pulled up seductively as if she wanted to challenge Vincent to a kiss. The moment was, as always, super hit. Because seconds before, as well as afterwards, they hadn't had a particularly friendly conversation. But especially after his absolutely inappropriate comment, the mood between them had fallen. Had she not sensed it, sensed that they were not alone? Why had no one been able to spot her when she had immediately looked around?
That wretched bastard. When was it going to end? Why did he have to ruin even the last few days of her holiday? She had been faithful to George after all. She didn't get herself into inappropriate situations. She was playing by the rules after all. At least on the surface. For her inner turmoil contradicted her actions. Survive this indescribable attraction for a few more days and then Vin was out of her life and thoughts. Forever.
Mary, Mary, what are you doing to us?

~

But this fucking snow! My wrist is sore. My dick hurts from all my self-love. As soon as these flakes are finally gone, I'll take what's mine. Time's up. I'm coming whether you like it or not. I'm coming to show you what's good for you. Go ahead and show your claws, it only turns me on more.

Day 18

Her holiday was slowly coming to an end. She wanted to enjoy the last few days, hours on the slopes. No matter how tired and sick she was. No matter how stormy it was. She had to get out! The weather warnings had already limited her runs. Mitch had gotten them the permits to attempt a run. In the spirit of experience, to practice their skiing techniques in the unpredictable weather. But that was all he allowed them to do. The wind was too strong, the snow was falling heavily from the sky. Visibility worsened with each passing minute. Like the storm before them, her body raged.

Her headache grew more intense with each passing minute. Everything inside her screamed that she needed a break. Her joints ached. It seemed they had no choice but to return to the mountain hut and wait out the blizzard.

But the return journey was no walk in the park.

As the door slammed into the lock, she felt the great disappointment of having lost another day. They should consider themselves lucky that they had made it back to the mountain hut in one piece and unbroken. The ride in the minibus had been risky and incredibly nerve-wracking.

Vincent cleared his throat behind her. She had completely forgotten he was there.

Hopefully it wouldn't be long before George and Maureen caught up with them. Until then, it was a case of ignoring him as much as possible and fighting the boredom.

"I'm going to do some reading." she finally said and escaped to her room. Out her window she saw the white swirls, heard the wind rattling the windows. The trees swayed back and forth. Some branches gave the appearance of snapping off at any moment.

Marisa cursed softly as the lights went out and an eerie silence followed. She grabbed her mobile phone and used its torch to feel her way around the room. She walked carefully down the stairs into the living room.

Vincent was lighting several candles. Apparently he had spent the time thinking of essentials while she had been hiding in her room. She was surprised that he had found so many. The room took on a pleasant glow. Cosy and romantic. Just the sort of thing that didn't suit them.

"I hope the emergency generator kicks in soon. Otherwise, it will be cold... "

Marisa frowned. How cold could it get already?

"Get out the rummy cards. I'm going to look for some alcohol. The next few hours are going to be long. Maybe we can warm up from the inside."

Vincent had one or two other ideas about how they could keep warm, but didn't say a peep. He fetched some cards and games from his room. When he came back, she had indeed found a couple of ominous bottles and put glasses with them. She smelled the first bottle and frowned. Then she saw him in front of her. In the flaming light of the candles, so stunningly attractive, with his hair wild so that she just wanted to slide her fingers through it.

She took the first sip, shaking at the taste, at the strength, and poured for him. She handed him the glass, their fingers touching lightly. As if burned, she withdrew her hand and drank her glass. Maybe she could drink herself into unconsciousness. Then she wouldn't have to struggle live with her jumble of emotions.

Vincent stayed away from her as much as possible. The small living room table was barely big enough to put enough distance between them, but it was a start. He took the glass, tasted the alcohol. It wasn't enough. His mind had only one thing on his mind. He couldn't take his eyes off her.

He drank more.

They played and drank until the first candle went out. Vincent stood up, groggy from the offensive swill they had drunk. He was not to touch another drop. It hadn't helped to take his mind off her anyway. On the contrary, he wanted her like never before.

Marisa watched him from the floor. She no longer had the strength to sit down on the sofa. Her head was spinning. Her stomach was full of fizz.

At least she no longer felt sick, she thought contentedly.

But her attraction to the man standing in front of her had not disappeared. If it was possible, she felt all the more attracted to him.

Shit. Shit. Shit.

Marisa had to distract her hot thoughts.

"George and Maureen ... did something happen to them?"

Vin looked at her from his side. He had decided to keep as much distance from her as somehow possible. This topic helped him focus on something other than how he could undress her and make love to her here on the soft carpet for hours.

He blocked his thoughts. She seemed genuinely concerned that her fiancé hadn't arrived back yet.

"You're comfortably ensconced somewhere, with candlelight and wine."

Shit. He hadn't really meant to say that.

"He wouldn't cheat."

Why did he have to say that? What exactly was he trying to imply?

Vincent remained silent. Her faith in this man was unfathomable. Her faith in this relationship was so infuriating. He wanted to shake her. But he didn't dare touch her in the smallest way right now.

"I wouldn't be so sure about that. He's had his eye on her all along. The way he's always looking at her and chasing after her." He admitted honestly. He settled down in front of the sofa, he had missed the seat and seemed a hundred times closer to her than before. He did not move away from her. His body did not listen to his mind. "And now they most likely have the whole night ahead of them. No electricity, no heating. Just candlelight and body heat."

She looked at him warningly. What irony. Weren't they also in the same circumstances right now. Here everything was poop safe and innocent.

"And that would immediately tempt you to betray someone? Look around, we're in the same situation. And I'm not jumping down your throat unrestrained."

"I'm not stopping you."

She took a deep breath and faltered. Her heart pounded to her throat at his reply. The table between them was fortunately directly in the middle. That would stop him should he approach her further. And what would stop her?

Marisa crossed her arms in front of her chest dismissively.

"Stop." she warned him coldly. "Please."

"Because you don't want me? Or because you actually think you and George have a future? Because you're afraid to face the truth."

"Just stop. I don't want to talk about it anymore."

Vincent thought nothing of it. His patience forever at an end. And the alcohol let itself be noticed.

"If you really loved him, my closeness wouldn't affect you like this," he said softly. He watched her lower her gaze. Her eyes full of emotion.

"If you loved him, you wouldn't have reacted to me when I kissed you. Deeply and sensuously." he reminded her again of that fateful day. Her memories came back in one fell swoop. She had not forgotten how she had reacted to him. And he to her. Her stomach turned at the thought.

He was right, but she wasn't ready to admit it yet.

"As if you have any idea of love."

"I know how I'd treat you if you were my fiancée." He ignored

her attack on him. He cornered her.
"Do you?"
Vincent pushed the table out of the way with one hand so he could see her properly. Panic rose in her eyes at his action. She wanted to jump up and run away, but the alcohol in her body weakened her reactions. After a few seconds, her heart calmed. He stayed in his place. He did not pull her into his arms as she had thought. He did not touch her in any part of her body. He remained true to his word.
Then why did she feel so disappointed? Why did she feel anger rising inside her instead of relief?
Vincent had sworn to himself that he would not come near her again until she wanted him too. The guilt was clearly written all over her face. He could not do this to her. Yet she looked so overwhelmingly gorgeous in that light candlelight. Her hair was so loose and wild that he wanted nothing more than to run his fingers through the strands, undo her hair tie and let the long brown hair fall over her shoulders.
He was lost.
"I would..." He began, his self-control wavering. "I would stroke your cheek gently, with my thumb. My fingers down your neck. I'd rest my head against your neck and breathe little kisses, up to your ear. On your cheek."
Marisa opened her mouth in shock. Her mind was screaming at her, demanding that she not listen, that she silence it. Her mouth could not produce a syllable. Instead of standing up, seeking safety from herself, she leaned back against the sofa and looked him straight in the eyes. Into his sweet blue eyes. Her breathing weak, halting.
Vincent swallowed as he took in her gaze. It killed him how far she was from him. Still.
"Your scent is beguiling." he continued. "I want more.... so much more... My other hand slides slowly under your jumper where I feel your hot skin. So soft .... so gentle. My mouth searches yours; my lips taste your sweet lips.... Sweet and sour..... You lay your head back slightly as you open to me. .....

Willing and hot.... Our tongues play ..... tease..... Drive our passion forward. I touch your chest ..... draw little lines down over your belly ..... to your belly button ...... and on... on ..... down."

Marisa felt dizzy with excitement, with anticipation. She breathed loudly, biting her lower lip in extreme excitement. The storm raged inside her.

Kiss me. Hold me. Do all that you just said and more. She begged him inaudibly.

His voice faltered. His breath rapid. His gaze so dark.

She swallowed dryly and waited for his words. Her head leaned back. Her eyes closed.

Abruptly he stood up and looked down at her. He lifted her and carried her up to her room without further ado.

Everything was spinning, the movements like a roller coaster. And she felt sick. She squeezed her eyes tightly shut.

Just don't throw up.

He was silent for a long while. Her breathing slowly calmed. Her face relaxed. A smile on her lips.

"But I'm not your fiancé. And never will be." he whispered softly, annoyed.

And then he let her sleep it off in her bed.

~

They were at the mercy of the storm. The rain continued and continued. It had taken them completely by surprise how the heavens had opened with a force, and they were soaked to the skin from one second to the next.
Vincent looked at Marisa. She at him. And they just laughed. They both looked like wet rats, it was one of the funniest and most light-hearted moments in their relationship.
They had been out for a walk, and now he was pointing back the way they had come. He knew they were not far from the gazebo where his parents had a property with an arbour. They could linger there for a few hours until the worst was over.
It was a small cottage, with a small attached kitchen and a single room used for everything. It had a few comfortable pieces of furniture. A table, a sofa and two armchairs. During the winter they stowed all the seat layers and blankets and so on on the sofa. It wasn't particularly inviting or warm, but it gave them shelter.
"I hope it stops soon." said Vin as they both looked out at the large window from the arbour. His hair was still dripping, though he had already rubbed a towel over his head. They had taken off their wet jackets, but that had been useless. For the rest of their clothes were also completely soaked.
Marisa looked at him. And only for a split second did she hesitate. Then she put her warm hand to his face, stroked his lips with her thumb. Immediately he responded to her tenderness and Vincent brought his mouth down on hers. His lips cool from the rain, but his hand warm as he gingerly placed it around her neck to pull her closer. His kiss was sweet,

his closeness beguiling.

He stepped back from her, breathing heavily. He looked deep into her eyes. Questioning, uncertain.

Marisa took his hand and put it under her jumper, on her skin. Then she kissed him unabashedly, with a lust she had suppressed for weeks. The fear of not knowing what to do or where to touch him was gone. She followed her desire, responded to what pleased her. Marisa felt dizzy with excitement, with anticipation. She breathed loudly, bit her lower lip in extreme arousal. The storm raged inside her.

He wanted to pull back, didn't want to rush it. But she brought him to his knees. Her mouth found his. Their tongues played, teased, drove her on. He touched her breasts, her belly and lower. She almost lost her mind at his caresses. But she did the same to him, she had the same power over his body as she felt where she could touch him. Where he responded to her the most.

Vincent stopped, completely out of breath.

"You have to really want it. If it's too fast for you...."

Marisa shook her head and looked him straight in the eye. Into his sweet blue eyes. Her breath weak, faltering.

"Kiss me."

Vincent swallowed as he met her gaze.

He only had so much strength to hold back. It was unbearable, her kisses, her hands were beguiling. He had tried everything to stop her. He had tried for weeks to resist her.

There was no going back.

~

They only arrived in the early hours of the morning. Together. Cheerfully.
George lay quietly in his bed beside her. Didn't say a word.
Marisa did not move. Her head was pounding. Too much alcohol. Too many emotions.
In a few hours she would have to face those feelings. Not now.
Mary, Mary, what are you doing to us?

~

Finally. Ah.
I can't believe my luck. I can't wait till you suck me off again. I'd better hang on. I'm addicted to your wetness between your legs. You were a dream. I want to fuck you again. Ah.

~

Day 19

They had not frozen to death in their sleep. So, they hadn't needed body heat after all. Everything was back to normal. Everything was back to the way it was before.
Or was it?
The snow lay high in front of the door, but she could hear from afar how the snow shovels had already set to work. Soon they could walk to the big alpine hut and have breakfast.
George was his dear self. He was helpful, attentive and totally friendly. He inquired only curtly how she had survived the evening and night. Not a syllable did he mention Vincent.
Or Maureen.
And at that moment Marisa was glad. She didn't want to discuss any of them. Didn't want to lie and didn't want to be lied to. The fact was, she was feeling a little frail. Whatever she had found in the cupboards had not been good for her. How had she been able to drink so much? What all had she said or done?
For fuck's sake... she shuddered at the thought of last night. Pure panic set in. What exactly had happened on the carpet in front of the sofa? How had she made it to bed? She had no memories apart from his hot words and her thoughts.
The conspiratorial blush crept into her face. She lowered her head, hoping no one recognised her guilt and panic. As much as she didn't want to, she had to talk to Vincent and ask what had happened.
Shit.

It couldn't happen fast enough for something to get out. All morning she had had to sit impatiently in the alpine hut, waiting. No sign of Vincent. No way to finally settle her guilty conscience. Or to have earned it.

The slope remained closed until the afternoon. Marisa could have cried. Her holiday was coming to an end in two days. Was that it? Was this how her holiday was supposed to end? No more skiing? No more talking or arguing with Vincent?

Mitchell arrived first, with good news. Her head instantly stopped hurting. She was glad to finally get out, if only for a few short hours. And to talk to Vincent.

There he was at last. Had he been hiding all this time? Where had he been all this time?

Divided into her groups, she had never been so happy. Once at the summit, she let the other skiers go. Vincent navigated them down the mountain. When it was her turn, she stared at the map for a long time. And then she found the courage to approach him about it.

"Vin. Wait a minute."

He looked at her quizzically. His demeanour cold, dismissive.

Oh shit, had they actually slept together and now he had no reason to show interest in her? Had his curiosity, his desire been satisfied?

"Last night..." she began uneasily, getting no further.

"There's nothing more to say. What's done is done."

The colour drained from her face.

"Shit. Did we... I mean, did I...?" She looked sick at the thought. He couldn't bear her disappointment in himself, the reluctance.

"No." he interrupted her, taking a deep breath in and out. "I didn't touch you, like I promised. So you could stay with your George."

Her emotions totally confused. Her mind on the brink. Her heart lost.

So what exactly had happened? How had he been able to get her so excited? With words alone? Why hadn't she fought back? Why did she still want more?

"But we were... we were..... Why not?"

She felt an emptiness, as if she had lost something she had never had.

What had it meant to him? Was he making fun of her right now, how easy it had been to seduce her? He obviously hadn't felt the same desire she had. Otherwise he wouldn't have been able to just walk away.

Shit.

The alcohol had gone to her head. She had let herself go. She had not been able to think, only to feel. Luckily Vincent had had enough self-control for both of them that nothing had happened. She was grateful to him.

Or angry at him for being able to resist her. One or the other.

"Remember this. When I make love to you, I want you to be conscious and remember every single second afterwards and not regret it."

The tingling in her belly was back.

Joy came to her.

Her mobile phone vibrated. Several times.

Vincent gritted his teeth. Just when he had had her complete attention, he interrupted her.

George.

"You'd better look at your mobile. Don't want your George to think you're cheating."

She frowned. She didn't want to read his message at that moment. Wanted to finish the conversation right now, but properly. And honestly.

Her mobile phone continued to vibrate.

However, she looked out into the landscape instead.

Really out.

Quietly, without continuing to talk.

Her combativeness subdued.

Her soul soothed.

"Just don't say anything more now." she pleaded softly. Because right at that moment, she would have admitted that all his doubts echoed in her just the same. If he cornered her now, she would have to face the truth. She couldn't, or was that exactly what she was doing at that moment?

Vincent accepted her wish, felt her wrestling with herself. He felt her defences weakening little by little. After a few minutes, he too overcame the cold and really saw the mountains, smelled the purity in the air, saw the woman beside him.

Then, as if waking from a trance, she folded the map back up, put her gloves back on and shut the door on her regret.

"I don't love him." she informed him soberly.

Marisa turned to Vincent to see him and be honest for the first time. With a matter-of-fact announcement, she continued.

"I don't believe in true love anymore. I'm not 17, 18 anymore." That wasn't surprising. But the next part was hard for her to admit. Had never accepted it before. "George and I are not right for each other. I know that. So I settle for the next best thing. To love a child, my child, unconditionally. That's why I wanted to marry George and not risk our relationship again."

Vincent fell silent, affected.

"So, it was for his sperm and not his attractive personality after all." he finally said.

And this time she laughed sadly.

"Yes, exactly."

"Well, that's settled then."

Was it?

"Are you calling off the wedding now?" His eyes cold, his gaze direct. After all these revelations, there was no question in his mind that she should even think for a second about a future with George.

Marisa met his gaze. Her answer unclear. If she saw Vin standing in front of her, it was a guaranteed yes. But he wasn't really here in her life. The day after tomorrow he would be out of her life forever. For a second time. And that was as it should be. All this time, nothing but nightmares and bad memories had plagued her. There was a reason why she never wanted to be with him again, why she had never forgiven him. But in all

the turmoil, she had completely forgotten to hate him for it. Her mind hadn't had the capacity to deal with that too. Which was just as well. She never needed to relive those last moments with him back then. As soon as they had all departed, her old, steady life could begin again. The boredom. The emptiness.
She did not want to be alone. But was George still the solution?
"There isn't." He shook his head in disappointment when she still couldn't agree. "He's up to something. He's not the one for you."
She had had enough. She came and came to no conclusion.
"Fine. If you really want to hear it, I promise I won't marry him. I won't do any more online dating or dating. I'll stay single and childless for the rest of my life."
"That's a totally childish reaction. And not at all what I want for you." He could have screamed. Why was she making such a fool of herself? She could win over hundreds of men. He saw day in and day out how the other skiers in her group looked after her alone. Mitchell, Johnny. Why didn't she see how desirable she was?
"You for me? Like you have any interest in me!"
Vin gritted his teeth angrily. She was driving him crazy.
"I'm no more right for you than you are. Haven't you realised that yet?" His breath came fast and his eyes sparked fire. "I want for you to find all that you seek. I want you to find someone and you can have children. But I can't give you that. I won't marry you."
She stared at him in shock.
"No one asked you for that."
And yet she felt as if he had pulled the rug out from under her. As if all this time, after all, she had been inwardly hoping that her ex-boyfriend, her first boyfriend, had shown up here in the mountains to rescue her. Like in a novel, he would fall head over heels in love with her again, take her out of an unhappy, hopeless relationship and ask her to marry him. She would have said yes immediately.
You fool.

You are so stupid that you haven't even realised it yourself.
Damn you. Come to terms with the fact that you weren't the love of his life. And never will be.

Neither knew what to add at that moment. Too much had already been said. Too much was up in the air. Too little could be changed.

Marisa looked back at the mountains. Her beloved mountains.

"Let's just ski." she said resignedly. As she put her sunglasses back on, tears ran down her face. She ignored them and wiped the tracks away with her gloves. As if they had never been there.

Vincent saw them. The tears too. He had said everything he had in him. He had tried to open her eyes. But had no solution. He was not the answer.

So, they did what suited best. They went skiing. The wind in her face briefly reminded her of the wet tracks on her face, the cold burning her cheeks. She sucked in the air deeply, inhaling and exhaling deeply. For a few seconds, if it was possible, she closed her eyes. She reacted quickly and skilfully to bumps on the slope. She felt the tingling in her stomach when things got tight or tricky. Then she felt alive again. At least for those few hours in her beloved mountains.

At the end of the descent, her head was a little clearer.

She finally looked at the many messages.

A mixture like her feelings.

Are you having fun on the slopes?
You dirty whore.
Get back to me when you're on your way to the mountain hut.
Did you fuck all night?
Missed you last night.
I want to strangle you with my bare hands.
See you soon xx

She breathed quickly. The photo came much later, when she was already back in the alpine hut and had recovered from the nasty words. She almost didn't open it because she wasn't sure she could take another threat.

The transmitter was anonymous. As it always was, and yet different. So was the photo. Her fear vanished.
This time it was a photo of George.
And Maureen.
Clearly cheating.
Ah.
I'm sorry.
She wasn't upset, she wasn't sad. She felt nothing. Just emptiness. A glimpse of her bleak future.

~

Life was beautiful. At last, all the hurdles had fallen. There was no longer a big question mark in their relationship. At last she could let herself feel and let herself love.
The days, weeks held the most beautiful moments of her life. If she had thought she was in love with Vin before, now she knew she loved him. More than anything else in her life.
It wasn't just sex, it was the time she got to spend with him. But the sex only made it better. The sneaky kisses while they crammed in the library together. The long walks during which he told her about his dreams. His ideas of studying psychology at university so he could analyse other people and their actions. His curiosity to see why some people kept making the wrong decisions and others could never make up their minds. They speculated about their friends and relatives. What kind of people were they? They laughed together and were relaxed.
All this painted their world so rosy. So beautiful. At that moment, she was sure he loved her too. There was no other way. He was by her side, he hadn't broken up with her after the first time, as others had predicted. He was with her. Completely and totally with her. They found a way to see each other regularly without jeopardising his final exams. She helped him prepare for his qualifying interview at the university. She went with him to the campus to see his new accommodation, where he would be living from October. They made plans how often they could see each other on weekends. They planned the summer.
How had it all gone so wrong?
Marisa put her arms around her torso and squeezed so hard it

hurt. Maybe the pain would stop her from thinking any more about what came next.

Day 20

Marisa was silent. Was she the kind of person who always made the wrong decision? Or could never make up her mind? She wondered if Vincent had ended up graduating in psychology. What had he said? He worked in law enforcement. A whole different strand. Had he switched to law?
So many questions she hadn't been able to ask him in the end. Whereas he really had asked a thousand questions of her. She laughed lightly to herself. She had not taken her chances to get to know the man Vincent properly. Slight remorse kicked up.
What she would not regret were her adventures on the descent. Her group this year had been unique. They had fitted together well.
Mitchell looked at her quizzically as she came down the mountain for the last time. Taking off her gear for the last time and packing onto the minibus as they waited for the others. He handed her a hot drink.
Cocoa.
How well he knew her.
She smiled at him. And totally unexpectedly, he gave her a hug. A hug that lasted longer than intended. He hugged her tightly. Vincent joined in at that moment. He ignored the strange feeling that came over him when he saw her closeness.
"I'm sorry." said Mitch ruefully.
When they broke away from each other again, she looked at him in confusion.
"What are you sorry for?"

Mitch looked directly at her and then at Vin, who was watching him intently.

"For constantly pairing you with him."

Marisa laughed at his remark. It was a liberating laugh, genuine and warm. Her eyes shone and she felt the joy inside her. Her first step of liberation.

"He kept up well." She gave him a loving look. It gave him the rest.

"I'll see you later at the après-ski party. Vincent."

~

"You guys go ahead, we'll be right there."
Marisa stopped by the door and so did George.
Maureen and Vincent made their way to dinner. They wanted to eat early before all the seats were taken. With the farewell party to follow, the large, splendid alpine hut would be full. This party was one of the most popular occasions where people could really let off steam. No one would have to get up early tomorrow to get to the slopes. No one had to save their strength to master difficult and risky loops the next day. Today was a celebration of all they had accomplished. No broken legs or arms, fast stretches, steep, smooth ones. They had exceeded their own expectations and pushed boundaries. The journey home tomorrow would be so hard for some.
As would she.
George looked at his fiancée, slightly annoyed, as he had hoped to spend the last few hours with the blonde beauty. He hid his annoyance behind his sweet mask. As always.
Marisa hesitated for another moment. And then she made the right decision.
"George, I think we need to discuss something before we go to the party."
For a split second, fear ran across his face, but he had regained his composure immediately.
"Of course, darling. What do you want to discuss?"
Marisa pulled her phone out of her jeans and showed him a photo.
At first George was unmoved, but when he realised he was in the picture, with Maureen, some emotions came up.

"Where did you get this from? Were you stalking me?" His first reaction was rash and he immediately regretted it. He changed his tactics. "That was.... That..... I had been drinking. I was upset."
She put the phone away again and stopped him immediately.
"I don't blame you." she said quietly and he stared at her in surprise. "But I think it means an end for us. We should break off our engagement."
This time the panic on his face was clear. He widened his eyes and shook his head violently.
"No ... no ... no! I'm sorry. I didn't mean to hurt you. I ... I'll make it up to you. I - "
"George. It's over. Not because of the photo, or your interest in Maureen." she explained further. Her voice so damn quiet he could have screamed. "It's over because ... you and Maureen, it's been going on all three weeks, I'm not blind. But I'm not jealous either. This image, this evidence, leaves me cold. I don't feel protective of our relationship or possessive of you. I feel ... nothing."
"You feel nothing?" His anger broke through. Her words had cut him deeply.
She was surprised at the anger in his eyes. Of course, she had never seen him like this before. He stepped close to her, his gaze fixed directly on her. His body language threatening.
She swallowed.
"Do you want me to make room for him? Is this about him?" He had forced the words through his thin lips, the distance between them narrow. She couldn't dodge out of the way easily; the wall was right behind her. She had to take a step to the side to get past him.
"No. It has nothing to do with Vincent. It concerns only you and me." she replied strongly.
"Oh really. What happened here the night you were snowed in? Did you kiss again? Did you fuck?"
His reaction scared her. Yes, he had a right to be upset and offended. But she felt uncomfortable in his presence. At his

vulgar expressions.

"No." she weakly tried to resist.

"Don't make me laugh. I'm not blind any more than you are. He's been waiting all this time to rip your clothes off your body. And you want it."

She tried to get out of the corner. But George kept pushing her towards the door, the wall, with no way out.

"How did you feel when he kissed you? Did you feel anything then?"

Alive.

She didn't speak it. She saw the moment when George wasn't *George* anymore. Recognized how he only saw red. Hate. Rage. Rage.

"You want to feel something? You want to feel something?"

His hand shot ice cold around her neck, and he squeezed. She had no time to react to him. He slammed his whole body against her, her head hitting the wall painfully. She tried to pull his hand from her neck. In vain. He had a strength that overwhelmed her. She fought back with her hands, her legs. But he was stronger.

He brutally ripped the jeans off her hips, leaving a long scratch on her side with his ruthless approach. And the pressure around her neck grew stronger. Pure fear rose in her. She couldn't breathe, she couldn't stop him ramming his knee between her legs so he could get at her. It twisted her eyes with pain, with panic.

Please don't, she pleaded in her head. Silent tears ran down her cheeks. He pressed his hard mouth to hers, forcing himself closer and closer. She froze. She turned, she twisted. She was defenceless. She saw black before her eyes when she could take no more breaths.

Silence.

An eternity passed.

And just as quickly as he had turned, he changed his purpose.

"You're not worth it."

Like a piece of dirt, he gave her trembling body one last

shove against the wall before letting go of her completely. Marisa's back bumped against the ice-cold wall. Then she sank powerlessly to the floor. Her torn jeans around her knees.

Her body weak, but so far unharmed. Her mind at work. She heard him ripping things out of the cupboards in the room. With the last of her strength, she pulled up the broken trousers, scrambled to her feet as quickly as she could and fled to the bathroom next to the door. She turned the key as many times as she could. Her hands trembled; her breath hitched. Her pulse was racing. She tried to calm herself. She listened tensely for his movements, his footsteps down the stairs. She held her breath as silence fell.

She knew he was standing outside the door, listening for the slightest sound just as she was.

After an almost unbearable eternity, he opened the door and left the mountain hut. The snow van hummed to life and sped away a moment later.

Marisa ran to the bathroom door, unlocked it and pressed herself against the front door. She put on every lock there was. She looked down at her trembling hands. Then she broke down crying.

~

He saw his whole life go down the drain. Everything he had dreamed of; everything he had planned, ruined. Everything ruined because of one night.
He could have cried, really cried. He had never felt such deep remorse. And anger. And hatred.
And fear.
"I don't know how it happened." she said softly.
"Of course you know how it happened or weren't you paying attention in Bio?" he snapped back coldly.
Marisa winced slightly at his tone.
"This is all your fault. Because you keep trying to seduce me everywhere." he was talking at it now. His emotions so jumbled that he didn't think for a second about what he was saying here or who he was accusing here. "If you weren't on my dick all the time, we wouldn't be in this shitty situation."
She didn't say a word. Yes, she liked being intimate with him. Yes, she had surprised him once or twice with her lust. But he did the same to her when he kissed her unexpectedly and touched her deeply.
"Shit. Shit. Shit." he started again, even angrier than before. Much more panicked than before as he considered again how his life was ruined. "Are you sure?"
"Yes." Her soft syllable was enough to cause him the deepest pain.
Vin suddenly stood still. He took a deep breath and exhaled slowly. His eyes full of anger.
"It's not too late to have an abortion."
Marisa shook her head instantly. She now found the same

anger he did.

"No, never. This baby is innocent. We can't just have it taken away like it means nothing."

"Mean nothing? What meaning does it have when you have a baby? You just graduated from 11th grade. No degree nothing. It would ruin everything for you."

"*You*? *Me*? Have you already pulled yourself out of it? We might as well face it together and give him something."

Vincent looked at her in shock.

"I'm going to college in two months. I don't want to pay child support. I want to start my new life. I want to have a career."

Marisa looked at him brokenly. She realised so many things.

"A life without me? Either way?"

Vincent did not avoid her gaze. On the contrary, he answered her questions, her worries, with a nod.

"Yes..... I'm not the girlfriend type. I want to be free."

She felt sick. Her heart could not have broken more than it did at that moment. Somewhere deep inside, she found the strength not to get down on her knees and beg him. She straightened, her shoulders pulled tightly back, her eyes clear and cold.

"You're free again. Congratulations."

And with that, she left him standing, never to be heard from again.

Until now. Seventeen years later.

~

FUCK!
Fuck, fuck, fuck! Fuck you!

~

Midnight, a new day....
Day 21, the last day

It struck midnight. New day, new luck.

It took her a few hours to pick herself up. Her shoulders taut and her eyes clear, she looked at herself in the mirror.

Maybe it had all just been a dream?

The brown eyes looked back at her silently and emotionlessly. Her face was still as dull and plain as before. Her body still just as unremarkable as ever. Her clothes comfortable, not fashionable. No longer torn.

Maybe you should call for help?

Marisa took a deep breath. The only thing new about her were the bruises on her neck. They were raw. But they would soon fade. A day or two and the whole thing would be forgotten. She wouldn't have to think about it anymore. She would be able to look forward to her new life. Her work, her colleagues. That was all she needed.

It could have turned out differently. She felt sick. She squeezed her eyes painfully shut to stop herself from letting the horrible moments play out before her eyes. It was no use.

It had been her fault. She had played with fire. She had upset him, and he had not been able to control his anger. Why had she even had to insult him? Who did such a thing?

You fool. He could have done anything.

Maybe you should report it?

Marisa had to distract herself. She was going crazy with her self-doubt and memories otherwise.

It was a long way to the popular alpine hut. A place where she had made good memories. A place where many people would be. She could find refuge there. No more thinking about it.
Maybe you should talk about it?
Vin.
He was sitting at the bar, a big beer in front of him. He looked gorgeous. Sexy.
When he saw her walking towards him, his eyes did not leave hers for a second. Her heart was pounding up to her throat. She wanted to throw herself into his arms and just let herself feel. She wanted to find security, in his hold, protection.
Vin saw only her. This woman with brown eyes and long brown hair. Like then, only more mature, more like a woman and even more irresistible. In her tight jeans, the thick jumper and the scarf around her neck. He wanted to pull her close and kiss her to the ground. But she seemed so unattainable.
She stopped in front of him, nervous and unsure. What now?
"It's over." she said tersely. "With me and George."
Vincent did not move an inch. Let the words sink into his consciousness. Then slowly he stood up and approached her. His eyes dark, hot. His hand gripped around her neck.
Her breath caught. She wouldn't have wanted anything else. Wanted only him, always had. But her emotions were unstable, assaulted. She was broken.
She took a step back, pain written all over her face.
"That's not what I'm here for." she declared. Her whole body shook. But she could no longer separate her panic and arousal. It would not be a good idea to give herself to him today.
Instantly he closed himself off to her and his gaze became cold, forbidding.
She felt the deepest remorse.
"So why the hell are you here?"
He turned back to his beer and finished it. He waved to the bartender for another. She didn't know the answer to his question.
She hadn't wanted to be alone. She had wanted to be near him.

She had wanted to be with him. But not like this. Nothing superficial.
"I have no idea." She ran a tired hand over her face.
Vin just shook his head slightly. Disappointed, annoyed. Confused.
In the corner he spotted a pretty brunette. He raised his glass in her direction and she smiled back. Marisa looked away. Let him have fun with the next best girl. It left her cold. It all left her cold. All her emotions had been used up today. It had been a mistake to come here. Vin couldn't help her. Wouldn't help her. She had to deal with her fate alone.
Just like she did then.
Before she left, there was something she needed to know after all.
"You never asked about what happened afterwards."
He stopped his flirting for the moment. This subject was uncomfortable. Something he had never wanted to think about again.
"No. I won't."
She walked around him to block his view of the other, and so that he would see her. Just her. One last time.
"You just abandoned your pregnant girlfriend like that."
"You could have had an abortion. You tried to push me into a relationship I wasn't ready for."
She endured the coldness, his reluctance. She fought her own guilt.
"I didn't get pregnant on purpose."
"You wanted to hold me."
"That's absurd." She didn't believe her ears. She was disgusted that he could have even thought such a thing. "I was hopelessly in love with you."
Marisa looked into emotionless eyes. His concentration already on something else. He didn't hear her, didn't want to be reminded of those dark times. Of his failures.
An incomprehensible emptiness spread through her as she realised what this last day, this last conversation meant for her

and Vin. She would never see him again. She felt as if she had lost him a second time. But that was not the case. You couldn't lose what you never had.

She swallowed dryly. Her throat ached.

"It really hadn't meant anything to you?" she finally concluded. Resignation spread through her.

"It was just sex. Good sex. But I didn't - don't - have the time or the will for more." And again, he sought eye contact with the other woman. He rose slightly to make it clear that for him this conversation was over.

Marisa had to finally accept it now. Her first great love was a lost cause. And she had wasted all these years trying to find someone even remotely like him. What a mistake that had been. At last, she saw it.

Her heart in a thousand pieces. Not because her engagement had broken up. Not because her ex-fiancé had almost raped her. But because she had again had her head in a pointless novel where Vincent was concerned.

"Fine. I just want to correct one thing. I wouldn't marry you."

With those final words, she left the whole resort behind. So did Vincent McDormant.

~

After the holidays

Marisa could not sleep. Over and over again she thought back to that night, felt his hand around her neck. Her throat tightened until she awoke from sleep gasping for air.
It had been her punishment. For her failure. She had failed him.
Just as the policeman at the station had made her understand. She had been the stupid one. She had broken the rules first. She had betrayed him.
You're saying you cheated, but your fiancé didn't blame you? Yes.
And you're saying that you spent the next few days, weeks, then night and day with the same man you had already cheated with? Yes.
You also received threatening messages on a regular basis? Yes.
And did not report them? No.
How many photos have you been sent? Several.
Did you report these incidents to management or the police? No.
Did you talk to anyone about this? No.
To clarify again, you broke up with your fiancé because he was leaving you cold? Yes.
And the other man played no part in this event? .....
Did he actually rape you? No.
Did he sexually harass you? No.
And you want us to arrest your ex-fiancé for doing what? ....

She had embarrassed herself to the bone. No one had taken her seriously in her complaint. Why should they? Her story, her experience was meticulous compared to real victims. It was not worthy of a trial. Clearly they did not care how great her fear had been. They couldn't help her with that. They did not examine her wounds, the bruises around her neck, the deep scratch on her hip. It had not been a serious case.

How had she ever been able to claim that she had been sexually assaulted? He hadn't.

The next day she revoked her complaint against George Rashdy.

~

The room smelled of sweat, of nerves and guilt.

The room was small, plain and angular. The tables stood in their measured places, properly straight. The judge's wide, polished wooden table overlooked the rest of the room. From there he saw everything.

The accused, the innocent.

First there were many loud, pleading voices. Factual, convincing arguments from the lawyers.

Then a short, nerve-wracking silence.

The judge gave his verdict.

The guests, acquaintances and innocent people breathed a sigh of relief. Tears of joy rolled down their cheeks. There were hugs.

On the other bench, anger and disgust grew.

The judgement had identified who was to blame. Who was the guilty party.

Justice still existed.

~

This room is so fucking perfect. So straight, as if life were so fucking perfect.
The stench alone pisses me off.
And why does my lawyer have such a weak baby voice. No one can hear what he's saying. Speak up! Show them I'm innocent! Jeez, say something!
And their faces.
Don't look so scared! Like you're gonna pee your pants when I look at you.
Now spit out the verdict. Let's hear how you believed all their heart-warming stories. I'm a man who can't be trusted.
Cunt.
Shit. Ruined everything. All this time, I've been playing patience and love like a complete idiot. I had the perfect plan. Lost everything because of her. Shit. Shit. Shit.
I should have fucked her brains out. Then she wouldn't have been able to think or say a word.
That wasn't the end. You wait, you faithless bitch.
Get a hold of yourself. And remember, the game goes on.

~

Day X

And that must have been how she ended up in this miserable situation. Chained to a radiator.
And her ex-fiancé an absolute tyrant.
She couldn't have known that, could she?
Maybe she had had her head so full of memories of her first great love and couldn't cope with the constant confrontation with Vin that it had simply escaped her that George was totally deranged.
And even if he had been, would this day have been any different?

18:26

Marisa was perfectly content with her life. Admittedly, the first few days after the eventful skiing holiday had been difficult. However, she had had little time to wallow in self-pity because her holiday was over and work was waiting. This completely distracted her from her heartbreak. She could hardly think about Vincent, or about that fateful night in the mountain hut. She didn't miss his voice at all, or her fiancé. She was not devastated that she would never see him again or that she had almost been raped. All her attention and strength had to go into her work.
And she loved her work. She still remembered Vincent's thoughtless comment when she told him she worked in a nursery. Yes, she liked children. She wanted children of her

own. He just knew that. He had known that when he had dumped her when she was 17.

Shit. Her thoughts refused to be controlled today. That never happened before. Or at least not often. Or really only after work. In her flat, in her bed. All the time.

She took a deep breath. No more of that. He's gone. He's a womaniser. He's no good for you. Just for one night.

She didn't even get to experience that.

Because of George.

She felt sick at the thought of him. Of her ex-fiancé. For heaven's sake what had gotten into him that night? How had he been able to suppress his true colours, his real temperament so well all this time? She had been blind, stupid.

And Vin had been right.

Damn.

Her thoughts ran in circles.

Marisa shook off any thinking, grabbed a few of the rubbish bags piled up at the entrance door to her nursery and carried them outside. The fresh air did her good, even if the rubbish smelled unpleasantly of dirty nappies.

Back at the door, she hadn't noticed the dark figure beside the driveway by the trees. She unlocked the door again when suddenly she felt a cloth over her mouth, and she was brutally pulled back by her hair.

Panic came up. Her thoughts chased back and forth in confusion.

"Shhh. Mary, it's me. Did you miss me?"

She stiffened instantly as she recognised his voice. She felt sick, her head spinning. She almost lost her balance when she realised George had sought her out. And how!

Was he now going to finish what he had started in the mountain hut?

"Take it easy. Stop struggling." he warned her coldly. He was stronger than she was. Any movement, any struggling seemed useless. He only pulled harder on her hair, pressed the cloth over her mouth even more. She could hardly breathe. Her eyes went black.

"We're going to go into your beloved nursery like good boys. Without alerting anyone. Call all your minions to the first floor. They haven't really cleaned up there yet, have they?"

Marisa shook her head in horror. There was no way she was going to let him in, firstly, and secondly, expose her poor staff to this crazy man. She tried to get away from him again, but her bold defiance only angered him and he banged her head against the sharp edge next to the entrance door instead.

Marisa hesitated for a brief moment, but knew it was futile. At least they would be safe for the next few minutes if they were not near him.

She did as he instructed. Feverishly, she tried to find a solution. She had to notify the police. But how?

"Leave them alone. Please. They are alone in the room. They didn't see you. We can go and leave them out of this." she pleaded again. It fell on deaf ears.

"Of course, darling. No problem, darling."

His words sent an icy chill down her spine. That was why she hadn't come to see it. He had always said yes to everything. He had always been so fucking friendly. Shit.

George pushed her relentlessly down the hall, up to the stairs to the first floor. One more time she tried to stop him from wrapping the other employees in this drama.

She turned abruptly and kicked him in the stomach with one leg.

"Lock the door. Call the police."

He was surprised enough that he hadn't seen it coming and stumbled back two or three steps. But he hadn't fallen, hadn't felt any pain, or if he had felt pain, it only made him feel worse, and he charged at her full force.

Marisa tried to run away, spinning away from him as fast as she could. Her hands tied so tightly and uncomfortably behind her back left her little balance. He grabbed hold of her legs, and they landed crashing on the stairs. Her shoulder bore the brunt of it, and she knew instantly how she had dislocated her

shoulder. But she felt pain everywhere, her cheek, her knees.
In her struggle she saw Rachel come running out of the room to see what was wrong. Shock leapt into her face. Uncertainty. Panic. Fear.

"Lock yourselves in. Police!" she screamed breathlessly once more as George carelessly and roughly climbed on top of her and slapped her face. Tears burned in her eyes. But a load fell from her heart when she just saw Rachel disappear again. Keys in the hole, furniture moving, shrieking with excitement.

"Shit. Shit!" George shouted in anger.

He pressed her down hard on the stairs once more, when he was sure she wasn't going to get up so easily, he jumped off her and fetched his backpack towards him. With haste and obvious annoyance, he tore open the tape and covered her mouth with it. Then he carelessly dragged her up the remaining steps into the room next to the penguins. A smaller room where the children played with paints and plasticine. Or other activities where they got completely dirty.

With the last of his strength, he pushed her towards the window, in front of the heater. With some fumbling and swearing, he managed to tie her to the heater with several extensions. Careless of her injuries. Marisa fought the sinking feeling in her stomach. The pain sent little white dots before her eyes. But she would not make a sound, would not give him the satisfaction of showing her discomfort.

Then, exhausted, he dropped to the floor a few feet away from her and just laughed. Hysterical, out of control. Only after a few incredibly disturbing moments did he get up and walk to the door to the penguin room.

Marisa tried to hold him off, couldn't move. Couldn't talk. She watched helplessly as he made his way to the other nurseryers. Her breathing shallow, her eyes wide.

"Open the door, please. I just want to talk to you." he asked kindly. Just as kindly and hypocritically as she had only known him as her fiancé.

No reply.

George rattled the doorknob in frustration. The lock couldn't be that good after all.

"I'm not going to hurt you. I don't give a damn about any of you. You're just unlucky Mary made you work late. It's all her fault."

"The police are on their way." came an anxious voice.

Marisa thought of Lara, who had just started working for her. A lovely, child-loving person. She was full of energy and positivity. What would this mess do to her enjoyment of life?

George gritted his teeth angrily. Nothing, absolutely nothing was going according to plan here.

Fuck.

Then Marisa heard nothing more. No matter how hard she tried, she couldn't make out what he was doing. Had he fled? Had he given up because the police were on their way?

She somehow tried to get into a comfortable position in front of the heater as she listened intently. With luck, she was able to peel the tape off with her fingers enough to breathe easier. She barely had any feeling left in her fingertips; the cable ties laced so tightly around her wrists. Her shoulder was the worst. The muscles twitched, complained, forced her to her knees.

As if in a trance, she looked at those thin plastic lines. How could they be so effective?

~

20:12

So not really. She couldn't have done otherwise, even with the knowledge that he was totally batty.
Time ticked away. Silence. Too much time to think. To realise.
Marisa took a deep breath in and out. Don't panic. That wouldn't do any good. She had already noticed that in those first few hours. Her wrists didn't want to be moved back and forth any longer either. The wounds were already deep, the mere thought of touching the thin plastic cable turned her stomach.
The sirens in the background were only barely perceptible at first, then they grew louder and louder. She felt hope, great relief that all this would soon be over.
She was not the only one who had noticed the sirens and blue lights.
George came back into the room calmly and expectantly. He had not run away. Oh no. He had used the time to close the narrow driveway and exit to her nursery. Accordingly, the police cars could not drive directly into the yard. They had to stop in the street. The view up to the house where Marisa had set up her nursery was obscured. Security measures so that crazy people like George couldn't just watch little children. Next to the narrow driveway was the garden for the children, but it was surrounded by large trees and thick bushes. A few metres away from the driveway was the exit, the small car park for the parents had always been far too narrow and small, especially with the little manoeuvring space. In front

of the exit, from the road, you could see the front of the big traditional house. But not much. The windows were decorated with art pieces and stickers. And the penguin room was at the back of the building, that you couldn't see from the exit or driveway.
George had chosen the best rooms. As if he had planned it all that way. Really?
Why?
"Why don't you just let us go?" she asked cautiously.
He looked down at her jerkily. He had been so deep in thought that he had completely forgotten, she was there. He saw the tape hanging from her cheek. He didn't care right now if or what she said.
He took a sharp knife out of his pocket and arrogantly bent down to her.
"Mary, Mary, what are you doing to us?" he whispered teasingly. She recognised the song, knew the syllables by heart. Did it mean that he was …? "No. You've already ruined everything anyway. It can't get any worse."
The blade shone brightly in the light. Her thoughts distracted. She didn't want to provoke him, needed to consider her words or actions carefully first.
"How did I fuck everything up?" she probed slowly. None of this made sense. If he had just wanted to overpower her, why all the drama and her employees in the other room.
"You and your fucking rules." He hissed in her face. The sharp point pierced into the skin of her neck without further ado. She didn't dare swallow.
Her mind was working. What was he talking about?
"You didn't want a romantic relationship. You didn't want sex before the wedding." she defended the only decisions that could conform to any rules.
George laughed coldly. The blade far from her skin again. She took a deep breath in and out. He seemed unpredictable at that moment. Her head was pounding, she could hardly concentrate on this conversation. And yet she wanted to ease

his hatred a little and escape this whole miserable situation.

"I'm not talking about our dull engagement after all. It was all just part of my plan." he replied honestly, his eyes twinkling with disappointment. "Your pretentious rules for your nursery. You and your security measures. No parents in the nursery, no acquaintances. A husband though, who should have been allowed to enter."

Marisa couldn't understand why it would have any effect on him whether he could visit her at work or not. Why did he want to enter the nursery? Her mind ran amok. Was he a paedophile? Oh my goodness! Had Vincent been right all along that something was wrong with him, and she hadn't seen it? Was he trying to get close to little children?

"You wanted to get close to little innocent children?" She contorted her face in disgust, not paying attention at that moment to how much she could upset him with her reaction. That fact sickened her. "You despicable bastard."

From far, far away she heard the ground floor phone in her office.

George angrily grabbed the tape and sealed her mouth.

Then he walked slowly down the stairs. It was time to deal with the police.

~

A negotiator had years of training behind him. They practised the riskiest and most unpredictable scenarios. One planned and implemented various negotiation techniques in talks. Every word, every proposal had to be considered and thought through. No action was allowed to be spontaneous, and one had to reckon with arbitrary behaviour of all participants at any time, including the hostages. It took patience, it took a good understanding of the criminal's psychology. In such situations, emotions were unpredictable, could change from one second to the next, from doubt to anger. From crying to freaking out.

A crisis navigator had to be able to anticipate the situation before the next statement or act and make a decision within milliseconds that hopefully resulted in the least amount of personal harm. In a critical hostage situation, the spokesperson had to be able to make a decision quickly and confidently. Fear and hypersensitivity were terrible enemies of a successful and safe negotiation.

There was no guarantee that the situation would end well. But one had gained enough experience, had the confidence in oneself, that one could prevent this delicate situation from coming to a head.

Vincent McDormant was the deputy crisis navigator.

~

21:01

The police cars completely closed off the road in front of the nursery, the several police cars were parked in front of the entrance and exit. A few of the police officers set about exploring the perimeter of the property and sealing it off. Others were working on the exit to open the gates.

So far they only had the phone call from the young women who had been detained in one of the rooms. One of the policewomen spoke to her patiently to reassure her and talk her well. She asked necessary questions to make sure where the hostage taker was at the moment.

Meanwhile, Vincent stood with the active police officers who had produced a detailed map of the building in front of them. He put on his stab waistcoat as he listened intently to the information the policeman had gathered this far.

"Officer 9843 Hector Young at your service sir, according to Rachel, a twenty-four year old nursery teacher, there are four female hostages in the room on the first floor, northwest of the building. Only one point of entry through the door, which they have locked and barricaded with furniture, two windows with an unfavourable view from the side street blocked by height and trees, the second window facing out to the back garden. We are currently trying to get the neighbours to let us see from their building. But the angle might be too acute. One of the hostages, erm -" The younger policeman looked at his notepad for precise details. "Maggie, 58, is suffering from chest pains, has trouble breathing. Panic? Suspected heart attack?

Officer 3879 is talking to her now to find out the exact medical circumstances. The other women are unharmed."

Vincent nodded. He glanced at the map, memorising everything he was told.

The emergency doctor was standing by; the ambulance too.

"And where is the hostage taker?"

"He's on the move. According to Rachel, he's on the loose in the nursery, he has access to all the rooms."

Vincent looked at the map again. There were several access points from the ground floor. Each room had a patio door. It would be possible to gain access to the ground floor and catch him unaware. The hostages, as long as they were locked in the room, were substantially safe. It was worth a try.

"What do we know about him?"

"Male, white, early to mid-forties. Tall, slim."

Vincent looked at his watch. The hostages had been in this situation for two hours, thirty-five minutes. It was time to release them. Their stress levels are at their highest and most unpredictable.

"Do we know what he wants?"

Hector shook his head slightly and checked his notes again.

"According to Rachel, the man had broken in around eighteen thirty in the evening and had taken her nursery manager by surprise. On his way to the other women, the manager stopped him and they were able to lock themselves in the penguin room. After they had run away, he tried to enter the room. He said he wasn't interested in hurting them."

"So, all the hostages escaped into the room?"

"No. The manager is in the room next door -"

"He has unfettered access to the hostage?" he interrupted the young officer. Suddenly his attention was on an emergency situation. "Why didn't you say so immediately?"

Vincent ran straight to the policewoman 3879 to take the phone from her hand. It was now a matter of resolving this precarious situation as safely and quickly as possible. He had wasted enough time talking to this officer who it had not occurred to him to tell about the hostage who was in imminent danger.

"Rachel? You're talking to the negotiator, Vincent McDormant. How are you doing?"

"Can you help us? Maggie's really not well. And my poor boss - she had blood all over her face."

Vincent took a deep breath.

"Do you know where the criminal is at the moment?"

"He's in the next room. He's talking to her."

"Apart from blood on her face, did she have any other life-threatening injuries that you could see?"

"No. I don't think so. I mean he hit her full on and they landed crashing on the stairs. But then I ran away. I didn't help. I just did what she said. I didn't -"

"You did exactly the right thing. Because of you, help is here now and we will find a safe way to free you all." he interrupted her wild rant. Fear turned to doubt. He had to avoid her trying to play hero.

"Rachel? Rachel? Step away from the others a bit."

She cried audibly. The whimper was almost louder than her whisper. In the background he heard a few other frantic voices frantically talking at each other.

"Rachel, is there access to a phone in the rooms?"

She sniffed. But soon she had regained her composure. Enough to understand and answer his question.

"The phone is in the office downstairs. But it's portable and we use it to talk to parents from the room."

"Okay, thanks. I'll pass you back over to my colleague Jennifer. Rachel, you're doing great. You've helped us more than you think now. Now help your co-worker."

Vincent handed the phone to the officer and walked back to the police van. He demanded the phone number of the nursery, and all the background information on the nursery director.

Now it was a matter of finding out why this crazy man had broken into a nursery and held 5 women defenceless.

He typed the landline number into the phone. At his ear

the phone, in front of him Hector Young, who was looking intently at his laptop screen. He picked out the most important facts about the nursery and summarised them neutrally for Vincent.

"This house was converted into a nursery five years ago. There are 150 children enrolled here from the age of 6 months to 4 years. There are 15 nursery teachers employed here, as well as the cleaning lady and cook. The owner and director of the nursery is 34 years old, comes from Frankenberg and -."

Click. Someone had lost weight.

It was time to talk to the hostage-taker.

~

21:21

The phone rang incessantly.
George took all the time in the world to go down the stairs. He had to make sure he didn't stand in front of a window or door. He had seen them point their guns at hostage-takers in films. He wasn't really that bad. He only had a few knives on him, but still he didn't want to risk it. He was in no hurry to talk to the police. He didn't feel like talking about his spiritual well-being. He wanted to sit quietly in a corner and think about what to do next.
Or would a talk with them be helpful in getting what he had wanted for so long? What he had longed for so much that he could no longer think clearly?
He walked into Marisa's office and stared motionlessly at the phone. Had he had any choice but to force his way into the nursery?
No.
It was all Marisa's fault. Mary, Mary.
He grabbed the phone and ran back up to the room. His anger was directed at his ex-fiancée.
With a cold smile, he crouched in front of the woman, who hung with her arms twisted on the radiator. Her forehead smeared with blood and small beads of sweat. Her laceration had stopped bleeding. She was breathing hastily, as the tape showed. Her brown eyes ice-cold.
The shrill ringing cut through the icy atmosphere.
George pressed the button to answer the call and lifted the

receiver to his ear.

Silence.

"Hello, you're talking to the crisis navigator. My name is Vincent. I am willing to negotiate with you."

George pressed the button and hung up again. Marisa looked surprised and worried, at the phone in his hand. Why had he hung up? Why wasn't he willing to talk to the policeman? What had he said? He couldn't have been a good officer if George had hung up again immediately.

Then total chaos broke out.

George stood up abruptly. His back turned to her. Then all at once he started laughing loudly. And laughing. His eyes fixed on Marisa again.

His eyes wide and wild, he literally doubled over from laughing.

"I can't believe this. I can't believe it."

And then a little more composed as the phone began to ring a second time.

"Well, this whole thing could get interesting now."

He answered the call with the broadest but iciest smile ever.

"Vincent, good to hear from you."

~

"..... The owner and manager of the nursery is 34 years old, comes from Frankenberg and her name is Marisa Keach."
Vin paused in his actions. His head was going crazy again, he had been thinking about her every day, now was not the moment to think about his ex-girlfriend or their last meetings. He looked as if struck at the young policeman who continued to search the internet for information and details.
The prolonged sound of the ended call rang out on the other end of the phone.
Fortunately, the hostage-taker had chosen the moment to hang up. That had given Vin a second of retrieval. Immediately, and without a hitch, he focused on his task.
A 34-year-old woman was in danger and needed his professional help. A crazy guy had broken into her nursery to hurt her. To sexually abuse her, to blackmail her. He needed to find out why and what he was up to. He had to get in touch with him and negotiate with him. This man was someone who was disturbed. Someone who knew where she worked. Someone who had ignored the other staff. Someone who knew her?
Shit.
Vin ran back to Jennifer, who was still reassuring Rachel and the others. He waved at her that he really needed to talk to her. Jennifer handed him the mobile phone.
"Rachel, listen to me. I need you to remember exactly what all you heard or saw right now."
"I can try. I don't know if I-" Her voice faltered again.
"You can. You've helped us so much already. Just a little more.

The man who attacked your boss. Is the man someone you know or recognised?"
"No."
"Did your boss address the man?"
"I don't remember. ...Yes."
"Did she use 'you'?"
Rachel breathed weakly. The pressure was incomprehensible. She wanted to block out all thoughts of what she had seen. At the same moment, she wanted to be able to help this policeman out. His questions seemed important and crucial.
"I don't know. In the room, next door when she's alone with him, maybe, but we can't hear her, always just him and his rage."
Vincent had to ignore that statement for the moment. He couldn't think about how the man would take out his anger on Marisa. And why Rachel didn't hear any other voice.
"Did she use his name at any point?"
Rachel shook her head in disappointment. Helpless, sad that she was no help.
He was losing hope that he had any chance of finding out who the man was. Maybe his idea was absurd. Maybe he had become so entangled with this man and couldn't focus on anyone else.
"Did he say her name? Did he know your boss?"
Rachel felt the tears welling up again.
"No, I .... he saw her on the stairs.... She had fallen so hard."
She could see the scene clearly in front of her, but describing it in words was difficult. She felt sick at the thought of the shrill scream she had let out. The bone crunching sound when Marisa had landed on the steps with the man on top of her. It shook her.
"Okay, Rachel. This is not a problem -"
"Yes, it is. I remember. I know. It was quiet for so long we didn't know if he was still there or what happened to Marisa. And then he came up to our door. He shook and twisted and kicked her so loudly. We were so afraid he was going to smash it. And then he got quiet again and talked to us. He said he didn't care

about us at all. …. We're just unlucky that Mary made us work late. It's all her fault."

Vincent felt a chill run down his spine.

"That's fantastic, Rachel. Rachel, you have been the biggest clue to us. Thank you, thank you so much."

Vincent handed the mobile phone back to the other policewoman and hurried to Hector. His next task, and that of the other policemen, was to research this person. He should find out everything and more about him. Find out his address, search his flat and find reasons why he had attacked Marisa Keach in her nursery.

He himself grabbed the phone one more time.

Mary.

What were the chances?

He knew a person who called her that, even though she didn't actually like it. A person who had always been a thorn in his side. A person who had bothered him from the beginning. He had convinced himself that his annoyance had only been a kind of jealousy. Now, however, he was no longer sure.

~

"Sir, yes I am the deputy negotiator. Yes, the situation is under control at the moment. We know who is responsible for it. Sir, yes."
Vincent listened intently, answering patiently.
Until he had to interrupt the conversation.
"I know both persons of this crisis situation. The hostage and the hostage taker."
Silence.
"How exactly do you relate to them?"
Vincent remained professional.
"Marisa Keach is an ex-girlfriend. George Rashdy is her ex-fiancé. We just spent a ski holiday together. He knows me."
Silence.
"Step down. I'll send a replacement."
"With regret, yes, I understand you must remove me from the crisis situation, sir. But I can continue the negotiation."
"Out of the question, McDormant. You are emotionally involved in this mess. You know better than I do that letting emotions get involved is not a good grounding."
Vincent gritted his teeth in annoyance. Yes, he knew that.
Damn it.
He couldn't stand by, and watch Marisa linger in the arms of a psychopath and do nothing to help her.
Shit. Shit. Shit.

~

"Vincent, good to hear from you."
George carelessly tore the tape from her mouth. Her lips dry and sore.
Marisa looked up wearily. The pain in her shoulder had weakened her. She fought fatigue, tried to suppress nausea. She most likely had a mild concussion. On top of that, she no longer had control of her right arm, her shoulder dislocated.
But now she stopped. Her head jumbled. Was she hallucinating?
George smiled back at her.
"Yes, darling, you heard right. Your ski partner, your crush is our dear negotiator. He'll get us out of this mess real quick and easy as pie."
He puts the phone back to his ear.
The smile immediately faded from his lips as he listened to the policeman on the other end. Instead, his face became angry, his hands clenched into fists and the knife straightened.
"Then undo the whole thing. I don't give a shit that Vincent knows me. That's exactly why I want him in charge of the negotiations. No one else. Otherwise, you can forget the whole thing."
He walked over to Marisa and in his anger he raised the knife and cut deep into the flesh on her forearm.
She had wanted to be strong, had not whined about her shoulder, her head. But the cut had happened so quickly, so deeply, that she cried out in agony.
Only then did he hang up the phone.

~

The shrill sound made everyone's blood run cold.
Hector had put his phone call to the hostage-taker on speakerphone. Everyone had heard George's answer. The young officer had tried to negotiate with the other. George had refused out of hand. It had not been his fault, for George it had become a game. In his crazy mind, this situation had just improved a hundredfold. But Vincent saw in the latter's eyes that he felt guilty for it. Marisa had had to suffer because of him. He would never forgive himself for that. Later, when all was well and safely over, he would have to talk to him.
Five minutes later he had called his superior again and received permission, or rather urgent orders, to conduct the trial.
Vincent turned back to the police officers, who got to work on the internet, checking social media, dating sites and police records together. He waited impatiently for a report. Something positive. Something that would help him with the persuasion.
He needed to turn off his shock, his fear. George was a typical lunatic who acted randomly. There was no protocol for Vin to follow. He had to let George guide him and take every opportunity for softening. It was of the utmost importance to contain the personal damage.
Personal damage. Stay neutral. Keep your distance. Not thinking about the fact that it was Marisa.
Marisa.
Stop. Think. Act.

~

22:42

He laughed coldly. But he did not hang up.
George stood tall and unmoving over Marisa, who hung curled up against the radiator. Her arm limp, the cut bleeding. He looked blindly at the blood as it gradually ran down her arm to her elbow. Drop after drop landed on her white blouse. He was mesmerised by the colours. By what he had done.
"Mary, Mary, what have you done?" he whispered coldly. She looked at him in disgust. She felt dizzy.
"I didn't do anything to us." she countered coldly. She couldn't imagine being able to feel more pain. She didn't care at all what he was doing to her. She just wanted an end to this insane situation. And sleep.
Just sleep.
"Nothing? You and Vincent. What the hell is he doing here as a cop? Did you know that? Have you been seeing each other since we broke up? Are you a couple? Are you fucking?"
This time she laughed at his accusations. They were ridiculous.
"Yeah, sure. Vincent and I have such a passion for each other."
George didn't like her tone at all. He pulled her hair so she would look him in the eye. She stopped instantly.
"Since when?"
"Since never." she said with more respect this time. Maybe she wasn't ready to feel more pain after all. Her eyes rolled as she tried to focus her gaze on him. "We don't fuck."
George stared into her face. She seemed to be struggling to stay conscious. He frowned at her. Unsure if he could believe her.

Fucking didn't matter.

He had more important things to deal with.

He pressed the button on the phone to put an end to the annoying ringing. He couldn't concentrate at all with the noise.

~

"McDormant. We found something."
"You're not going to like it.
Vincent saw the two police officers coming towards him. They were holding various plastic bags of evidence they had seized from his flat.
His laptop.
"This guy has hired a lot of security. He uses the latest technology as far as online security is concerned. His accounts are almost inaccessible, but he hasn't thought of a what -"
"First things first. We have five hostages, two of them in critical condition."
The officer nodded ruefully and opened the emails.
And Vincent saw pictures of himself and Marisa on the piste. Photos that made it seem that Marisa and Vincent had rather a closer relationship than had been the case. After the initial shock, he remembered his task.
"Where did he get the photos? Did you track down the source?"
"Originally the photos came from a mobile phone number. He hadn't saved the name of the sender, instead it came under: Bland Womaniser M."
Vincent knew who he was talking about. He couldn't believe he had got Mitchell to snap those photos behind her back and then send them to George as well. For what purpose? Why hadn't he talked to Marisa?
"Did he forward the photos?"
The policeman cleared his throat in embarrassment. His superior was clearly in deep conversation with another woman in those photos. He saw what George had also seen. But neither had any idea what had really happened.

"Yes. Most of the photos were sent to a certain 'Mary'."
Vincent took an exasperated breath. Shit.
"But not from his private account. He used an anonymous number over the internet. Even more, he installed an elaborate program where he could pre-program it when the messages were sent."
The bastard.
What had he wanted from her?
Vincent reached for the phone. He had to talk to this guy. How could he hide the disgust he felt for this person?
"There's more."
Vincent was silent and waited.
"It wasn't just the photos of you - I mean, he didn't just send the photos. There were hundreds of text messages in his outbox."
He opened a document where he had copied the messages into it. Again, he knew for a fact that they were about Vin and the hostage. He didn't want to be in his shoes.

You dirty bitch. When I catch you, I'm going to fuck the smile off your face.

You incorrigible whore. If you can't learn from your mistakes, I'll have to show you how to painfully repent.

How was your day, dearest slut?

Hours on the road with your crush. You disgust me.

Did you think about your fiancé for a second?

Why so shy? Aren't you going to answer me?

Shall I visit you in your bedroom later?

Vincent had to turn away from the words. He had seen enough. His blood was boiling. Now he understood her haunted looks whenever she had looked at her mobile. That was why she had run like mad out of the common room those times. Only now did he understand her panic when he got close to her.
Too late. He had watched like an idiot as a psychopath systematically destroyed her. He, who had years of training in psychology of the insane, had not seen it coming. He had been so desperately fixated on feeling nothing for her that he hadn't realised anything.

SUSANN SVOBODA

Shit.

~

"George. You asked for me."
He didn't quite manage not to let his contempt shine out of his voice.
George recognised the latter's voice immediately, his dislike too. Good.
He didn't want special treatment. He wanted the truth.
"I did. At last we can discuss one or two things properly. All of us. Mary, say hello to Vincent, darling."
George put the phone on speakerphone. He looked at the woman promptly. His eyes icy cold.
"Mary." This time it was more of a threat. She gave it up. She couldn't fight both the pain and the embarrassment.
"Vincent."
His heart stopped for a second. Then he was in control again. Had to be, couldn't give in to the feeling of panic. The best he could do for her right now was his best.
"Oh how nice, like a little reunion. And this time we can really be honest with each other. Did you fuck my fiancée?"
"Ex-fiancée." she brought out coldly. He just looked down at her coldly.
Stupid bitch.
Vincent was glad to hear her fighting spirit. And that she insisted he was her ex.
Keep it up, MK.
"No."
George got angry and slapped the flat of his hand on one of the small tables. Everyone winced.
"Stop lying to me. We all saw the way you looked at each other."

"If there had been more, wouldn't you have been sent more compromising photos? Couldn't you have been given more ammunition to haunt Marisa with?"

Marisa had hit her head, feeling sick, but she heard exactly what Vin was implying here. His hatred and disapproval were clear as day.

The other policemen around him, looked at each other worriedly. McDormant was too involved in this. Was he the negotiator or stirrer?

Vincent felt the stares and turned away from them. He knew exactly what he was doing here.

He had had to make a decision ten seconds ago. He had been faced with the dichotomy of this negotiation. He had been forced to take a side with which he could identify himself and also convince George that he was genuine. He would not be allowed to contradict himself, he would not be allowed to waver, he would not be allowed to change his views. This decision would facilitate and further the negotiation.

"It was you? You sent me those sick messages?" She straightened up as much as she could in anger. A sharp pain shot through her arm and shoulder, but she did not flinch. She was so full of anger she could see blindly. "You've been singing in my ear all this time, in your sleep? You bastard!"

Vincent held his breath tensely. Her reaction had been stronger than he had expected. He had to jump in immediately before George reacted to her challenging words.

"I have no interest in Marisa. Ask her. She's not my type."

The other just laughed hard. Fortunately, that statement had distracted him from Marisa. Marisa was also distracted and disappointed.

Right. Kick me when I'm already down.

That was *not* important right now.

"Yeah, I know what you mean. She left me cold too. I talked her into the idea that it was best that we waited until we got married. But actually, I didn't have the slightest interest in fucking her. She believed it."

George laughed.

Marisa turned pale. If that was possible, there wasn't that much colour left in her face. All these revelations were getting to her. Did they just have to talk about her sexual inabilities? She would like to sink into the ground right now.

No, stay strong. Stay awake!

"But you've been getting it on with Maureen, haven't you?" she only countered in disgust.

"Oh yes. *I* actually have to apologise to our Vincent on that one." He tilted his head, as if in remembrance. "She was good. I couldn't keep my hands off her. But I did try to create so many opportunities for you to be together. My photographer had really resisted playing along in the end."

Marisa furrowed her eyebrows in annoyance.

"Who did you get involved with? What's wrong with d-?"

Vincent had to respond. Marisa was too upset. His tactics were failing.

"George. One of your hostages needs medical attention. I want you to release her. In return, you can make a reasonable demand."

Marisa broke off. She took a deep, stressed breath. She was fed up with it all. Her pain was unbearable, but her employees came first. She tried to sort out her thoughts.

"Maggie? Maggie has heart problems. She's 58. Oh my God, George, you have to let her go. George, enough of this crap. She's completely innocent. She's got nothing to do with your craziness. Nobody does. You owe me this!"

"Shut up!"

George brought his knife to her neck. She fell silent immediately. The cold on her wounds hurt more than the actual cut. She wailed softly, her teeth chattering.

"George?"

In one fell swoop the conversation had turned, its joviality gone. The memory of the hopeless situation he was in came flooding back. He had forgotten all about the others. He had forgotten that there was no easy way out of this.

Shit.
"George, no further injuries -"
He pressed the button to hang up. He had to think.

23:16

Vincent held the mobile phone tensely in his hand. A trial could take hours. He knew that. He had more than patience to deal with it. He knew that. He had more techniques and ways he could use to stall. He knew that.

Jennifer assured him that the four women in the penguin room were safe. Tired, exhausted, impatient. At least calm enough. But he knew that their attitude, their state of mind could change at any moment. Calm could turn to anger. A controlled situation could turn into total chaos.

He could not relax.

"McDormant. This is police officer 6726, Christopher Stimson. He has something to add to the situation."

Vincent looked impatiently at the man in front of him. His manner was meek. He could not look Vincent in the eye.

"Stimson?"

"About a month ago, charges were filed against George Rashdy for sexual abuse and domestic violence."

"Show me." Vincent held out his hand for him to read through the file himself.

"I didn't process the report and I didn't open a file," Christopher replied.

Vincent shot him a look that was unmistakable.

"Details. All of them."

"Her story was weak. He would have pushed her against the wall and touched her indecently. Allegedly, he'd choked her cruelly. It wasn't rape. She had had an affair herself and he had been angry with her. In the end, she herself admitted that it had been her fault."

"Her fault?" Vincent's jaw dropped. An affair? The kiss? Her kiss, his advances had caused George to lose his control and show his true self. Shit.

"I remember it because it was a weird interview. What I had noticed was her scarf. She had her scarf on all the time, even though it was so uncomfortably hot in the office. Now I wonder if maybe the guy had left marks."

"You didn't investigate her?" His accusation shone through.

The policeman swallowed nervously. Now in retrospect, her story didn't seem so incredulous or irrelevant. He felt dirty.

"There should be no interpretations or questions from a policeman, a law officer. The way I hear it now, she told you clearly about her experience. The first thing you should have done was to look at her wounds and then arrest this scumbag. I will report this misconduct. This whole thing could have been avoided if you had done your job without question."

Vincent turned away from the officer who had been taken away. Himself, he was struggling with his anger. An anger directed at George.

But worst of all, and most inhibiting, was the blind anger at himself. He saw her right in front of him, with exactly the same scarf around her neck. That night, when she had come to the bar so late. He had misunderstood her, he had thought of only one thing. And had insulted her so much afterwards that they had parted under bad circumstances. The next day he had not been able to apologise to her, she had left early. All these weeks he had been regretting his missteps and looking for a way to forget her.

And then this complete idiot had not taken her complaint seriously.

It made him sick. This George was completely baseless.

With a condescending wave of his hand, he sent the other policeman away.

He had to get this hostage all out of this situation in one piece.

Now.

~

23:38

The phone rang. Over and over again.
George had just been restlessly pacing back and forth for the last few minutes. He was aggressively banging the flat of his hand against his own head. Talking to himself, admonishing himself, cursing himself. Argued with himself.
"I don't want to talk to you anymore!" he finally shouted into the phone.
A contradiction. He had answered the phone. He wanted to talk. He was confused.
His actions were most erratic at this point.
Vincent had to act. Make an offer he couldn't resist.
Take it slowly. He had to get the idea himself.
He needed to feel like he was in control.
"George, maybe we should talk about this face to face. Why don't you come out and we'll discuss what exactly is bothering you."
He shook his head fiercely, even though Vin couldn't see it. He knew what his silence meant.
"And Maggie? Can we talk to Maggie? We want to make sure she's all right."
George hesitated.
"They're fine. You should be worried about Marisa."
Vincent froze.
"What did you do?"
"Nothing more. She looks a little pale. Hey, Mary. Why so quiet?

Don't feel like messing with me anymore? Is that because you know I'm going to win?

"Fuck you."

Vincent breathed a sigh of relief. She was still there. And ready to fight.

He waited patiently. His self-control shone through.

"Why don't we make a deal, Mr Negotiator?"

"What do you propose?"

"I come up with the idea here and you get the credit. Gladly."

George smiled with icy eyes. He squatted down in front of his ex-fiancée. The latter's eyes reflected the same coldness. But she looked a little sickly. Even he could see that.

"I'll release the other hostages." Vincent nodded in agreement, already knowing what he wanted. "In their place, I want you here in nursery. Like you said. It would be better already to discuss these problems face to face."

The other policemen around him began shaking their heads and making gestures for him to end the conversation immediately.

"Agreed."

George hung up.

"No, out of the question. I will not support that decision. You're not going in there. You're too invested."

Vincent did not hear the arguments, already preparing himself spiritually for the exchange. His face-to-face negotiations brought certain risks. But also advantages. He had to focus on the benefits. He could not allow himself to be distracted by the others.

"Vincent, this is a mistake." His superior and friend put a hand on his shoulder. His eyes insistent as he took him aside. "Obviously there's more hatred between you and this man than you initially mentioned. This cannot end well."

"We need to avoid personal injury. We get four hostages in exchange - that's what I'm thinking about. Once I'm inside the nursery, I can get him to let Marisa go and give himself up."

"How, what are you going to do differently than on the phone?"

"I can stop him from continuing to take his anger and resentment out on her. And I can gauge his moods better. Eye contact is important when the criminal is unstable. You know I'm right."

He looked up at the first floor in the house. Everything was lit up. He had turned on the lights in every room. He wanted to see everything.

"Besides, I need to see how badly she's hurt."

Still not completely convinced, he arranged for Vincent to be fitted with a covert microphone and bug.

~

00:04

George ordered the four young women in the adjoining room to move the furniture off the door and unlock it. When no one stirred, he cut Marisa loose from the heater and dragged her outside the door. She could barely walk, her legs asleep, her wounds numbingly painful.

He tied her arms behind her back and she cried out involuntarily. Those darned cable ties cut deeper into her wrists. Her obvious pain made the others do as he asked.

When they opened the door for the first time since early evening, they saw Marisa first. Her blouse was soaked with blood, her forehead still crusted with blood. But worst of all was her skin colour. She looked like a ghost.

And then they saw the knife at her throat, and George right behind her.

Rachel drew in her breath in shock, the others started crying and got scared.

"Quiet! Quiet. Or I'll slit her throat." Quiet lashes persisted. "Take each other by the hand."

They hesitated no longer. With quivering limbs, Rachel reached for Maggie's hand, just as the other two girls held each other. Nerves raw, fear inhibiting.

"Look at me. Back against the wall." His orders were obeyed inch by inch. "Run down the stairs. Slowly. Wait at the bottom." With the last of their strength, they followed his instructions. Rachel slowly pulled the others down the stairs with her, her eyes always on the others and George, who followed just as slowly. Marisa pressed against her.

One by one they pressed their backs against the walls until they reached the front door.

George positioned himself behind the door, close enough that he could open and close the door. But also so that Marisa could be seen and how he was threatening her.

Finally, the door was opened, the four women ran to freedom and Vincent entered instead. Hands in the air. Door locked immediately.

00:35

He had years of experience in these scenarios. He had the self-control like no other policeman. He had successfully conducted hundreds of negotiations. His actions controlled and calculating. He was the best at his job. He knew how not to show weakness. Damn, one had practiced this very situation. How to save a friend, someone you knew.
But the moment he saw Marisa and the state she was in, his practised mask slipped. For a split second, panic gripped him at how much she had suffered and the numbing thought that he could not help her.
Her eyes fixed directly on him, a look he would never forget.
For weeks she had dreamed of an unexpected reunion. A hundred heart-warming moments had been represented in her romantic mind. Not once had it involved a hostage situation and bloodstained clothes. What did she have to look like? What would he think of her? Shit. This was not how she had wanted to see him again. For a split second, she felt all his emotions mirroring her. Like a blink, the moment was gone again.
Then Vincent straightened his shoulders and looked away from her. As much as he wanted to pull her into his arms, there were one or two other hurdles to overcome.
George smirked at the worried sight. He pressed the knife deeper against her neck. He gave the same instructions as to the nursery teachers before. He made a gesture to move towards the office. He had fleetingly pushed the furniture

aside so that it was easy to reach the heaters. Slowly but deliberately Vincent had to walk into the office and tie himself to the heater with the cable ties.

George checked his loops and tightened them. When he was sure he couldn't get away, he attended to Marisa, who stood beside him swaying and sweating. For a few seconds she had toyed with the idea of running away, or kicking him, or screaming. But she lacked even the strength to stand properly. Then he did the same to Marisa. With his ungentlemanly movements, he accidentally pressed on her deep cut on her arm, causing her to draw in a sharp breath. She had a hundred little spots in front of her eyes. She sank to her knees almost falling, her arm limp and the muscles twitching spasmodically and painfully at her side. She was as white as a sheet.

Vincent watched the older man as he stooped to the front door to make sure everything was well locked, and no one could enter unexpectedly. The knife still in his hand meant it took longer to lock everything. Vin took advantage of the moment to approach her. Marisa had leaned her head against the radiator, exhausted. She barely managed to keep her eyes open, but his nearness, his very existence, awakened excitement in her that she hadn't felt in a long time. She found a last bit of strength and looked at him.

He needed to examine her wounds, he needed to know that she had no life-threatening wounds. But he had no hands free.

"Where are you hurt?"

"That's where you start?" she countered, "Not 'I told you so'."

Vin glanced fleetingly at the other man, who was still dealing with the door and windows.

"I have a few other things to say."

"Like what?"

He was torn about how to respond to her. He should insist that they just talk neutrally about her wounds and he reassure her professionally. But she didn't need him to speak well to her. She was combative and feisty. And she was no ordinary hostage. She was not a textbook example. She was his ex-girlfriend.

MK.

"Why didn't you tell me what that sick guy did to you while you were on holiday?" he began now, completely incensed, and he moved closer to her. His voice low but loud and clear. Her eyes wide and tortured at the thought of that night. She was embarrassed that he had found out about it. "Why didn't you show me the news? Why did you suffer alone?"

"You weren't very welcoming."

"I'm sorry. I wish I could have helped you. I wish you could have opened up to me."

This time his voice changed. He was shaken, remorseful. So close to her.

She had suffered more damage to her head than she supposed after all. For at that moment, she felt very close to him. For those few seconds, her excitement was greater than the pain. It did not last long enough. The twitching in her arm snapped her out of the moment.

"I let you down then. I can't -"

She felt sick.

"Let's talk about it later." she said quickly. This was not a subject she could discuss.

"I was only thinking of you."

"Do you think I'm going to croak any minute? If not, tell me later how much you love me and you want to marry me." Her voice weak, a small smile on her lips as she could barely keep her eyes open.

"I didn't mean to - "

"Well, you two lovebirds."

George smiled coldly, but there was only hatred and distaste in his eyes. "How nice that you can finally be close."

Vincent had to look away. His worries were eating at his focus. He had to finish. Marisa would not hold out any longer.

"Why are we here?" began Vin, negotiating.

George sat down on her swivel chair, exhausted, and twisted back and forth.

"You didn't like the look of her."

Vincent looked at him, unimpressed.
"She needs medical attention."
"No. She's argumentative enough."
"Because you make me sick." she retorted. She fought the desire to just close her eyes and sleep. She had to pull herself together, no way was she going to show him how much she was wavering. And even less did she want Vin to see her struggling not to burst into tears.
George didn't like her attitude. Did she think because her lover was there now that she could defiantly come to him? In one movement he grabbed her hair and aggressively pulled her head back. He leaned right into her face and his look was warning enough.
"George!" Vincent jumped up, but the zip ties, those effective things, kept him from being able to protect Marisa. He could only watch as he tortured her.
George drew his knife sharply along her neck. He ignored every word, every question from Vin. He saw the sharp blade leave a thin red line. The blood dripped. He was in a trance.
"George. Whatever you have done, we can find a solution. George, your next actions, the choices you make, will mean your own fate. If you continue to hurt Marisa, I can't help you. Can't negotiate with you."
She breathed haltingly, remaining as still as possible. Her instinct was to pull away from him as much as possible, but instead she didn't move an inch, allowing him to cut her with the knife. Her eyes fixed on him, direct and unafraid. She challenged him.
She swallowed nervously.
"I'll ask one last time. What happened between you?" His gaze just as direct on her. His concentration only on her reaction.
Vincent's body tensed. A hundred solutions bounced back and forth in his mind. He had to make the next decision. Anticipate how George would react to which response. He had to choose who to protect.
"We already knew each other, before the holiday."

George paused immediately. His surprise so great that he stepped away from her.

Marisa's heart was pounding in her throat. Her adrenaline so high, the pain so deep, she couldn't think straight. Relief swept through her limbs.

"I'm all ears."

"She's my ex."

Her ex-fiancé couldn't believe it. What?

"Explain."

With every crisis situation, one always arrived at a crossroads. His coldness, arrogance gone. Remorse and honesty instead.

Vincent straightened up as much as he could. From the corner of his eye, he saw Marisa's condition worsen. Her eyes barely open, her body limp beside the heater. The sweat on her clammy skin.

"Marisa was my first girlfriend. Seventeen years ago."

"Do you still love her?"

George looked at him intensely, his eyes narrowed slightly.

She heard Vin finally speak the truth. It finally came out what had connected Vin and Marisa all this time. She noticed how his attitude towards her ex-fiancé had changed. In the beginning, their conversations had been icy and aggressive, challenging and ruthless. Now the complete opposite.

Marisa realised how Vincent was able to change his tactics, his technique, just like that. Who would have thought that after 17 years he was still analysing other people? So, he had been following people's psychology after all. Good for him, she thought contentedly. His life had made sense after all, according to her.

"Do you love her?" repeated George impatiently.

"You never forget your first love. Part of it stays with you forever."

Marisa felt like she was in a dream. She no longer knew if this situation was real or in her head. His words were too unexpected, not true to the truth. George, however, seemed to believe everything he said. He listened to him intently.

With a happy smile on her lips, she finally gave in to the urge and closed her eyes. Vincent saw the moment when she lost consciousness. He noticed at the same time how George followed his conversation. He seized the moment.
"What do you mean?"
George sat down on the chair in front of him, without giving much thought to how cold-blooded his movements were, he wiped the knife on his jeans. The blood, Marisa's blood, was on him and he didn't care one bit.
Vincent had to push those dark thoughts far away from him.
"She was my first... and last friend. No one after her was like her. No relationship, no affair was comparable to what we had. As teenagers." Vincent remained calm and serious in his statements, his eyes tracking George's every word. His mind interpreted his reaction at each assertion. "Marisa is compassionate, quick-tempered and sincere. She is real, her love is real."
"You didn't have an affair?"
"I kissed her. Nothing more." His honesty finally came through. "I wanted more; I can't deny that. But Marisa kept her promise to you."
George was silent. He was lost in his own thoughts.
The crisis navigator did not hesitate for a moment. He straightened up, wanting to take advantage of the moment of familiarity.
"I need to feel her pulse. I need to make sure she's okay. George? A hand loose is no danger to you." His request clear, but friendly.
The other looked up, then at the motionless woman by the radiator. Then at the knife in his hand. Without much thought, he cut a loop. It stopped threateningly in front of him. He didn't quite trust him that much.
Vincent stepped as far as he could towards her, stretched his free arm and put his hand to her neck. Her skin cool, damp. He waited half an eternity until he finally felt the pulse under his fingers. Faint, but it was there. Tenderly he stroked her

forehead, the loose strands of hair from the sticky wound. The skin so damp and cold. His fingertips ran gently over her cheeks. He examined her wound as far as he could. Her arm looked funny lying limp against the radiator. Until he realised it was her shoulder hanging down. It was a dislocated shoulder; he knew from his own experience how painful that was. Only then did he discover the deep gash in her forearm. He tried to move closer, the open area was still bleeding. No wonder she lay powerless on the floor. She was losing more blood with every minute she was here.
"That's enough."
George gestured for Vincent to step back again. He did not let go of Marisa.
"She needs help, George. Bandages, snacks. We need to help her."
"Where am I going to get that?" he said defiantly. He had thought of everything, but injuries had not been anticipated.
"This is a nursery. There will be biscuits and first aid kits here." Vincent quickly looked around the room. Everything was carefully lined up and tucked away. On the other side of the desk and shelves, was a small anteroom adjoining the next room. It looked like the kitchen. "The kitchen."
George hesitated. Then reluctantly he walked through the small anteroom and to the kitchen, not taking his eyes off Vincent. Carelessly, he rummaged around in the cupboards. He found some juice and a few biscuits. Next to the cooker he found first aid kits. He grabbed one and threw the things he found towards Vincent. He tried to get the bandages out, but it was impossible with one arm tied tightly to the radiator.
"George. I need both arms."
The other shook his head coldly.
"George. I want to help her. I have to help her. My job is to protect everyone from Harm. You have to protect yourself from making her condition worse."
He hesitated a moment longer. Everything seemed so hopeless and futile at that moment. He thought convulsively. Then he

fetched a pair of scissors from her office, he stood behind Marisa and pulled her head up, the knife at her throat. She didn't move, completely unconscious. Vincent had to look away.

"One false move and I'll end her suffering." His eyes wild, Vincent didn't doubt his threats one bit. George shoved the scissors in his direction.

Then Vincent made quick and deft work of treating her wound. The pressure, the movements caused pain and Marisa stirred. She opened her eyes, tired and suffering. She saw Vincent nimbly wrap her forearm. Then fastened it with a plaster.

"Hi." she said softly. Her eyes shone for the first time since he had stepped into the nursery. "It wasn't a dream after all. You're here."

It broke his heart that he couldn't return her smile. He had to think of her well-being, of the unpredictable hostage-taker. His joy was unimportant.

He concentrated on holding the carton of juice to her lips. His face serious.

Despite the situation she was in, she felt deep anger rising within her. This man had the most infuriating self-control ever. He was always so fucking restrained. She could have shaken him. A smile, a little fucking smile would that have been too much?

The sugar brought her distraction. Yummy. She felt her strength come back a little. She straightened a little and felt the knife against her neck.

Ah, shit. George. Hostage. Danger. Pain.

She realised why Vincent didn't have time to flirt with her.

"That's enough. She's awake again. So just aggravated assault again."

Among other things, Vincent thought to himself. But yes, thankfully Marisa was feeling better at that moment. Some colour crept back into her cheeks.

George forced Vincent back to the heater. He put the cable tie back on, this time without help from George, who was still standing over Marisa with the knife.

1:12

The blush on her face didn't stay for long. Time ticked away.
"Why are we here?"
George paced back and forth impatiently. He ran his hand over his head in agitation. With that question, he turned abruptly, holding the knife threateningly in Marisa's face.
"Because of her! Because of you! Because of this whole fucking skiing holiday!" His anger exploded at the thought. He looked at her urgently, Vincent ready to jump should George dare make a short-circuited move.
"George. I hear you. Neither of us enjoyed the holiday. It was torture."
"The time, patience and friendly posturing I had invested in this relationship. I spent every spare minute trying to win her over." His anger was coming through again now, his frustration. The knife raised. "I had it all planned out, had her in the palm of my hand. She stayed away from you as long as I reminded her regularly who she wanted."
"By sending her threatening messages?"
"I had to remind her of her promise. It worked. She stayed by my side."
George eased away from her. He continued to pace the room, upset.
"But you dared to break up with me. You dared to say I was leaving you cold. Fuck you, Mary! As if this arrangement had anything to do with sex." He laughed out loud. "But I showed you that night."

She didn't want to remember the hours of pure fear. The panic, the helplessness of being completely at the mercy of a stronger man was terrible. She had had nightmares for weeks. That evening had been one of the worst experiences in her life. Even now she could not stop the trembling.

George cast his gaze over Vincent in a flash. He wanted to see him suffer as much as Marisa.

"I enjoyed my time with her. She tried to fight back, but it was useless."

The crisis navigator was silent, planning the next move, having to bring the madman back down to earth. The ex-boyfriend, the man, was furious. The man wanted to punch him in the face so he wouldn't get up again.

"So if you didn't care about sex, why did you want to marry her? Money?"

George looked at him in wonder, as if the answer wasn't obvious. He spread his arms wide and turned slowly in a circle. "I needed her for her nursery."

Marisa leaned her head against the radiator. Her strength was failing.

"He's going after the children," she muttered coldly. Her disgust spoke for itself.

"Shut up. I'm not a child molester. Can you trust me to do that?"

She just stared at him. The look on her face said it all. She would gladly spit in his face if she still felt any strength and vigour.

"Look around you. I could trust you with anything right now."

He shook his head in annoyance. He had already said so much, why not the truth.

"Marisa and her hundred rules! She won't let any parents or acquaintances into her shit-loving nursery. I had to get her to marry me first so I could finally be allowed into that special circle too. Into her office. Into her realm."

Vincent watched every step, every movement. He stood ready to intervene, he didn't sit down. He didn't move. He waited for the right moment.

"And then?"
George looked at him. This time with pain in his eyes. This time with remorse and the utmost regret. Frail. Sad. Human
"Then I could finally see my daughter again."
Silence.
Marisa opened her mouth in surprise, immediately thinking of all her children registered here. None of them had listed him as the father. She hadn't known he had a child. That he had been married. Vincent had been right again. He had a past.
Vincent gathered his thoughts, had to get George to talk, to distract him from his anger. What was even worse was sadness. The expression on his face was anguished. These emotions brought involuntary behaviour in some hostage-takers. His pulse was racing. The knife was still in his hand, he was too close to Marisa.
Shit.
"What's your daughter's name?" she asked cautiously. Her eyes sincere.
"Clara."
"In the penguin room." she added softly. She smiled slightly. "Clara is very bright. She loves to play with the dolls."
Marisa had tried to add a few positive experiences to distract him. She saw a little innocent girl in front of her, with brown hair put in two braids. And mostly she was wearing a pink ballerina dress. She was so sweet and thoughtful.
Her well-meaning remarks backfired.
George gritted his teeth angrily. He walked slowly towards her. "I don't know all that because I'm not allowed to see her anymore. Because of one night, because of one slip, one moment of anger and my wife cut me out of her life. Because of a few minutes I am no longer allowed to visit my daughter, hold. I am cut out of her life and you make it impossible for me to see her. Because of you I have lost everything."
Vincent had to intervene.
"I know how you feel. Losing a child, losing hope for a future with the child, gone, just taken from you." He spoke sincerely

to her, his voice controlled. "I lost a child too. I know how you feel."

George paused, the knife at Marisa's throat. Her eyes wide, her breathing brisk. She saw it was going to end any moment. For her. The anger, the hatred clear in his eyes. Then the turmoil, the remorse, the grief.

"Oh really. How fitting."

"I never met her or him. Everything had gone well in the pregnancy; we'd only seen the ultrasound three weeks before. And then the miscarriage. The visit to the sterile, depressing hospital. Still clinging to the hope that the blood, the pain meant nothing. Hoping that today's medicine was good enough to save our baby."

Marisa looked down at the floor, stricken. Her heart broke at his words. She could feel the pain right then. She felt the fear, the hope. He described the day as accurately as if he had been there. He hadn't been there .... had he?

George listened intently, believing the quiet, sad words.

"We were robbed of the chance to hold the baby. To love our baby unconditionally. The loss, the emptiness. The stark change from anticipation to the deepest grief. I can understand that. "

No one moved.

Vincent felt that this was the beginning of the end. His heart began to pound.

"George, I can help you. I can talk to the lawyer about how well you responded to our negotiation. How you kept your agreements with the other hostages. And how you allowed me to examine Marisa. I can help you. .... But not if you hurt her. You don't want her life on your conscience, do you?" His words came through to him slowly. The knife trembled, his hand so tense. "You can see your daughter again in a while. You'll have to pay a fine, for the last few hours. But if this gets out of hand now, if you lose control now, you'll have to spend the rest of your life behind bars. Your daughter will never know you."

George hesitated.

Silence.

Fear. Hope. Anger. Grief.

The knife fell to the floor. Vincent withdrew his hands from the loose loops he had failed to tighten the second time. He stepped behind George. With one foot he kicked the knife out of reach. He grabbed one or two of the cable ties, his gaze focused and serious.

"Mary doesn't bear all the blame."

~

1:59

The words were hardly spoken that Vincent recognised his mood and intentions. Too late.
George swung with a force towards Vincent and rammed his whole body against the negotiator. With a crashing sound they crashed into the shelf in their office. Books, folders, paper fell down. Vincent grabbed George's upper arms to push him back with more force. In his rage, George overcame the younger man and found in himself a strength he did not normally possess. He pulled him back with him into the anteroom where Marisa was panicking, trying to reach the knife. If only she could finally cut those cable ties....
George threw himself with all his weight against Vincent and they both landed on the floor next to their feet. Her ex-fiancé felt a rage that blinded and deafened him. Her ex-boyfriend avoided the worst of the blows to his face, with his nimble movements.
With all her might, wherever it came from, Marisa George kicked his head. He hadn't seen it coming, he'd been so caught up in the rush that he hadn't seen anything or anyone but Vincent McDormant.
Even so, her kick made him let go of Vincent out of surprise, the distraction was only split seconds long. With a fury he had had to suppress for weeks, he stood up and walked towards Marisa, hands clenched. Fire in his eyes.
Like a good negotiator would, he had anticipated this move

and Vin jumped up and grabbed the man around the neck from behind and kicked him viciously in the back of the knee. He crumpled and the pain and shock gave Vincent the upper hand. Immediately he had forced him ungently to the floor, his hands twisted behind his back, his knee between his shoulder plates.

At the same moment the front door crashed to the floor.

"Police. Police. Don't move."

Several policemen in protective gear entered briskly. Weapons in hand. They instantly arrested her ex-fiancé on the floor, who was crying bitterly.

Vincent turned to Marisa, with the knife he freed her from the heater as carefully as he could. Her wrists were bloody, her arm weak. Gently he lifted her arm into her lap.

She was free.

Their eyes crossed, a thousand words, a hundred emotions all at once. He just wanted to hold her at that moment, to kiss her. But his training spoke against it with every syllable. She was and remained the hostage he had to protect, even if from himself. He wanted to tell her so much, explain so much. But he did not know where to begin.

"What do you remember?"

"I only remember -" She broke off. So many things had been said. All this time Vincent had had the upper hand. A success he had earned. His strategies had worked. Whatever he had said had been right.

And yet she could not suppress her anger.

"It was clever to exploit our past to get him around. Heartless and calculated."

Vincent wanted to answer something, wanted to deny that this had all been a callous tactic. Yes, he had had to remain neutral as a negotiator. But had he been?

"Callous? You were lying half unconscious on the floor. He had cut you so deep you were bleeding out. I had to intervene."

"But not with our baby." she hissed back, disappointed. "How did you even know all those things?"

"I had come back." he replied quietly. "The day that ... I was in the hospital. Your father told me everything that had happened and how you were much better off in Simon's arms. Didn't he tell you about our cold conversation?"

Marisa stared at him. Her head was pounding, her muscles twitching. Everything was jumbled. He had been there? He had talked to her father? He hadn't mentioned a word of it. Never. Why not?

"Simon?"

"Yes, your new boyfriend. You didn't wait two weeks before you found yourself a new one."

"That doesn't give you the right to take advantage of her in such a cold-blooded way."

Finally, the emergency doctor arrived, the medical help she needed right now more than this pointless argument. He didn't get to say more. He thought it was crazy that they had to argue at this moment. Instead of embracing and rejoicing.

The emergency doctor stepped past him to get to his patient. He wasted no time and set about examining Marisa on the spot.

Vincent stood half apart, his gaze still locked on hers.

An officer approached him to discuss the procedure, the night, the endless hours.

"I still have to make my debriefing statement. I can't-"

Her face was pale, weak from all the excitement, she rested her head against the radiator again and smiled weakly.

"Take care, Vin."

"MK..." His voice pleading. She closed her eyes.

It was over.

~

Marisa doubled over in pain. It paralysed her whole body. She felt sick, dizzy. She became frightened. Within a few hours, the cramps intensified, contracting her abdomen in agony. She made it to the bathroom where she discovered the blood.

In her panic, she called her father and mother. A little later they were at the hospital.

There was not much they could do. Despite the fact that they had just seen her ultrasound. Despite the fact that they had told her everything was going well.

She cried when they told her she had lost the baby. Much later she found out it had been a little girl. The curettage was painful and brought a lot of heartache. It made everything clear and final. She felt so alone. As if it had only ever happened to her. How unfair! What had she done wrong? What had she done that her baby couldn't take it?

Emotions poured in on her incessantly. Guilt. Fear. Grief.

And relief.

~

Two weeks later

The world was healing.
Her new entrance door to her restored nursery looked great. Solid, clean and impassable. Her security cameras had just finished being installed. From next week, she would open her doors again. By Monday, everything had to be forgotten so that she could finally sleep again. She had to be able to stand confidently in front of the parents and say that there would never be another incident like this and all her children were safe here. It had been a sad event. Something out of her own control. People could confidently register their children with her again. And work here.
Marisa Keach watched the man descend the ladder again. The camera was mounted right next to the entrance, so she could see exactly who was arriving and leaving the building.
They had done a great job. The cleaning company had thoroughly cleaned all the rooms and the furniture and fittings had been replaced by the insurance company.
She was ready. So were the majority of her employees, thankfully. And half of her children were re-registered for Monday. The rest needed time. A lot of time.
And in time, she wouldn't feel so lost. So broken from the loss. The thought of not seeing Vincent again almost killed her. In the same breath, she was glad. Now she could finally focus on her career, her children. She could heal, forget and just not feel anything. That was also positive. She didn't need his cold eyes and distaste.

"I sanction these security arrangements."
Marisa's heart stopped for a few seconds. There was no mistaking his voice. Everything in her awoke. She was as nervous as a teenager in one fell swoop. It took her a moment before she turned to face him.

The laceration on her forehead had been as good as healed, if you looked closely you could see traces of yellow marks and find a small scar. Her arm seemed better, but her cardigan covered her scars.

His hair was wild, his eyes as blue as she could lose herself in them. He was wearing normal clothes again, jeans and a jacket. He no longer looked like the crisis navigator who had saved her life.

But had also destroyed her life completely in the first place and had talked her into his negotiations in an ice-cold way. *Don't forget that, MK!*

For a moment there was silence. As long as she had dreamed of seeing him again, she had also remembered all the reasons why it was better not to see him again.

But try as she might, she could not remember any reason exactly.

The other man now approached her and discussed the last details with her, showed her how everything worked. As innocent as the whole thing was, Vin watched intently. He didn't trust this guy. He had a bad feeling-.

He stopped his thoughts. What the hell was wrong with him? Years of training and suddenly he saw psychopaths walking all over the place, especially if they were men who were around Marisa. Hadn't he said the whole thing before? His senses were totally confused when he had her in front of him.

Jealousy didn't suit him.

After the man had packed all his things into the van, they were alone again.

"The house looks very different in the light."

Ouch. That wasn't the best start to a stress-free conversation.

"What brings you here?" She ignored his false start.

The new front door opened, and Rachel came out of the nursery. She immediately recognised the man in front of her, even without a stab waistcoat and mobile phone to his ear. First worry, then joy and gratitude on her face.

For a few minutes they chatted amiably while Marisa stood uneasily by. He could talk so easily and freely with other women. He laughed blithely and his eyes sparkled. Had he ever looked at her so openly and happily?

Stop it! None of this matters at all. She admonished herself as her thoughts betrayed her.

She reminded herself that she still had a lot of work to do and no time for pointless, unpromising conversations.

Finally, Marisa arranged with Rachel the next tasks and what the other nursery teachers should do before finally saying goodbye to Vincent herself.

"I'll be right there to help you." Her gaze impatient, her mind totally confused as to what to focus on. Those blue eyes. Oh man. "So, why are you here?"

"I'm here to check on your well-being. Routine visit." That was exactly why he was here, as usual. He had so often visited victims afterwards to chat with them, to tell them how much they had helped him. It was routine for him.

But today that routine fell flat.

Marisa looked at him quizzically. And said nothing, still bitter. She looked uneasily at her wristwatch. His presence was unbearable. He looked stunning in the daytime. But his behaviour had been unforgivable. He smelled so good of aftershave. But he had let her down then. He was her first great love. And always would be.

But every time she saw him, she was reminded of that day in the hospital. And now he had passed that memory off as his own.

He was offended by her impatience.

"Do you have an appointment?"

"Yes, an appointment." she replied curtly.

His look showed pure disapproval.

She turned to him with a jerk. Her disapproval just as obvious.
"Do you have anything to say about that?"
Vincent gritted his teeth. He wanted to say more than something, he wanted to shake and shake her. Her eyes sparked fire. He was on thin ice.
"Did you meet him at the gym too?"
"Well, here comes the telling off at last. Routine visit, my ass. You couldn't pass up the opportunity to come here to tell me that you told me so right away."
"And once again, you couldn't wait two weeks to find a new boyfriend."
Marisa couldn't believe it. She saw red!
That bastard. That fucking bastard. How dare he?
She looked around uncomfortably, worried that her employees had seen her here arguing with him. She pointed angrily to a small outbuilding where the nursery teachers spent their breaks. It was out of sight and earshot. She ran ahead, after a short while he followed her in. Locked the door behind her. Ready for her wrath.
"I can't believe I should be defending myself now, too. My life, my choices. You left then and never got back in touch. Now we've had no contact for years. You couldn't care less who I'm seeing or not seeing."
"Not when I just saved you from a psychopath you were going to *marry*."
"I would have married him too if you hadn't kissed me."
"So, all this has been my fault? Are you saying that you didn't want it too?"
Marisa fell silent, concerned. Somehow they had left out the real problem and were talking about a completely different subject.
"You can't have it both ways. You don't want a relationship with me, fine. But then equally you can't expect me not to look for someone I can be happy with."
Vincent said nothing in reply.
Marisa hesitated.

"That night ...... this whole, long experience has left scars. I'm scared when I open the door. I'm scared when I close the door..... But I can't let that fear win." Her words sounded powerful, frighteningly honest. "I promise you I won't go online and meet wild strangers. I'll be careful."
"I can't ask you to do that." He admitted resignedly.
"You'd never know if I'd stick to it." She shrugged slightly.
"Quite the opposite. I know what a promise means to you."
Silence.
For the first time they were aware that they were alone. In a secluded room, with no connections. It became uncomfortable.
"Why are you really here?"
Vincent ran his hand through his hair, tired and uncomfortable. His gaze on the hard floor. He seemed almost shy.
"We should have sex."
Marisa almost laughed out loud. But his demeanour was funny. His words so unrehearsed. Not at all like the negotiator. Not at all like the Vin she knew.
"I think if we do it this once, then we can put it out of our minds. And move on with our lives. I mean, my thoughts, my head -"
He realised he had been talking without stopping. And what nonsense. Maybe she didn't have the same fantasies at all. Maybe he had just told himself that she was interested. He was suddenly not sure what he was doing here. She had just been in a crisis situation, why should she-.
Marisa did not think for a second. She stepped up to him and pulled his head down to hers. Her kiss was hot. She held nothing back. Her lips were soft and sweet. She pressed herself against him, feeling him respond to her on the spot. His hands framed her neck, and he pulled her closer. His desire revealed, his tongue teased her to the extreme. She could barely stand, wanting to drop to her knees. The pleasure came crashing down on her. Her pulse raced; she was floating. His hands

wandered down to her cardigan, went under her jumper. Her skin so hot, so soft. He pressed her against him, wanting more, to feel all of her. She responded to his touch, laying back in her head as he kissed the back of her neck. His caresses were driving her crazy. He sucked lightly on her skin. She moaned softly. It took her senses away, she wanted to kiss him back. Wanted to arouse him as much as he aroused her. She lifted her arms to wrap them around his neck and pull him against her.
Her careless movement brought an unexpected sting to her shoulder, and she jerked back.
Vincent sensed her surprise and broke away from her.
His eyes so dark, his breathing unbridled. A few more minutes and he would have totally lost control of himself.
Marisa didn't feel any different. She turned away from him, took a step back. She was filled with lust and desire. That kiss had taken them both totally by surprise.
She swallowed nervously. Sex. All he wanted was sex. She knew that. She knew exactly how it would end and how broken it would make her. And yet she couldn't think straight.
"It really couldn't have been dinner first?"
They both laughed at her comment.
Vincent ran his hand through his wild hair. This woman was driving him crazy. He was ready to relax his rules a little.
"I'm staying at the Saxony Hotel. They also offer dinner. And breakfast. Come at eight."
With these words he left the outbuilding.

~

No, she would not go there.
No, she wouldn't drop everything for him.
No, she wouldn't give him that satisfaction.
Yes, she was going to sleep with him.
Shit. Damn.
No, she wouldn't get all dressed up for him, though.
Marisa chose jeans and a blouse. With the wound and the bandage on her arm, her shoulder at that, making some movements still impossible, she had no choice. She wouldn't put on extra make-up or style her hair. She went as she was. Plain, boring Marisa.
Who was totally excited, like a teenager and could hardly keep her thoughts under control.
Deliberately late, she entered the fine hotel, making her way to the bar without hesitation or further thought. It was too late to turn back. It was too late to save herself.
He stood at the bar, his back to her. His jeans fit perfectly, his top tight and showing. Oh man.
Could they skip dinner and get it over with?
With as much confidence as she could manage, she stood at his side and ordered a glass of wine. Somehow she had to calm down. Alcohol might have been a help or a hurdle.
When Vincent turned to her, her heart stopped. Everything inside her was full of butterflies. The excitement was almost unbearable. She looked him straight in the eye. He leaned towards her and gave her a soft kiss on the cheek.
And she almost fell to her knees with excitement. But she remained standing.

"At last." he whispered in her ear. She got goosebumps at his nearness, at the warmth of his body. His voice so excitingly hot.

A single word that said so much.

Careful to keep a safe distance from her, and not touch her by accident, he directed her to the restaurant. Slightly disappointed that he actually wanted to eat first, she walked with him to the table he had reserved. She didn't feel hungry, at least not for food.

Finally they were seated and Marisa could relax. The worst was over. She was here, had greeted him. What other hurdles did she have to get through? The sex.

She felt sick. Could she still do that? Did he have great expectations? In any case, he had gained more experience than she in this field, what if she wasn't the least bit good enough? Shit.

Vincent didn't seem to notice her nervousness, or address it. Instead, he steered the topic to completely neutral conversations. And she found herself gradually relaxing.

She was interested in how he had become a crisis navigator. All those years after originally studying psychology, he had also trained as a police officer. Also gained a Masters Degree in Criminology. Years later, he was the expert in his field.

Their conversation was easy. Like before, they could talk about anything and nothing.

"George has made his confession."

Marisa looked at him quietly. She had not expected this abrupt change of subject.

"What drove him to do all that?"

"One night. He had lost control of himself for one night with his ex-wife. He had been of the opinion that she had cheated on him."

That sounded familiar.

She put a trembling hand to her mouth. Hadn't she herself been the bad one here?

"He had been disappointed by everyone. He just wanted to be

happy."
Vincent shook his head.
"He can't force his happiness. He can't rape his wife and stalk her afterwards to see who she's hanging out with."
Marisa was speechless. It all sounded like déjà vu, only with herself in the lead role. Guilt was setting in.
"He had been right." she said quietly. She agreed, but her guilty conscience was bothering her.
"About what?"
"I had cheated on him. I had betrayed him."
Vincent propped himself up on his arms and leaned towards her. He saw her dilemma, could literally read her guilt.
"No, you didn't even touch me." he insisted earnestly. He could remember that painfully. She had not come near him. It had driven him out of his mind. The days near her, the long nights in the room next to her.
"Actually, it did. Every time, in my head. In my dreams. I wanted you to kiss me."
She dropped her gaze.
Silence.
He didn't know how to act. One touch and it was over with his self-control. Did she want the same thing he did? Was she reacting to him because she wanted him or because she was still suffering the effects of her experience with George? He could not, and did not, read her.
"Had she cheated on him?"
"No. Even after all this time after the break-up, he found no evidence that she was with anyone else. All the photos and videos he had taken of her had been innocent."
She looked up, confused and unsure.
"How could he have taken those photos of us? He wasn't a good skier. He couldn't have followed us."
Vincent realised that she had obviously forgotten that detail from the night of the hostage situation, or other things had been more important to focus on.
"He had blackmailed Mitchell. He was the ladies' man who,

unfortunately, also enjoyed himself with married women. George saw him one night, with the manager's wife, and used that information to get Mitch to always assign us together as ski partners and then follow us."

She shook her head in disappointment and shock.

"No wonder his mood seemed so depressed at the end and so cold. He could barely look me in the eye." she explained to herself. And then the next thought. "And that's why the last photo was of George and Maureen. He was trying to help me."

Vincent looked at her in surprise. He hadn't seen the photo during his investigations. She hadn't shown it to him either. Neither had any of the messages. She had wanted to carry everything on her shoulders alone. He leaned back. From this close, he could smell her shampoo. It distracted him from the conversation.

"Why did the attack come only now?"

"His wife had left him, and he began to threaten her emotionally with ice-cold messages... as he did you. With his extensive IT knowledge, he was able to hide his IP address, and pre-program messages to send then when he was by your side. And hers originally.

After a few months came the realisation that it was him. She sued for a no-contact order. And three weeks ago, she got sole custody. That was the straw that broke the camel's back."

"So cunning." She felt cold at the thought of all he had ruthlessly done to his wife and to her.

"He had the whole thing really well planned out. Once you married him, he would have had open access to the nursery. One day he would have disappeared with Clara."

"He really just wanted to see his daughter."

Vincent nodded his head slightly. He played with his glass. His thoughts, his fantasies elsewhere right now. She looked adorable. Her hair in a knot, as always. Her eyes so brown and clear, as always. And yet as if he had never seen her before.

"So, you were right. He didn't want to marry me." she finally said. She suddenly felt strange. His gaze went right to her skin.

"You didn't want to marry him either." he returned. His eyes sparkled. "There was nothing there to connect you."
He leaned forward slightly. With his index finger, he touched her hand ever so gently.
"Nothing that ...turned you on."
Her stomach turned. Her pulse raced.
She put her napkin beside her plate and rose resolutely. He looked up at her.
"Room number?"
Vin stood up too, right in front of her. So strong and attractively sexy. Marisa bit her lower lip at the sight of him, at the desire in his eyes.
He took her hand and slowly but deliberately pulled her with him.
The lift took half an eternity to arrive. They stepped inside. How could five floors take so long. His hand in hers was not enough. It was all so absurd, so crazy.
Marisa laughed softly and Vincent turned to her. At that moment he had never seen anything more beautiful than the gleam in her eyes. He smiled back.
They made it to his room. Vincent switched on the light.
Suddenly unsure, nervous or just caught off guard by the whole thing, he just looked at her.
"Is this a good idea?" he asked suddenly.
Marisa frowned for a moment. Then she just kissed him, holding nothing back. As if she still had the strength and the mind to leave now.
Vincent needed only a millisecond to react to her hot kiss. He had to restrain himself, had to find some self-control, but her touch was so arousingly beautiful. Her tongue played with him, exciting him to the extreme, he pressed her against the door, framed her face with his hands and deepened the kiss. Marisa felt dizzy. She was glad he had her in his hold. She ran her hands under his top and felt his skin. Wanted to see more of him, feel more. Vincent's hot lips wandered down her neck, he too found his way under her blouse, to her breasts. She

made soft noises the longer his caresses lasted. He detached himself from her a little, completely out of breath, his gaze full of lust and desire, which only excited her more. He took his time undoing the little buttons on her blouse, carefully and agonisingly slowly brushing it off her body. He saw the bandage, and he kissed her arm so tenderly that she could hardly stand it.

"MK." he breathed into her neck.

Without a second thought, she pushed him onto his bed and did the same. There was no stopping her now. There was no more endless self-control here.

Finally.

~

It was dark in the room, fortunately. She could hide her dilemma and confusion in her mind.
It had been unique. They had been good then, but now... He had learned a lot. The bad thoughts wanted to come up and ruin this moment. Why couldn't her mind at least allow her three, four hours where she didn't have to think about anything else?
"Do you sleep with all your victims?"
Vincent propped himself up on his elbow. His gaze on her, hot and seductive. He couldn't look at her enough. Her hair wild now, her skin so soft and revealed.
"That wouldn't be professional."
"Of course not." she teased him. And yet she felt she was one of many.
"I tried to stop us."
"Not very hard."
His eyes looked at her in confusion. Suddenly he wasn't sure he'd misread her signals.
"Shit. I wasn't trying to take advantage of you. I -"
She stopped him with her lips. Teasingly, sincerely.
"Don't think. Respond."
She looked up at him. The dark desire in her eyes. She stroked his bare chest tenderly, down to his belly button, lower.
He said nothing.
Instead, his lips came down delightfully on hers. His kiss possessive, deep. She responded to him without thinking. At least for the moment. He loved her over and over again. Until at last they fell into an exhausted sleep.
After all this time, she had longed for his body so much that

she had completely forgotten who Vincent was.
Vincent McDormant was *the* man for a night. But not for life.
In the early hours of the morning, she slipped out of his room.
And was devastated.

~

He should be glad that the situation was the way it was. It should be a load off his mind that she had made the decision to leave. It would have been really complicated and stressful if he had had to tell her in the morning that it had only been sex. Otherwise, it was always him who had to think of an excuse. He had left many a warm bed without saying anything. He always had a reason in the back of his mind why he would have to leave the next day.

He should really be glad that Marisa was no longer there.

Problem solved. Life could go on. They had slept together once, or rather several times, and now they knew what it was like again. They went on.

The problem was that this had never happened to him before. Or rather only once before, that he couldn't forget the sex. And the woman too.

Once, 17 years ago.

~

She stood motionless by the door. Her new camera by the entrance had worked. She saw that it was Vincent standing outside her nursery in the middle of the day, on a Saturday at that. What she couldn't understand was why? And whether she wanted to open the door....

Marisa gave in at the second ring. She stepped out to him, not letting him in. Just as the rules had intended. Which had almost cost her her life, but in the same breath meant that a little innocent girl had been protected.

The man in front of her did not look particularly thrilled. The fact was that he looked really pissed off. His look changed instantly when he saw her in front of him. For the moment he saw her naked and completely surrendered beneath him. Her brown eyes so warm and full of lust.

It hadn't been enough.

"Good to see you." she said dryly.

"Really? It doesn't look like it at all."

"Bet that?"

Before he could stop himself, he kissed her on the mouth. Her lips so sweet, so tender. She was quite surprised and grabbed his arms to keep her balance. This man! What was he doing to her. After a few long seconds she was finally able to think clearly again, and she pushed him away from her. With a heavy heart.

This time his anger won, and his eyes were dark.

"Another date?"

She shivered. One kiss and she wanted to give him everything. Even her dignity, her pride.

"We only agreed on dinner."
"And breakfast." came his bitter reply. He didn't seem to like it when someone stood him up. She hadn't meant it that way. She had wanted to protect herself from all this.
She swallowed.
"What's the problem here? Is it that you couldn't leave first, like you're used to? I'm not like all the other women," she replied strongly and convincingly.
As if he didn't know that.
"I didn't leave to hurt your ego." She finally added, just as coolly as he.
"Oh no?" He wasn't sure why he was so angry with her. So disappointed.
I am losing myself in you. Her heart cried out in despair. She tried to ignore it, not wanting to admit it had got to her again. But it was already too late. She needed time, space, needed to be alone to lick her wounds. He should finally leave. Every additional minute with him cost her strength she no longer had. Especially after a sleepless, exciting night.
"We did what you suggested. We drove it out of our system."
"Just me? Did you only tolerate it because of me?" He looked shocked in her face. That statement had cut him deeply. Much deeper than he would have expected.
Her look was direct. She didn't want to hide anything. Just as little did she want to tell him the truth.
"No. I wanted to."
"Wanted to? Only in the past?" He had to be tired or sick. He took her every word hard. What did he care about all that?
I will always want you, she replied silently.
He ran his hand through his hair, annoyed and impatient.
"Can't we talk about this like two adults? We just need to communicate more."
"Bring in more plain language?" she said mockingly. "Fine. You don't want a relationship, I do. You don't want to feel anything, I do. Plain language enough?"
He ignored her sarcastic remark. Her words didn't really hit

home. Everything in his head, in his mind was jumbled and he couldn't make sense of it.

"This is about sex. Lust, pure lust. Which you feel as much as I do. Don't you?"

His eyes so clear and so sexy. His closeness was unbearable. His words were the problem.

"Why don't we meet here and there for a few months, and both enjoy it? Six months or so."

At his own words, he realised that he lived two hours away from her hometown. Quickly in his mind he counted up the few ways he could see her at the weekend. On top of that, it could happen that he was called to an emergency or that she was ill. Then it would only be maybe twenty times in six months that he could see her. Twenty seemed a very low number.

"Or a year." he added thoughtfully.

"Did you just do the math in your head of how many times we would sleep together?"

She stared at him, stunned.

He fell silent, concerned. Maybe. He might as well move ...

Shaking her head, she drew her eyebrows together.

"Stop negotiating with our relationship." she admonished him. Though she was slightly flattered. "The only thing there is to negotiate is the wedding date. Not with you, absolutely."

Vincent looked at her. She was a great woman. He just wanted to pull her into his arms and kiss her to the ground. He had never had to work so hard to make love to a woman.

"We've done it before, haven't we? A few weeks, months - "

"No! We were more than sex. We had more than that. Have you forgotten how much time we hadn't spent in our beds? And how we had spent that time?"

He shook his head. Of course he hadn't. Not a moment had he been *able* to forget.

"I can't give you more. I don't want to hurt you." He admitted honestly. She closed her eyes for seconds. Her heart in ruins. Every time she thought there might be more, there was hope

for a relationship, he brought her back to earth, ice cold. She had to get away. Had to pull away from him. Yes, he would hurt her. Hurt her.
"I know that." she admitted quietly. "That's why I snuck out of your hotel room this morning. I just want everything. Dinner, breakfast ... lunch now and then."
Silence.
Marisa had to stay strong. As much as she felt drawn to him. As much as she wanted to slide her fingers through his hair and press her lips to his mouth.
It was over.
"Go, Vin." she urged him. Her gaze neutral, her pain hidden. "If fate has its way, I'll see you again next time we go skiing."
She tried to smile, though everything inside her broke.
"With your new guy?" His voice cold. His eyes almost hurt.
Marisa was silent, swallowing dryly, her heart racing.
"It's going to take me a long time to get over all this ... over you. There won't be anyone new for a very, very long time. If ever."
She made a move that for her this topic, this conversation had come to an end. She wanted to get back into her safe nursery. She wanted to start licking her wounds. And then on Monday she would have her hands so full that she wouldn't have time to think about him. Now was the time to go.
Vincent hesitated. His anger still clearly written across his face. He couldn't sort out his thoughts. He was all over the place because of this woman.
"Marry me." The words were out before he had calculated all possible directions for the conversation. Everyone involved was shocked. Panic and excitement erupted all at once.
She turned very, very slowly back towards him. Not with joy, but with shock.
"Stop! Please." she pleaded. "You are so confusing today. Your offers, your actions so confused. Don't you realise yourself that you're not making sense?"
Vincent gathered enough composure to explain his offer.
"You'll never find anyone on the internet who loves you."

She stared at him. What the hell? First a proposal and now a failed explanation. Why didn't he just stab her in the heart with a knife and take pleasure in rubbing salt into the wound? What was going through his head?
Her confusion and shock changed instantly to hostility. She had to protect herself somehow from more pain.
"No one will ever be able to love me?"
"My point is ... if you're all about a superficial relationship.... if you're all about kids, then I'm ready. We can start a family."
"No." she replied unequivocally. Surely this was completely insane and insulting.
"I'm offering you what you wished for George. And you say no?"
Marisa couldn't believe what they were discussing. And what's more, he seemed genuinely surprised that she refused his proposal. She wouldn't marry him after all.
"Out of pity? Because I'll never find anyone? I'm not worth loving. No one will want to be with me. Do you actually hear what you're saying?"
He looked at her in confusion. He had indeed lost his mind.
"You want children. Longing for them. I can give you that. We already know we are compatible."
Marisa's heart broke into a thousand pieces. How could he so icily bring up her past again?
"Go." she demanded weakly. Tears threatened her.
"MK?"
"I was able to give you just that back then. *You* abandoned *us* and didn't give a damn about us. Please go."
This time she managed. This time she was strong and consistent.
She turned briskly but confidently away from him to go back to her beloved nursery. She did not look back. Didn't want to know how angry he had been at her reaction. She herself did not have the strength to look him in the eye. She had felt so comfortable in his arms, had just let herself go for a second. Why hadn't she protected her heart from this heartbreak?

Why did she have to fall just as far as she had 17 years ago?
At least this time she had the foresight that he was not good enough for her. She didn't want a superficial relationship anymore.
She wanted more. Much more.

~

Would she ever find her way back to her old life? She had no interest in looking for a date or smiling after another man. The last few weeks had proven to her that her selfish plans were not necessary to survive. Instead of making herself happy, she could put all her energy, time and money into her nursery. Here she had hundreds of children to love and nurture. All of them needed her support to have a safe and happy start in life. Even the parents sometimes needed more time and good coaxing. That would be enough for her. That was safest.
Her heart had no room for more.
Vincent only broke her, and he caused a craving in her that she could not fill. A craving for his endless love for her. Yes, he was right. In bed they were more than compatible. But she didn't want to spend the next few months having fun, only to wake up alone one morning. Like he did this morning.
There was a knock.
Marisa paused. She wouldn't get rid of him that easily, today. She would not find her peace again that easily. She didn't move.
"I wasn't ready for a baby." he said into the camera. He knew she could hear him. He hoped she did. And would let him in. "I wasn't ready for my first relationship, my first girlfriend, ... to be the love of the rest of my life......... I panicked, scared. In my eyes, our baby was an obstacle to our future ..... to my future, my career."
His eyes were full of remorse and disgust.
Marisa opened the door, not looking him in the eye. She wanted to hear what he had to say. Wanted to know why they couldn't be together, then and now. She couldn't let him in, she

walked past him towards the outhouse. She hesitated before opening the door. The last time, she had almost kissed him to the ground and made love to him on the spot. He remembered the same moment. And that she had simply left afterwards.

He followed her in silence. She stood at one end of the room; her arms folded in front of her chest.

"The way you think of it, I didn't abandon you. I couldn't forget you. I came back and found you in the hospital. Your father was so angry with me. Understandable. I'd gotten you pregnant and dumped you. Unforgivable. He convinced me to leave without even talking to you. Without even apologising."

"My father never mentioned a word of it."

"I don't blame him. You were in better arms. Your parents, Simon -"

"Did my father tell you about Simon?"

Vin nodded. Even today he felt the deep disappointment that she had been able to find a new boyfriend. Just like that. She shook her head slightly. Thinking of her beloved father.

"He wanted to make sure you didn't get close to me. Or he wanted to hurt you. Or both." she finally replied. She could imagine exactly how her father had wanted to take revenge on the young man. "Simon didn't exist. At least not to me. It took me years to even smile at a boy, let alone want to be with someone."

As if a heavy weight had been placed on him, a thick fog lifted from his heart, from his cloudy thought.

"I understand why you look at me with hatred in your eyes. I understand why you want nothing to do with me. I'm sorry it had to end this way."

Marisa put her tired hands in front of her face. Thick tears in her eyes. Pain in the heart.

He wanted to approach her. The sad sight of her was unbearable.

"Vin...." she began slowly. "When I saw you again, it brought back all those emotions, that pain. That heartbreak of my first love, the disappointment...... But the worst feeling that came

over me was guilt. Seeing you reminded me of how guilty I had felt in the end. And still feel."
"The miscarriage is not your -"
She shook her head. Her disgust on her face.
"Guilt-" Her voice broke at the acknowledgement of her failure. A tear formed on her cheek. She cleared her throat slightly and gathered strength. "Guilt because I was relieved. More than anything, I was relieved that I wasn't pregnant anymore. That I didn't have to drop out of my A-levels after all. This feeling of guilt was like a burden that I just couldn't carry. And I took that anger at myself out on you. I'm sorry. I should have been honest from the beginning, and admitted to myself and to you that I absolutely didn't want a child at 17, 18."
They stood silently in front of each other. Honesty was good. He breathed slowly. The memories of his first and only girlfriend were still as fresh as they had been then. But they no longer hurt so much at that moment. Marisa stood before him again. She had become a woman who knew what she wanted and what she didn't want. A woman who had built and run her own nursery. She was unique, sincere and adorably sweet. And she stood before him.
"I have to leave tomorrow." he finally said. His statement carried regret. "I'm staying in -"
Marisa stopped him.
"It's okay." she interrupted him carefully. She searched for a strength within herself that she didn't have. She had to let him go. It was easiest that way. "I don't need to know where you live."
He looked at her. Her eyes tired. Her posture taut. He wanted to put a hand on her shoulder, but she eluded his proximity. He was so confused. It needed a script.
Please go, she pleaded with her tortured look.
"Why not? You could come and see me when you're out."
"You should go now, Vin. We've talked it all over." she replied instead. Her body shook. She just wanted to collapse on the spot and let her pain run wild.

"Why?" he asked again. His look exasperated. He moved closer to her again. Wanted to feel her, shake her. What was going on now? Had one night really been enough for her? Did she not want more?
"Do you love me? That night ... you said I was your first great love?" She deflected from his question. Had to know.
"I thought you were unconscious... "
"So, it was all a trick after all."
Ah.
A hot tear rolled down her face unhindered. She wiped it away angrily. Shit. Why didn't he leave already?
Panic. At the sight of her. Panic at all she had been through.
"You're not fine. All this stress with George and your pain is not okay. You need help. I can't leave you on your own."
"No. No. *This* is not okay. You're breaking me." She looked up. Displeasure written across her face. Disappointment with herself. She shook her head. "I should have shown more dignity, kept more self-worth. But no, instead I went to the hotel, and I let myself be seduced again, and then I open the door for you too. *Twice.*"
Marisa was angry with herself. He frowned. Who wasn't making sense this time?
"I'm breaking you?" He was deeply shaken at her words. Didn't want this. Wanted her to be happy. He couldn't just walk away. He tried to get closer to her but she stepped away from him.
"I'm losing myself in you...... I'm falling more and more in love with you." she admitted angrily. "And everything inside of me wants to beg you to stay."
Her feelings revealed before him. Pain, anger, hope, rage. A jumble of emotions. And he saw more in that moment than he had ever wanted to see.
Vincent just stared at her.
For half an eternity, no one did anything. And she knew that with her revealed feelings she had finally driven him away. She had had to tell him. She didn't want to repress it or play games.
He made a decision. One last time.

His gaze did not leave her face for a second as he approached her. He took her head in his hands and kissed her gently, probing. Immediately she was on fire. Immediately she tried to fight it. But his closeness, his aftershave were beguiling. She loved his caresses. She was floating. She returned his kiss with raw emotion flowing within her. He did not pull away. He took it all in, soaking up her love.
"MK." he whispered against her lips.
Her breath hitched. Her head was spinning. She couldn't think straight while he held her in his arms. She had to push him away from her. She had to gain distance. But she was afraid of making the right move. Once he left, he would never come back.
He stayed. He did not run away from her revelations. He looked at her. Looked at her properly.
"Years of training. *Years*. And I've never been able to read you. Haven't been able to understand how and why you react to me." he whispered back. He didn't let go of her. He needed to feel her, needed to make sure she could hear him. That she could understand him.
And forgive him.
"I couldn't understand your feelings because I didn't want to accept my own feelings myself. Now I know what those emotions meant..... I couldn't analyse you.... You are .... You are a reflection of *my* feelings. I didn't know what that would mean.... didn't know what or who I was looking at..... You and I. Both head over heels in love, lost."
His kiss so gentle, so sweet. She trembled. She thought she understood him. It seemed to make sense. Her fogged mind came to the surface. Hope was spreading. Again... had she learned nothing?
Be still, mind. Keep hoping, my heart.
Vincent reluctantly let go of her for a moment, his eyes so warm. The butterflies in her heart awoke.
"You actually turned *down* my marriage proposal."
She bit her lower lip, unsure of how much she had just

embarrassed herself. Just one little kiss and she had landed in his arms. His gaze saw her innocent gesture and his breath quickened.

"I - you." She swallowed. "What?"

"My marriage proposal. You turned it down."

"Rightly so." This time she won. "I hadn't finished negotiating."

He smirked.

"You're making yourself out to be a good crisis navigator." He joked, then cleared his throat nervously. "Seriously. I don't have any practice at this." he said sheepishly.

"I hope not."

He laughed. She took a step away from him to concentrate better. What was happening here right now? Was he making fun of her or were all her dreams about to come true? She was so confused by his kiss, his apology, his mere presence.

"MK. Marry me." This time his tone was loving and sincere. His eyes happy and straight on her, she looked shocked at him. Her eyes slightly widened. She was no longer breathing. He had better hurry before she passed out at his words. "I should have guessed when I offered you more than six months.... In my head, I was ready to move here so I wouldn't lose two hours of commuting time to get to you faster."

She didn't move an inch. She was paralysed. Really? It took her a few seconds to regain her voice and her mind to answer him. "Vin, are you kidding me? Just then you only offered me your sperm."

"I'll give you more."

He kissed her, touched her, turned her head. His hands all over, his tongue teasing. Her response was mutual. Breathlessly, they drove each other up. Her pulse raced; her body vibrated. She could not resist him. Her mind vanished.

"I didn't want to believe it, but you were and are the only one who touches me. You never let me go. I was always looking for you."

Marisa levitated. Now all that was missing were the three magic words ...

"I love you, Marisa. Can you believe it?"
"Yes..... I mean, we did have dinner first." At that moment, his feelings seemed genuine. Convincing. He laughed again, and she with him. His kiss sweet and perfect.
"And your answer?"
She pushed him slightly away from her. She needed space, time, a clear head. At least some distance. Her eyes open, her heart excited. She breathed in and out deeply. He returned her gaze, without haste, without pressure. Just with love in his warm blue eyes.
"Yes."
Marisa smiled at him. Maybe she would marry him after all, and her silly girlish dreams could finally come true.
She stepped up to him and sealed her agreement with a hot kiss. He swayed at the lust that overcame them both. He was a little dizzy with all these feelings welling up inside him.
"And how many children am I agreeing to here?" His eyes laughing, his kisses on her cheek, on her neck.
"No.... I had been looking for the next best thing ... to love a child unconditionally." she said softly. She shivered. "Now I have you. The first best thing."
Vincent buried his head in her neck. Deeply pleased, relieved and happy.
"You told me so."
She raised an eyebrow seductively before showing him her own passion with her kiss.
"So, I don't need to buy a cat."
It had only taken 17 years to admit what they meant to each other.
Feelings no longer had to be silent. Feelings were finally allowed.

∼

Almost a year later

It looked magnificent. White, shiny and enchantingly beautiful. Just like in her imagination, in her memories.

Her arrival for her annual skiing holiday in Kilnovech had been as usual and now the excitement came through as she recognised the snow-covered mountain peaks and landscapes. Her heart soon flooded with her love for this place, the great anticipation of finally being able to ski here again.

From afar, she recognised her popular ski instructor. For a brief moment, the sight of him brought back sore memories, but also beautiful ones. So much time had passed since then. So much was in the past. It was a new beginning.

New beginnings were the best thing ever.

"Marisa...." His greeting rather shy and cautious. "Do you hate me?"

It was only when she put her arms around his neck and hugged him tightly that a hundred stones fell from his heart.

"Not at all."

Mitch hugged Marisa with relief written across his face. A few more wrinkles around his forehead from all the brooding and squinting into the sun suited him just fine.

"But you stay away from that married woman."

At his joking remark, everyone looked in his direction.

Marisa beamed amusedly at her husband. A deep tingle in her stomach at the thought.

Vincent smiled back, wishfully happy and cheeky.

∼

Finally. Again.
Fresh meat.

THE END

ABOUT THE AUTHOR

Susann Svoboda

Growing up in East Germany, I wrote my first stories as a teenager. In my lessons, secretly but perhaps not unnoticed, I scribbled my never-ending declaration of love for Gary Barlow, which soon developed into one love story after another on the backs of our English tests and worksheets. Having always been fascinated by England and its language, I preferred to use English names for my characters from the start.

Now twenty years later, I have found the time and courage to revisit these stories and also publish them.

Therefore, the original ideas and dialogue came from a dreamy young girl; but the present stories come from me as a mother of three young girls who will soon be fantasizing about their own idols. Together with my husband, we live in England and hope with these stories to give you something to dream along too.

BOOKS BY THIS AUTHOR

What Keeps Us Apart? (Part 1)

Lyle McClory was a successful writer. Melissa Jackson was a talented illustrator. They were the perfect match - at least for his books and her pictures. To top it all off, this was a once-in-a-lifetime opportunity to work for him. She couldn't have asked for a better career jump. He wrote bestsellers for adults, and imaginative stories for children. He was most certainly captivating his audience with everything he created.
He was also cold, arrogant and stunningly handsome. He sought his distance though and seemed to give his all to not be in the same room as her whenever possible. They spent more time fighting with each other than actually talking.
So why was she so drawn to him?

What Keeps Us Apart? (Part 2)

Melissa Jackson did not believe in love, even less so in marriage. So why on earth did she wake up with a ring on her finger? Yes, the famous author Lyle McClory had asked her several times to be his wife. Yes, she felt the most tantalising attraction to her now husband.
But no, this was not how she had planned her life to turn out. She saw herself as a plain, simple woman who had wanted to get on with her own business for as long as she can remember. Suddenly, she lost sight of that and worried about other unimportant matters. Why had Lyle chosen her to spend the rest of his life with? What was she doing in this high society?

Did she actually belong here?

What Keeps Us Apart? (Part 3)

Melissa McClory had found herself again. Finally, standing on her own two feet. Alone… She didn't miss her husband, didn't long for his strong arms at night. She could bear being apart from him, day in…day out. She had absolutely made the right decision to leave him.

And yet, she left the divorce papers in the back of her drawer, unsigned. She had too much on her hands right now, to worry about that small formality. Once her own company was running smoothly and successfully, she could read through the papers and then, only then finalise her decision. She didn't need or want Lyle McClory in her life anymore, did she?

What Keeps Us Apart Still?

Their fake marriage was over. All of their lies were exposed for all to see in the headlines every day. Melissa McClory felt compelled to take back her maiden name so that her own business would not go down with the hatred she was receiving. But fortunately, she had good friends by her side. Lyle was in her life, more or less. So why couldn't she be happy now that the truth was out?

BOOKS BY THIS AUTHOR

When The Past Destroys Hope

Jeff Knights already had his hands full - his farm was about to harvest and needed every single ounce of its proceeds to survive, and then Valerie Heffron showed up. The dolled-up millionaire's daughter who could buy anything she desired with her money. She was the girl he had wanted to marry.

And suddenly she was standing in front of him, completely without glamour and designer clothes. But he could see through her games. She was still the same, spoilt girl from back then. However, he had to admit that she was no longer a girl. She was an irritating woman who showed no intentions of wanting to leave his farm, no matter how often they got in each other's way.

FEELINGS MUTED

Printed in Great Britain
by Amazon